And now these three remain: faith, hope and love.
But the greatest of these is love.

—1 Corinthians 13:13 (niv)

MYSTERIES OF COBBLE HILL FARM

Digging Up Secrets
Hide and Seek
Into Thin Air
Three Dog Knight
Show Stopper
A Little Bird Told Me
The Christmas Camel Caper
On the Right Track
Wolves in Sheep's Clothing
Snake in the Grass
A Will and a Way

MYSTERIES OF COBBLE HILL FARM

A Will and a Way

JOHNNIE ALEXANDER

A Gift from Guideposts

Thank you for your purchase! We want to express our gratitude for your support with a special gift just for you.

Dive into *Spirit Lifters*, a complimentary e-book that will fortify your faith, offering solace during challenging moments. Its 31 carefully selected scripture verses will soothe and uplift your soul.

Please use the QR code or go to **guideposts.org/ spiritlifters** to download.

MYSTERIES OF COBBLE HILL FARM

A Will and a Way

GLOSSARY OF UK TERMS

boot • car trunk

chemist • pharmacist

croft • a small farm

crofter • one who rents and works a croft

cuppa • cup of tea

estate agent • Realtor

gimmer • female sheep

jumper • sweater

ramble • walk

rubbish bin • trash can

takeaway • takeout

wellies • Wellington rubber boots

CHAPTER ONE

One last tiny stitch, a snip of the thread, and the gentle application of a bandage brought an end to the lifesaving operation. Dr. Harriet Bailey removed her surgical gloves with a satisfied snap and tossed them into the hazardous-waste bin. A warm glow flooded her as she cradled the unconscious ginger tabby in her arms.

"You're going to be okay, Thomasina," Harriet murmured, smoothing the short fur. "You're going to feel so much better. I only wish you could have three lives, like your namesake."

Harriet smothered the doubt that suddenly flickered to life. While settling Thomasina in a recovery kennel, she mentally reviewed the procedure from beginning to end. The scene played as if she were watching a video, assuring herself she'd made no mistakes.

She covered the sleeping cat with a light blanket and adjusted the airflow on the built-in oxygen apparatus. "I'll be back to check on you soon," she promised, wanting to believe—as she always did—that the animals entrusted to her care were comforted by her quiet assurances even when the anesthesia hadn't yet worn off.

Instead of leaving, though, she rested her hand against the closed kennel door. She'd felt a profound connection with this cat since its first visit to the clinic. More specifically, from the first time she had picked up the chart and read the ginger's name.

Thomasina.

Immediately, Harriet had been transported to a long-ago visit to Cobble Hill Farm, the same beloved property that now belonged to her. She must have been about nine or ten when her family made the late-summer trip from their Connecticut home to this magical corner of Yorkshire where her grandfather, Harold Bailey, was respected by his neighbors, painted landscapes and animals, and, most important of all, made sick creatures well again.

Though Harriet and her family had made the intercontinental trip several times before and countless times after, a precious memory from that particular visit was reawakened when the ginger tabby came to the clinic.

"Is everything okay?" Polly Thatcher's distinctive Yorkshire accent brought Harriet back to the present.

"Everything went smoothly." Harriet smiled at Polly as she washed her hands.

The clinic receptionist, who'd quickly become one of Harriet's dearest friends, leaned against the doorframe of the surgery area. Narrow strands of her dark, shoulder-length hair were streaked with a pastel pink, a perfect springtime color that matched the embroidered touches in the knitted cardigan she wore over a cream-color V-neck top.

Polly shifted against the frame as she glanced down the hallway toward the reception area. Though her shoulders appeared tense, Harriet figured Polly was probably keeping an ear out in case the telephone rang or someone entered the clinic.

A few months ago, Harriet might have teased that Polly wanted to be sure she didn't miss a call from Van Worthington, White

Church Bay's detective constable. Last autumn, Van seemed to have won Polly's heart. But when he'd proposed too soon, Polly had declined. She wasn't ready to make that commitment, and their relationship ended. Neither one seemed happy about the change, and at first the awkwardness between them had been palpable.

Thankfully, the tension eventually lessened, especially with their concerted efforts to revive their friendship. Given the lilt in Polly's voice whenever she mentioned Van, Harriet believed their feelings for each other still ran deep, and she hoped they'd give their relationship a second chance.

"Do you want to call Courtney?" Harriet asked in a singsong voice, though she already suspected Polly's answer. "Or should I?"

Despite the receptionist's spunky personality and talent for making conversation with nearly anyone, Polly would only call Courtney Millington on threat of banishment from the clinic.

"No need," Polly replied. "She's here."

Harriet's stomach knotted as she met Polly's gaze. "Already?" She shut off the sink and dried her hands. "I told her we'd call once the surgery was over. What's she doing here so soon?"

Polly pushed away from the doorframe, scowling. "Your guess is as good as mine. She waltzed in as if she expected me to bow at her feet or something. It was all I could do to keep her from barging back here."

"Thank you for that." Harriet made sure her clothes were neat then tidied her hair. "Let's go face her together."

"Can't I stay here with Thomasina?" Polly begged. "Just until Courtney leaves. I mean, someone should be here when the cat wakes up, right?"

"Not a chance." Harriet caught Polly's elbow and tugged her toward the door.

When they reached the reception area, Harriet pasted on a warm smile and greeted the woman, who rose from her chair.

Courtney had been a rising star in the fashion world at one time, modeling the hottest new creations on the runways of Paris and Milan. According to Polly, she'd returned home one day about a decade before, with no explanation for her sudden departure from stardom. And she had been a thorn in many locals' sides ever since.

The gossip surrounding Courtney had faded away long ago. Still, no one seemed to know why she'd returned to White Church Bay. Only that she'd brought a haughty, condescending air that didn't go over well with those who remembered the ungainly adolescent who'd been an average student and a snippy part-time waitress at the Happy Cup Tearoom and Bakery.

Now here she was in the Cobble Hill Vet Clinic waiting room. She may have left the modeling world behind, but not the lessons she'd gained in style from her time there. Her impeccably made-up face was perfectly framed by a layered hairstyle with chic highlights and lowlights. Her tailored dress, constructed from a fabric designed with swirls of intermingled pink and lavender, fell from her angular shoulders to below her knees. Translucent purple sleeves accentuated a royal-purple clutch bag, while a filmy scarf hung at her neck. A large amethyst ring adorned her left forefinger, and silver bands encircled all the fingers on her right hand. Her sculpted fingernails sported diamond art.

In a moment of self-consciousness, Harriet tucked a stray hair behind her ear and glanced down at her long-sleeved T-shirt featuring the clinic's logo, and heavy-duty jeans. Insecurity gnawed at her stomach. She'd rarely been bitten by the comparison bug and had no idea why it should raise its ugly head now. Sure, Courtney's fashion sense was glamorous, but Harriet couldn't remember the last time she'd been intimidated by another woman's appearance. Hadn't she outgrown that years before?

"My cat is fine now, is she not." Somehow Courtney's domineering tone turned the question into a statement. "When can I take her home?"

"The surgery went as planned." Harriet gestured toward the hallway. "She hasn't regained consciousness yet, but we can go see her if you'd like."

"What I'd like is to take her home where she belongs."

At first, Harriet was taken aback by the declaration, but she managed to keep her tone even. "That's not possible. She needs to stay overnight for observation. We discussed that when you dropped her off this morning."

A conversation that had evidently fallen on deaf ears. Courtney had swooped in, plopped Thomasina on the counter, scrawled her signature on the necessary papers, and left without a second glance. Her tires had kicked up the gravel covering the parking area as she reversed her late-model sports car out of its space and sped toward the main road.

At least she'd returned with less ruckus.

"Is it absolutely necessary for her to stay that long?" Condescension dripped from Courtney's tone, which was surprisingly free of a Yorkshire accent, considering she'd been born and raised on the moors. Courtney had come back from her years on the continent with the polished tones of a BBC broadcaster, sprinkled with the occasional French or Italian phrase.

Needing a moment to gather her thoughts, Harriet lowered her gaze and tucked in her lower lip. Advice came to mind from an old boss at the Connecticut clinic where she used to work: *"Iron sharpens iron, and it takes a rock to strike a rock."*

He meant that an assertive person often responded best to a similarly matched response. From his perspective, such individuals considered anything less as unworthy of respect. That kind of approach wasn't Harriet's way, but she resolved to be firm with Courtney for Thomasina's sake.

"For her to have the best possible outcome, it is vital for her recovery from anesthesia to be supervised by a professional," she said firmly.

If Courtney insisted on taking her pet with her, Harriet couldn't stop her. Surely the woman wouldn't be so heartless as to remove a still-unconscious cat from the clinic.

Harriet met Courtney's glare while keeping her shoulders relaxed. She meant to show Courtney that she was not to be bullied, without rising to her level of aggression. "If you want her to be well, Thomasina needs to stay here until tomorrow."

Courtney didn't move. She didn't even blink.

Harriet didn't either.

The ring of the telephone interrupted the rising tension. Out of the corner of her eye, Harriet caught sight of Polly snatching up the receiver.

"Cobble Hill Vet Clinic, this is Polly." Her clear, crisp voice sounded louder than usual.

While Polly handled the call, Harriet gestured toward the hall again. "Do you wish to see Thomasina before you go?"

Courtney's vibrant pink lips quirked up at one corner in what appeared to be an amused smirk. "Since she's still sleeping, she won't even know I'm there, will she? Or do you believe animals sense their owner's presence under such circumstances?"

"Cats are amazingly intuitive," Harriet replied. Though many medical professionals believed unconscious humans could sense the presence of their loved ones, she didn't know if the same could be said for animals. However, she'd experienced moments that made her believe they did. "It's possible Thomasina will know."

The dismissive smirk remained as Courtney tilted her head in a condescending gesture. All that was missing was an exaggerated roll of her heavily made-up eyes.

Harriet chose to let the silence continue, broken only by Polly's one-sided phone conversation and the tap of the computer keys as she added an appointment to the schedule. She refused to be drawn into a pointless argument, especially since she sensed that was exactly what Courtney wanted. What did Courtney expect to gain from treating her cat's doctor with such low regard? Or to endanger her cat's life by dismissing sound medical advice?

Polly's phone call ended as the door of the clinic opened. A broad-shouldered man with pale blond hair and a scruffy beard entered the waiting room. Except for his clothes and the fact that he carried an electronic tablet, he might have stepped out of the pages of a history book about Vikings. He removed his tan cap as his eyes, a blue so light as to be almost gray, scanned the room.

"Why, if it isn't Garth Hamblin." Courtney dashed to the man's side faster than a nail to a magnet. A brilliant smile softened the sharp angles of her photogenic features, and the warmth of her greeting removed all traces of her earlier iciness. "Of all the places to run into you. Is our famed vet operating on your pet too?"

Garth furrowed his brow. "I don't have a pet. I stopped by to—"

"My dear Thomasina is in recovery now." Courtney wrapped both her arms around one of Garth's. "Though you may not have heard the news. My grandmother moved into one of those senior care facilities. It broke her heart that she couldn't keep the cat she'd raised from a kitten. And that broke *my* heart. I'm caring for Thomasina now, and she's been such a joy. I'm so glad I can have a pet these days. My schedule made it impossible before, with Milan one day and Paris the next."

"I'm sorry to hear about your grandmother," Garth said, his shoulders tense. "And her cat. I mean, your cat."

"What can I do for you, Garth?" Harriet asked in an attempt to rescue him.

He extricated himself from Courtney's grip and shifted his attention to Harriet. "I stopped in for a quick chat." He glanced toward Courtney as if keeping a wary eye on a dangerous predator. "Maybe I should make an appointment."

"This is fine," Harriet said, grateful for the interruption and determined to use it to her advantage. If he left now, she'd be forced to get back on Courtney's conversation carousel. On the other hand, Harriet doubted Courtney planned to leave as long as Garth was in the reception area. Not with the way she eyed the man.

"Why don't you wait for me in exam room one?" Harriet motioned to the first open door in the hallway. "I won't be long."

"Appreciate it." With a curt nod to Courtney, Garth strode toward the exam room without a second glance. The door clicked shut behind him.

Once it did, Harriet again faced Courtney, who stared at the closed door. Her brilliant smile had transformed into a frustrated frown.

"We were in school together, Garth and me," Courtney said, her voice almost dreamy. "I used to think…" She shook herself, as if ridding her mind of unpleasant memories. Or perhaps unrealized hopes.

Harriet glanced at Polly, who shrugged. Apparently, she was similarly puzzled by Courtney's mercurial behavior.

Regardless, Harriet had to maintain her stance on behalf of her patient. "Thomasina needs to—"

"Stay here overnight. I know." Courtney topped off her words with a dramatic flourish as she glared at Harriet. "Which means I have to rearrange my entire weekend on a Friday afternoon so I can pick up that cat whenever *you* decide it's convenient."

This wasn't the first time in her career Harriet had heard such complaints. Not every pet owner was a devoted one. But Courtney's retort coming so soon after gushing over her grandmother's cat in a futile attempt to impress Garth lit the fuse on Harriet's temper.

Thankfully, that fuse was a long one.

"We're open from eight to noon on Saturdays," she said in her most professional tone. "I'll call you later today with an update."

"Don't bother unless it's an emergency." Courtney retrieved her car fob from her purse and spun on her heel to leave.

"Courtney, wait!" The wheels of Polly's chair squeaked as she rolled back and stood.

Courtney turned, the familiar smirk back in place. "Don't worry about the bill. I'll pay it tomorrow when I return for my cat."

"It's not that," Polly replied, her tone bordering on indignation. "I wanted to offer to care for Thomasina for you this weekend. So you can keep your plans."

Courtney's eyes narrowed. "You want me to board her for a few more days? How much will that add to my bill?"

"Not a penny." Polly lifted her chin and returned Courtney's stare. "I'll take her home with me tomorrow, and you can pick her up here on Monday. Anytime between eight and four."

Courtney appraised Polly with open suspicion. "Why would you do that?"

"My parents are going out of town, and Thomasina and I will be good company for each other. And that way you don't have to worry about her care or rearranging your plans. It seems mutually beneficial to me."

Courtney hesitated. Harriet could almost see her wheels turning, as if she still suspected some kind of ulterior motive. Such a sad way to go through life—always being on one's guard, fearful and suspicious of others. Though Garth appeared to be the exception. She'd thrown herself at him, even though he obviously didn't reciprocate her feelings.

Harriet could understand why he didn't, but that was sad too. The steadfast love of a good man might soften Courtney's bristling nature, but that man was unlikely to be Garth Hamblin.

Not that he wasn't a good man, but his heart belonged to the animals he tended at the Yorkshire Coast Wildlife Centre, a nonprofit animal rehabilitation facility he'd founded. Harriet doubted he'd be interested in a woman who clearly considered her grandmother's elderly cat to be a burden, in spite of her attempts to lie about it to him.

"I'll take you up on that offer," Courtney said to Polly. Somehow her acceptance sounded as if she were doing Polly a favor instead of the other way around. Without another word, she exited the clinic. A few moments later, her tires kicked up the gravel in the parking lot once more as she sped away.

"I should say something to her about that," Harriet said. "Someone could get hurt."

Polly snorted. "She wouldn't listen, and she wouldn't care."

Probably not. But if something horrible did happen, at least Harriet would know she'd tried to warn Courtney.

The exam room door opened, and Garth peered around the frame. "Is she gone?"

Harriet couldn't help but laugh at his exaggerated expression of fear.

"Until Monday," she said. "Thanks to Polly volunteering to take care of Thomasina over the weekend."

"I heard," Garth said as he strode toward the reception area. "Courtney doesn't seem as fond of the cat as she wanted me to think. Not that I'm surprised. Her mother couldn't abide having a four-legged creature in the house."

Harriet chuckled. "Good thing for me not everyone feels that way, or I'd have to close my doors."

"Anyone with livestock still needs a vet, even if it's only during lambing season." Polly grinned at Garth. "And so does anyone wanting to save a kestrel that got itself attacked by a peregrine. I'll never forget that day."

"I won't either," Harriet agreed. Garth had once rushed into the clinic with a kestrel wrapped in his flannel shirt. The bird of prey would never fly again because of the damage from a larger falcon's talons. But it had found a good home at a small sanctuary near Liverpool with a retired master falconer.

That wasn't the first time Harriet had met Garth. She'd been introduced to him by Martha Banks, who ran a nearby hobby farm and rehabilitated injured wildlife. Garth counted on Martha's help when his center reached capacity, while Martha turned to Garth when an animal needed more care than she could provide.

"I'm guessing today's visit isn't an emergency," Harriet continued.

"Not exactly." He flashed an apologetic grin toward Polly before facing Harriet. "But it is confidential. I suppose I should have called to arrange a meeting, but I was driving past and swung in on a whim. I'm sorry for interrupting your day."

"There's no need to apologize," Harriet replied, curious to know what was on Garth's mind while also concerned that he wanted to exclude Polly. The receptionist had been with the clinic for years and knew everything that happened inside its walls. Her insights often helped Harriet navigate tricky situations with longtime clients. What could be so secretive that she must be excluded from their conversation? "I can assure you, however, that Polly is a trustworthy confidante."

"I have no doubt of it, but I'm afraid I must insist on speaking to you alone," Garth replied. "If the matter wasn't important, I wouldn't be here. Believe me, I mean no offense to anyone."

Polly returned to her seat, gracing Garth with a kind smile. "None taken. And our next appointment is in forty-five minutes, so you picked a great time to stop in."

"Then we can meet now?" Garth asked Harriet as he tightened his grip on his tablet.

"I suppose so," Harriet agreed. "Polly, will you keep an eye on Thomasina? She should be stirring in twenty minutes or so."

Polly pointed to a small monitor on her desk that was wirelessly connected to a camera pointed at the recovery kennels. "Right now, she's sound asleep. I'll go back there in a few minutes and give her a pat." She grinned. "After all, cats are amazingly intuitive, as you told Courtney."

Harriet responded with a smile of her own. "I'm sure Thomasina will appreciate that. Garth and I will be in the study if you need me."

As she ushered Garth through the door that separated the vet clinic from the main house, Maxwell trotted after them on his wheeled prosthesis. His back legs had been paralyzed years before when he was hit by a car. Officially known as the clinic dog, the little dachshund had stayed hidden behind Polly's desk during Courtney's tempestuous visit.

As soon as they were alone in the room, Garth took a moment to greet Maxwell then closed the door behind them and set his tablet on the desk.

"I'm about to show you something truly incredible. I can hardly believe it myself." His voice quivered with excitement. "But you must first promise me that you won't tell anyone. Not your aunt. Not Will. Not anyone outside of this room."

Harriet lowered herself into Grandad's old chair. First Polly. Now Aunt Jinny and Will Knight—the pastor she'd been dating for the past few months, who was the soul of confidentiality—were on the don't-tell list?

Caution urged her to be wary. Curiosity urged her to say yes.

She had no idea how to answer Garth.

CHAPTER TWO

Curiosity overcame caution.

"All right. I'll keep this between us." Harriet folded her arms on Grandad's antique desk as Garth brought up a video on his tablet. "And Maxwell has never spilled a secret in his life." The little dog parked himself beside her.

The grainy footage on the small screen was dated the previous day. The scene, in shades of gray, seemed to show patches of thistles among rocks and overgrown vegetation. The sun cast squat shadows across the limited landscape that could be seen through the camera lens.

"Is this from a game camera?" she asked.

"One that's motion-activated." Garth hovered over her shoulder at the side of the desk. "Watch for it."

A few seconds later, a weasel limped into view. It paused, lifted a front paw, and sniffed the air with its pointy nose. Apparently satisfied no danger lurked nearby, the long-bodied creature sprawled against the roots of a scraggly tree. Its rear leg was bent in an unnatural position.

"It's injured."

"That's why I want to find it."

"I hope you'll bring it straight here if you do. But why the secrecy?" Harriet moved the tablet closer, wishing the video was in color, and examined the animal's light-colored bib against its darker coat. "This isn't a common weasel, though, is it? At least, it doesn't resemble the ones I've seen before."

She'd provided vet care at the rehab facility to a couple of weasels that had been injured by larger animals. From what she could tell, those had a lighter brown coat and a whiter bib than the one in the video.

Garth pulled out his phone and tapped the screen. "Not a common weasel, no. It's an arboreal relative, the European pine marten." He held up his screen to show her a photo of a creature with a chocolate-brown coat and a bib the color of daffodils. Its black eyes were intelligent and curious. His voice grew more animated. "The last recorded sighting of a pine marten around here was over ten years ago. Do you know what that means?"

Harriet paused the video. The adorable marten seemed to be napping. "This little guy is endangered. Perhaps near extinction."

"That's why no one can know about this video." Garth paced in the narrow space between the front of the desk and the shelves on the opposite wall. "If word gets out, our moors will be turned into a circus with researchers and government officials and reporters. The chaos will scare it away. And if it's part of a colony—"

Harriet completed what he left unsaid. "The entire population might migrate somewhere else."

"Maybe a place that isn't as safe as wherever they're hiding now."

Harriet sat back in the chair. She'd read an online article a few years before about an endangered species of fox found on acreage destined to become a shopping mall. If not for a courageous whistle-blower, the vixen and her kits would have been killed by the developers. From their perspective, it was more economical to cover up the foxes' existence than to protect a rare species.

Did such things happen without anyone ever finding out? Probably.

"Where is this camera?" she asked.

Garth rubbed the back of his neck. "Not as far away or as secluded as I'd like. My guess is that something chased the marten away from its normal territory."

"Which could be anywhere," Harriet said.

"Yes." Garth picked up the tablet and tapped the screen. "The camera stops filming because the marten isn't moving. About an hour later, it starts up again. Watch this."

He handed Harriet the tablet as a second video began. The pine marten appeared to startle awake. His ears stiffened, and his nose lifted to catch the scent-carrying breezes. He tried to scurry into the brush, twisted to nip at his leg as if in irritation, then limped out of range of the camera.

"He's dragging his rear leg." Harriet rewound then paused the video and enlarged the image. "Going by the angle, it might be broken."

"That's why I need your help. I've spent most of the day searching for him without any luck. Another pair of eyes would be beneficial, as well as skilled hands in case he's in a bad way."

The fact that they'd gone from referring to the pine marten as an *it* to a *he* wasn't lost on Harriet. A simple switch, but one that deeply mattered. Any living creature referred to as *it* seemed of little more value than an inanimate object. That certainly wasn't true of the injured pine marten. His life had value, regardless of his status on an endangered species list.

However, whether this particular animal was a *he* or a *she* was difficult to determine from a video. In general, male mammals were bigger than their female counterparts, and this one's face seemed to have a masculine quality. Harriet couldn't point out the particulars leading her to that conclusion. But after all her years of working with animals, she'd developed the undefinable skill. Somehow, she simply *knew*.

What mattered now, though, was finding him. An injured animal was a weakened animal, prey to any number of predators. Unfortunately, their search faced difficult challenges—primarily that finding one small animal on the moors was akin to a search for a needle in a haystack.

"You realize he's probably nowhere near this spot now," she said. "If he had been, he would have sensed your presence and fled. As well as he could with that leg, anyway. Or he might have hidden well." Despite Garth's skills as a tracker and an outdoorsman, the marten could have been within mere inches of him.

"I thought he might leave a trail, since he's dragging his leg." Garth folded his arms over his chest. "At least I didn't find a body or any signs of a struggle. That gives me hope he's still alive."

Harriet set the tablet on the desk and mused over the news. She hated the thought of the small marten, who probably weighed less than five pounds despite its length, suffering from his injury.

"When I leave here," Garth said, "I'm going back to the moor to set up more cameras in the same general vicinity as the one that's already there. I'm praying he'll go past one of them. Or maybe, if there's a colony nearby, another one will."

"What happens then? Would you try to capture an uninjured marten?"

"Of course not."

"Not even to tag it?" A transponder tag, a common tool of animal researchers, would allow the pine marten's location to be tracked and monitored.

Garth spoke in a firm, unapologetic tone. "I have no obligation to tell anyone about anything I find on my rambles. And I have no intention of revealing a colony's secret location to the world."

Garth's adamant declaration didn't come as much of a surprise to Harriet. Though she didn't know him well, the time they'd spent caring for sick and wounded animals had created a bond between them. He felt genuine love and deep respect for those animals entrusted to the care of the wildlife rehab facility. His gift for gaining the trust of a wild creature or calming a skittish one surpassed even Harriet's, and she admired him for those abilities.

"Not too many people know this, but the center is being investigated because a former volunteer with a personal agenda filed a complaint," Garth said, reaching for the tablet. "We've done nothing wrong except let a proverbial fox into our henhouse, and the investigator knows that. But the process takes time."

"I'm sorry to hear that," Harriet replied. "Is there anything I can do to help?" Maybe she could write a letter in support of the center's good work or even speak to someone on Garth's behalf.

"Thanks, but we'll survive. And I understand if you don't want to get involved with the marten case."

"I'd like to help you search, but I can't be gone too long today because of my patient. I'm on night duty."

"Of course." Garth rolled his eyes. "Courtney's beloved cat."

His ironic tone caused Harriet to flash a small smile before her thoughts returned to the wounded pine marten. "I'll let you know if I can get away for an hour or two before Polly leaves."

Garth's features brightened. "Thanks, Harriet. I know I'm asking a lot."

"I hope we find him." Harriet pushed back the chair and stood. "Soon."

"So do I." Garth tucked his tablet under his arm as they headed back to the waiting room, Maxwell trotting at their heels. "Let me know when you're on your way, and I'll tell you where to find me. Until then, mum's the word."

"My lips are sealed."

Polly raised her head from her computer with a questioning glance.

Harriet responded with a quick smile then turned her attention back to Garth. "If I'm able to leave early, I'll let you know."

"That'd be great." He shifted toward Polly. "What's Fergus up to these days? I haven't seen him since our last class reunion. We keep saying we'll get together, but it never seems to happen."

"Mum and Dad say the same thing about him," Polly replied with a grin. Her brother Fergus worked as a race car mechanic. He followed the circuit throughout the UK and western Europe then renovated old cars during the off-season. "Next time I see him, I'll tell him you said hi."

"Thank you. Tell him to call me when he comes to town, and we can get a few of the other guys together. Maybe organize a game of rugby."

"He'd love that." The conversation was interrupted by the ringing of the telephone. Polly waved goodbye and answered the call.

Harriet stood by the desk while Garth headed for the door. As he reached for the handle, the door burst open.

A young boy, perhaps six or seven, rushed inside and ran straight into Garth, who reached down and grasped his shoulders.

"What's your hurry, my man?" Garth crouched so he was face-to-face with the red-cheeked child.

The boy tried to speak, but his ragged breathing prevented it. With a pained expression on his ruddy features, he stared at Garth with desperate blue eyes beneath unruly brown hair.

Despite the afternoon chill in the air, he didn't wear a jacket or a cap, only a long-sleeved shirt with green and tan stripes and brown pants. Fresh mud streaked his sneakers, an expensive American brand that Harriet recognized from living in an upscale Connecticut town. The laces were stuffed inside the shoes, as if he hadn't taken the time to tie them.

Or perhaps he didn't know how.

Harriet got him a glass of water. "Drink this," she urged. "It'll help you catch your breath."

He hesitated a moment then gulped the water while Harriet peered out the still-open door. The only vehicles in the parking area belonged to her and Garth. Now that winter had released its icy grip on their little corner of the world, Polly once again rode her bike from the village to the clinic. It was sheltered in the nearby barn.

Suddenly the boy choked and coughed.

"Took it a little too fast there, I reckon." Garth spoke in a soothing tone accompanied by a compassionate smile. He rubbed the boy's back until the coughing eased.

When Polly hung up the phone, Harriet caught her eye and asked in a low voice, "Do you know him?"

Polly shook her head.

Garth crouched to eye level with the boy. "I'm Garth," he said. "What's your name?"

Instead of answering, the boy inhaled sharply then stared at Harriet. "Are you the doctor? My mum needs a doctor. I can't get her to wake up. Will you come see her?" His voice choked as he swallowed a sob. "Please, will you come?"

CHAPTER THREE

Polly jumped up from her chair. "I'll see if Jinny's here," she said over her shoulder as she dashed out the door. Dr. Genevieve "Jinny" Garrett was Harriet's aunt, and her medical office was attached to her house, the dower cottage on the property.

"Her car is gone," Polly said when she came back in a moment later. "Do you want me to call her?"

"Please." Harriet knelt beside Garth and the boy.

"We're staying at Beckside Croft," the boy said.

"I know where that is," Garth said. "But I didn't know anyone lived there."

"We moved in last week. It's supposed to be a secret that we're there. But Mum won't wake up." He bent his head, and Harriet clasped his shoulder. "I know she's not really my mum, but she won't wake up."

Garth stood and took the boy's hand. "We can be there in less than five minutes." Without waiting for a response, he led the boy out the door.

"Wait for me," Harriet called after him, but Garth kept going. Thankfully, Polly had already retrieved the emergency bag. She pushed it into Harriet's hands and rushed outside with her.

"Jinny didn't answer her phone," she said, "but I left a message, and I'll call emergency services. Now go, and don't worry about anything here. I'll stay until you're back, no matter how late."

Harriet nodded her thanks then hurried after Garth. She slid into the passenger seat of his vehicle as he closed the back door. Like her and many other rural folk, he drove a Land Rover. His was a dull copper brown and had the Yorkshire Coast Wildlife Centre logo on both sides.

The moment her door closed, Garth backed out of the parking space and raced toward the main road. Harriet glanced in the back seat as she clicked her seat belt. The boy, seat belt properly fastened and his small body stiff with tension, stared out the window. His lower lip trembled, but he seemed determined not to cry.

"This is Dr. Bailey," Garth said with a glance at Harriet. He kept his tone light as he continued. "Our new friend is Jack. He ran across the moor from Beckside Croft. We're going the long way around, but these wheels will get us there faster than our legs could. Won't be long now."

Harriet twisted in her seat so she could talk to Jack. "It's nice to meet you, Jack." When he didn't respond, she added, "My aunt Jinny is the people doctor, and we're trying to reach her. I'm a veterinarian. Do you know what that is?"

He gave her a scornful look.

She exaggerated a grimace. "Then you know I take care of animals. But I'll do everything I can for your mum until the ambulance comes."

"Will you wake her up?" he asked, his voice so low she barely made out the words.

Her heart clenched at the question. Could it be possible his mum—or whoever the woman was to him—had died? Harriet shook away the horrible thought and prayed that hadn't happened.

"I'll do everything I can," she promised.

Garth made a sharp turn, and Harriet grabbed on to the door handle to steady herself. With her focus on Jack, she hadn't paid attention to their route. She scanned the surrounding landscape to orient herself.

"I think I'm lost," she said.

"The North Sea is beyond those trees." Garth pointed to a thick wooded area then slowed to turn onto a narrow track marred with ruts and bumps. "Beckside Croft is up ahead."

"I'm not familiar with it." Harriet had been racking her brain since Jack first mentioned the place, but she wasn't sure she'd ever heard of it before. Not that she should be surprised by that. Tucked-away houses were scattered throughout the Yorkshire moors, and it would take a lifetime for Harriet to find them all. Garth had mentioned he didn't know it was occupied. No occupants meant no pets to be brought into the clinic.

"Though it seems we're neighbors," she added. "At least as the crow flies."

"You are," Garth agreed as he slowly navigated between the ruts. "I'm guessing our new friend cut across that pasture to get to your place." He eyed the rearview mirror and slightly raised his voice. "Is that right, Jack?"

Harriet glanced back in time to see Jack give a quick nod and swipe his eyes with the back of his hand.

"I know she's not really my mum."

Those had been Jack's words. Did that mean he was adopted?

"It's supposed to be a secret that we're there." Jack had said those words too. Did he mean that he and the woman weren't supposed to be living at Beckside Croft? Were they squatters?

Harriet snuck another quick glance at the boy. Aside from the muddy shoes, he appeared clean and healthy. Those shoes couldn't have come from a discount store, and neither had his clothes. Though Harriet knew little about a boy's wardrobe, she recognized quality fabrics and workmanship.

If they were squatters, they were squatters with money. Or a knack for thrift-store finds.

"Stop!" Jack's sudden cry startled Harriet. "Please, sir, stop," the boy pleaded as he struggled to remove his seat belt and open his door at the same time.

"Jack, wait." Harriet reached back to grab him, wanting to keep him from getting out while the car was moving, but her seat belt stopped her.

"She's there, she's there." Tears flowed down the boy's cheeks.

Garth managed to stop the car. "I see her. And she sees us."

Harriet shifted to see through the driver's side window. A woman stood near a rocky incline. She was too far away for Harriet to be able to tell whether she was old or young, smiling or frowning, injured or well. But even from a distance, the stillness in her stance betrayed her wariness.

At that moment, Jack managed to get his door open. He jumped out and raced toward the woman. At the sight of him, she covered her mouth with both hands then opened her arms wide and broke into a stumbling run.

Garth turned his gaze to Harriet. "This is a better outcome than I'd hoped."

"An answer to prayer," Harriet said. "Should we go introduce ourselves? And let her know an ambulance is on its way?"

"I'm more interested in knowing what she's doing at Beckside Croft."

At his suspicious tone, Harriet tilted her head. "What's bothering you about her, Garth?"

"That video footage I showed you? The camera is less than a kilometer from here."

Because of her family's trips from her hometown in Connecticut to her grandfather's farm in Yorkshire, Harriet had learned at an early age that a cottage in England didn't always resemble a cottage in the United States.

For many Americans, the word *cottage* conjured an image of a small, cozy house. But in England, the terms *small* and *cozy* seemed to be relative. For example, Aunt Jinny's dower cottage boasted a steeply pitched roof, multiple chimneys, and swathes of ivy. It was long and rambling, with enough square footage to be a spacious family home and a well-appointed medical clinic.

But Beckside Croft would have qualified as the quintessential cottage in Harriet's homeland. It was a snug little house with ebony-paned windows, ivy-covered walls, faded shingles, and a stone chimney. The late afternoon sun, hanging low in the sky, cast shadows from a sheltering maple across the sloping roof and the wide front porch with warped boards and missing railings. Vines wrapped their tendrils around and through the slats in a weathered picket fence. Flowering weeds encroached past the borders of rose beds and other perennials.

After Jack jumped out of the Land Rover, Garth had parked beside a late-model luxury sedan. Now Harriet stood with him near the flagstone path that led to the cottage's entrance and waited for Jack and the woman to join them.

The two walked hand-in-hand, Jack dragging the woman forward as if eager to introduce her to Harriet and Garth. Though she smiled at his exuberance, her eyes and brows were pulled tightly together, as if she struggled with a headache.

She wore a flannel jacket with jeans and hiking boots. Several strands of brown hair, a shade or two darker than Jack's, had escaped from her ponytail and blew across her flushed cheeks. As they drew closer, Harriet guessed the woman to be in her late twenties, possibly in her very early thirties. A touch of mascara lengthened her lashes, and her professionally manicured nails were a tasteful mauve.

"These are my new friends," Jack said. "This lady is a veterinarian." He stumbled slightly over the syllables of the long word but managed to get them right. "I don't know what he does."

Garth handled the introductions, his tone reminding Harriet of the one he used when speaking to a nervous animal. "I was at the vet clinic when Jack came running in."

At his words, the woman pulled Jack into a side hug and let her hand rest on his shoulder. "I'm sorry for the fuss," she said with a too-bright smile. "As you can see, I'm fine."

Harriet shifted her gaze from Jack to the woman, amazed at the family resemblance. "You must be Jack's mom. It's so nice to meet you."

The woman appeared startled, and she hesitated before answering. "I'm Elena Hunter. Jack and I are here on a bit of a holiday." Again, the too-bright smile.

"Welcome to White Church Bay," Harriet said warmly. "Unfortunately, my aunt—she's a physician—was away when Jack arrived and told us that you had lost consciousness. My receptionist is trying to reach her, and we also called emergency services. Are you sure you should be up and about?"

Elena's face blanched, and her body wavered. She seemed to lean on Jack to steady herself while Garth clasped her elbow. "Please, no," she managed to say between deep gasps. "They must not come."

"I'm not sure we can cancel the call," Harriet said, uncertainty in her tone. "Besides, if you were unconscious—"

"It was nothing," Elena insisted. "You can see for yourself, I'm fine." Her shoulders straightened, and she moved to the other side of Jack, forcing Garth to release her. "I won't talk to them."

Harriet exchanged a glance with Garth, who pulled out his phone. "I'll see what I can do." He stepped away to make his call.

Elena placed a hand on her stomach as she took one deep, calming breath after another.

"But, Mum, you have to." Jack's eyes darted from Elena to Harriet. When he spoke, his plaintive voice pressed against Harriet's heart. "I couldn't wake her, Dr. Bailey. Please believe me."

"I believe you," Harriet assured him.

Elena knelt to hug Jack. "I promise I'm okay," she whispered. Her eyes, when she lifted them to meet Harriet's gaze, seemed both fearful and pleading.

"At least let me take your blood pressure," Harriet offered. "My bag is in Garth's vehicle. I keep a few people things in it for emergencies."

"If I say yes, will emergency services stay away?"

Garth had his back to them, and his voice was too low to hear what he was saying. But his animated movements led Harriet to believe he was doing his best to cancel the call.

"I don't know," she said to Elena. "And I'm not sure I'd be doing you any favors if they did. You should see a doctor to make sure you're all right."

"Perhaps I will. But not until after our holiday." Elena hugged Jack again and straightened to gaze toward the road to Whitby, the nearest large town.

The rolling hills made it impossible to see the road from there, but they would be able to hear the siren as it neared the cottage. Harriet strained her ears, but only heard Garth ending his call and the usual birdsong.

"I convinced them you're on your feet, so they're not coming," he said.

Elena blew out a huge breath in relief.

"Promise me I didn't do the wrong thing here." Since meeting Elena, Garth's suspicious attitude toward her seemed to have lessened. Now he appeared drawn to her, almost as if she were a skittish fawn in need of rescue.

"I'd have refused to see them. Their trip would have been wasted." The too-bright smile made yet another appearance. "Besides, you brought Jack back to me. Nothing could be more right than that."

Garth glanced around the cottage's exterior, which was in desperate need of a gardener to tidy up the landscaping and a handyman to replace warped boards on the porch and rehang the gate on its hinges. "Is there anything you need?"

While gauging how much upkeep was needed on the outside, Harriet couldn't help but wonder what kind of maintenance was needed inside the cottage.

Maybe too much for Elena to feel comfortable entertaining guests.

"I only need to be left alone," Elena said in response to Garth's question. "I do thank you for your kindness and your concern, but I need to get Jack out of his muddy shoes. And the sea breezes chill the bones when the sun drops past the treetops. I'm sure you want to be on your way before then."

"What about checking your blood pressure?" Harriet asked. "It won't take very long."

Elena was shaking her head before Harriet finished speaking. "It was simply a little dizzy spell. I'm perfectly fine now. Good day to you both."

As she gently led Jack to the front door, he waved back at them. "See you around," he called.

A few seconds later, both of them disappeared behind the heavy wooden door.

"I wonder who she is," Garth mused quietly. "And why she's so eager to get rid of us."

"Maybe she was embarrassed about causing a fuss."

"Maybe," Garth replied, though he didn't sound convinced.

A curtain moved behind one of the windows. Harriet couldn't tell whether Elena or Jack wanted to see without being seen. Her guess would be that Elena was watching to make sure they left.

Harriet touched Garth's arm. "We should go."

As they walked to the car, Harriet mulled over the afternoon's strange events. The fear in Jack's eyes when he stumbled into the clinic had concerned her. Still concerned her. And so did the things he'd said.

Why was it a secret that they'd moved into Beckside Croft? And who wasn't supposed to know about it?

CHAPTER FOUR

After they got back into his Land Rover, Garth asked Harriet if she minded taking a small detour before they headed back to the clinic.

"That sounds intriguing. Since Polly hasn't called with another emergency, I suppose I can stay away a little longer. I'll let her know though." Harriet didn't need to ask where they were going. He could only be taking her to one place.

During the drive back down the rutted lane, she texted a brief message to Polly. EVERYTHING IS FINE. PLEASE LET AUNT JINNY KNOW. BE BACK SOON. DETAILS WHEN I GET THERE. A moment later, Polly responded with a thumbs-up emoji.

Before they reached the main road, Garth turned onto a different track with even deeper ruts. It was abruptly blocked by a stone wall, even though the lane continued on the other side.

He gestured to the land, rolling green hills dotted with sheep and cattle, that was visible through the windshield. "All this used to belong to the same family that owned Beckside Croft. We're talking about three hundred, maybe even three hundred and fifty years ago. At one point, there was a generation with two brothers. When the father died, he gave each brother half the land, all neatly divided fair and square. Both boys should have been happy, right?"

"There wouldn't be a story about them if that were the case," Harriet replied.

"A story as old as time." Garth frowned. "As the years passed, the elder brother prospered. The younger, who preferred a life of ease to hard work, didn't. Petty squabbles between them became arguments, and one of those arguments became a physical fight. This wall was built, and they never spoke to each other again."

"Who built the wall?"

"Nobody knows for sure, though my guess is that the older brother had the resources and manpower to do so. By then the lazy brother had gambled away over half of his inheritance. Sometime later, he sold most of what he had left and moved to York. All that remained of the original farm for him to leave his children was Beckside Croft."

As Garth shared the land's history, Harriet studied the ancient stone wall that cut across the track with as much permanence as the severing of brotherly ties. Weeds with tiny white and purple blossoms clung to dirt-filled cracks and crevices, somehow finding a way to survive in such conditions.

In a way, the delicate flowers symbolized the tenacity of those who'd settled here all those centuries ago, finding a way to survive despite difficulties and obstacles. Her own family could trace their lineage back several generations but not three centuries. Interesting that Garth knew the origins of the wall.

"Is this story about your family?" Harriet asked.

"Indirectly." He tapped his fingers on the steering wheel. "My grandmother's brother married into the prosperous branch of the family, though by then they'd experienced their own economic troubles. All that's left of their original farm now belongs to Fern and Ivy Chapman."

Harriet's mouth fell open. The sisters, now in their midfifties, were renowned for their sibling rivalry. Harriet had met them the summer before during an annual antique festival, when Fern's misguided attempt to upstage Ivy had nearly ended in a tragedy.

"It doesn't seem like the Chapman sisters learned from their ancestors," Harriet said.

"Human nature is what it is. But that's not why I brought you out here." Garth gestured to a stand of mature trees and narrow saplings. "The game camera that recorded the pine marten is in that copse. Restless Beck is about twenty meters farther west. I plan to put more cameras there."

"Restless Beck? What's that?"

"*Beck* is an old word for a stream. It's not much more than a channel that runs to the sea, but long ago it was known to change its course every few years. That caused all kinds of disputes for the property owners who used the stream as a boundary marker. Hence the name." Garth unbuckled his seat belt. "Come on. I'll show you."

As they walked toward the copse, Garth explained how the different properties—Fern's and Ivy's farms, Beckside Croft, and even Harriet's own Cobble Hill Farm—lay in relation to one another. He described the most likely areas to search for the injured pine marten. Her head was spinning by the time they reached the camera.

Unfortunately, they found no sign of the marten.

At last, Garth dropped Harriet off at the clinic's front door.

As soon as she entered, Polly bombarded her. "Tell me everything. Who is that boy? Is his mum all right? What kept you so long?

Or do you want me to get you something to drink first? Coffee? Tea? Water?"

"Nothing, thanks." Harriet nodded to the surgery area. "How's Thomasina?"

"She drank a bit of water not long ago. I made a note of the time on her chart. Since then, she's been peacefully sleeping."

"Excellent." Drinking water was one of the signs Harriet watched for to ensure that an animal was recovering from anesthesia. "Let's hope she isn't too cranky when I wake her up." She headed toward the hallway and past the exam rooms.

Polly rounded her desk and scurried after her. "Don't leave me in suspense. What happened with the boy? And Garth?"

"He's okay now." Harriet washed her hands while choosing her next words. "As for Garth, he's on a kind of mission right now. I understand his need for secrecy, so I can't say any more than that."

"I won't deny being curious," Polly said as she handed Harriet a towel, "but I love that you're a secret-keeper, since I trust you with mine."

Except when it comes to what's happening between you and Van.

But Harriet understood Polly's hesitation to confide in matters of the heart—especially when Polly was probably as confused about her feelings for Van as anyone else. She'd once had a thriving dating life, but apparently, when a relationship got serious, untangling the complexities of romance didn't seem to come easy to Polly.

While Harriet checked Thomasina's vital signs and examined the incision for any sign of an infection, she told Polly about the strange visit with Elena Hunter and her obvious desire to be left alone.

"I finally got in touch with Jinny," Polly said. "In all the hubbub, we both forgot she went to Saltburn-by-the-Sea for the weekend."

"That's right. For that mental health conference."

"She said she'd try to touch base with you sometime tomorrow, but if not, she'll stop in after she gets home."

"Thanks for all that." Harriet checked the clock as she returned Thomasina to the kennel. Polly should have left twenty minutes ago. "And for staying late, especially on a Friday when you have plans."

"It's a movie with a couple girlfriends. We're going to the theater in Whitby with the dinner menu. Their black-and-bleu cheese-burgers are my absolute favorite."

"Will and I have talked about going there, but when they show a movie we want to see, we're too busy. And when we can go, they're playing something we don't want to see. But I keep hoping every-thing will line up soon. It sounds like a good time."

"It is." Polly's light tone didn't mesh with the downcast expres-sion that suddenly appeared in her eyes.

Harriet wished she could take away her young friend's heart-ache. But who was she to say whether Polly had been mistaken to refuse Van's proposal? Only Polly could know that.

"You run along and enjoy yourself." Harriet grinned. "Before I make you call Courtney with the update on Thomasina."

Polly's eyes widened as she backed out the door. "No way. I am so out of here."

A few minutes later, Harriet locked the clinic as Polly pedaled off, then she dialed Courtney's number on the office phone. To her relief, the call went straight to voice mail, allowing her to leave a short, upbeat message and end with a cheery goodbye.

Evening chores were next on the agenda. Harriet munched on a garden salad while Maxwell and Charlie, the official office cat, ate their supper in the kitchen. The calico had been rescued from a burning trash can and still bore the scars on what was left of her gray, ginger, and white coat. Like all the office cats who'd preceded her, Grandad had named her Charlie. He used to joke that keeping the same name for all his office cats gave him one less thing to remember.

After tidying the kitchen and changing clothes, Harriet returned to the surgery area, leaving both Maxwell and Charlie to their post-dinner naps in the reading nook.

Once again, Harriet removed Thomasina from the kennel, recorded her vital signs, and took a peek at the incision. So far so good.

"Would you like to try eating again?" she asked the patient. Thomasina had only taken a few bites when Harriet had offered her food earlier. Hopefully by now she was ready for a larger meal.

Harriet settled in a chair she'd retrieved from the supply closet and placed Thomasina in her lap. She held the bowl of food steady while the cat sniffed it then took dainty bites.

The day had been long and stressful, but those quiet moments, when she could give physical comfort to a recovering animal, made up for the hard ones. Especially when those moments connected Harriet to her grandfather's compassion and love for animals.

She'd often spent time with him in the clinic or on his farm calls when she and her mom and dad came for their annual visits. While her parents visited old friends and explored the countryside, Harriet often opted to stay at Cobble Hill Farm. She'd learned so much as Grandad's little shadow and, under his guidance, gained extensive practical experience that gave her a head start in several of her veterinary courses.

Whenever Grandad invited her to join him in the kennel recovery room to "sit for a while," she wasted no time in grabbing a pillow and a blanket. They'd walk together through the dimly lit clinic and arrange her bedding near the post-op cages or in their special corner. Once Harriet was situated, Grandad would remove the furry patient from its kennel and place it in her lap. Unless the animal was the size of a retriever or a shepherd. Then the dog sprawled between the two of them.

Either way, the recovering animal experienced some much-needed love and companionship. Grandad believed the interaction, though it amounted to little more than an hour or so of togetherness and stroking the animal's fur, aided the healing. And he'd explained to Harriet that it helped the veterinarian as much as the animal.

When Thomasina had finished eating, Harriet shifted to a more comfortable position and cradled the cat in her lap. Thomasina purred softly, her eyes closed in a light doze.

"You're a special girl," Harriet whispered as she stroked the ginger fur. "Not just because of your name, though it makes me nostalgic for long-ago days. I remember as if it was yesterday when Grandad and I sat here with a ginger kitten who was a quarter your size. Her leg broke when she jumped from the top of a tall dresser and landed wrong. Grandad set her leg, and I even helped with the cast. That evening, I curled up next to Grandad with the kitten snuggled next to me. That was the first time Grandad told me the story of the original Thomasina."

The next afternoon, a drencher of a day, they'd watched the film adaptation of the novel. "This story has always been one of my favorites," Grandad had said. "It reminds me that faith is as important as science—perhaps even more so. A competent vet can save a lot of animals with science alone. But an exceptional vet also depends on faith." He'd also warned young Harriet that she might not like the veterinarian in the story. "Not at first anyway. But you'll like him by the end."

Harriet rested her head against the wall behind her and closed her eyes. Scenes from the movie played in her mind. Grandad was right about the veterinarian who'd lost his faith when his wife died. Now a widower raising his young daughter, he devoted himself to treating the local livestock but seemed to have little patience for pets. Before the tale ended, though, he'd rediscovered the healing power of love and faith with the help of an outcast and his daughter's ginger cat.

"It was a different time," Harriet murmured to the Thomasina in her lap. "Many people back then believed an animal was only valuable if it had a purpose, such as farm animals and working dogs. Grandad and I must have watched that movie over a dozen times. Because of him and Thomasina, I never wanted to do anything with my life except to follow in his footsteps."

Thomasina's purr softened as she drifted into a deeper sleep. Harriet stroked the soft fur and allowed her thoughts to flow from the past to the present and back again, finding a tranquil comfort in the rhythmic rise and fall of the sleeping cat's body against the palm of her hand. Her concerns over the wounded pine marten, over Jack and his fearful "mum," and Courtney's apparent disdain for the precious pet she'd adopted faded away as Harriet's own breathing matched that of Thomasina's.

Suddenly Harriet's head nodded forward, jerking her awake. Startled by the unexpected movement, she blinked and needed a moment to remember where she was. Thomasina stirred with a soft sound then gave a wide yawn.

"Still sleepy, huh? You're not the only one."

The cat stretched and then slipped from Harriet's lap. She let her go then slowly stood while stretching muscles that had gone stiff during her nap. Her phone buzzed, and she realized that was what had awakened her. She'd missed a call from Will, which she immediately returned.

"I'm outside your door," he said with a good-natured chuckle. "I bring gifts of food."

"I thought you had a meeting tonight." They'd had plans to go out to dinner at a local restaurant until Harriet had scheduled Thomasina's surgery for that day. Then their backup plan for supper together at Cobble Hill Farm had to be canceled when a last-minute meeting popped up on Will's calendar.

"It was shorter than expected, so here I am."

"Give me a minute to put Thomasina in her kennel, and I'll let you in."

Her day might have been long and stressful, but this was turning out to be a perfect evening. Will would want to hear all about her afternoon. Even though Courtney didn't attend church, he probably knew her and might have insights on how Harriet could establish a more positive relationship with her.

Harriet wished she could tell him about the injured pine marten and her promise to help Garth find it. She also wanted to know if Will was aware of the new occupants at Beckside Croft. Perhaps, as minister of the local church, he could pay a visit to Elena and Jack.

Once again, Jack's quiet words about his mum and their secret assaulted Harriet's heart.

Harriet's practical side cautioned that the relationship was none of her business, but her imagination clung to the mystery of the little family.

What exactly was Elena's relationship to Jack? His adopted mom? A relative or a guardian?

"I might know a way to find out for sure," Harriet murmured to Thomasina as she settled her into the kennel. As soon as the door was latched, Harriet opened her phone's internet app and typed *Elena and Jack Hunter* into the search engine as she walked to the back door. A cursory glance through the results caused her to frown. Though Hunter was a common enough name, none of the Elenas or Jacks were the Elena or Jack now residing at Beckside Croft.

When she got to the door, Harriet closed the app and pocketed her phone. She'd try again when she had more time, but for now the mystery remained.

A mystery that Harriet might not have known about if it hadn't fallen into her lap. But now she was determined to solve it.

CHAPTER FIVE

Saturday morning began before sunrise when Harriet was called to the Atkins farm to assist a cow with the birth of her first calf. When Harriet and Mr. Atkins emerged from the barn, the sun had risen above the horizon. Harriet crossed her arms on the top rail of the fence and appreciated the brightening of the sky as the earth's nearest star ascended.

A new life and a gorgeous sunrise. Was there any better way to start a day?

"Glad you could come out this early," the elderly farmer said. "The missus keeps telling me it's time to get out of the cattle business, but I'm not ready to say goodbye to them yet. Difficult births like this one make me wonder if she isn't right. Then I see that newborn calf standing on his own legs next to his mum and I hear the good Lord saying, 'Not yet.'"

"It's a blessing that never grows old," Harriet agreed.

When Harriet was ready to go, Mrs. Atkins presented her with a lemon pound cake to take back to the clinic with her. One of the perks of being the local veterinarian was that Harriet got to sample all kinds of goodies.

After the lingering goodbyes, Harriet slid into the Beast, the green Land Rover that had been part of the estate she'd inherited from her grandfather. Thankfully, she'd been in England long enough now that she'd mastered the art of driving on the "wrong" side of the road and the idiosyncrasies of the Beast's clutch.

Soon she was back at Cobble Hill Farm. After a quick shower, she fed Maxwell and Charlie while enjoying a slice of the pound cake with a cup of her current favorite coffee blend. A few minutes before eight, she slipped through the door separating the kitchen from the clinic.

Polly was already seated at her desk, and Harriet handed her a plate of pound cake and a fork. "From the Atkins farm, where the herd has grown by one adorably gangly calf who was incredibly reluctant to leave the comfort of his mama's belly."

"These are the days I'm most thankful I'm the receptionist and not the vet." Polly held up a bite of the pound cake as if making a toast. "I get the benefits without losing any sleep."

"But you miss the miracles," Harriet replied.

"Not all of them," Polly countered. "Which reminds me. Janette Philbin called after you left last night to see about an appointment for Gideon. He has a cough. I added them to the schedule, though it may mean staying past noon." Saturday was usually a half day for them.

"I don't mind staying a little late. I have a soft spot for that little guy."

"Don't we all?"

Gideon, a five-month-old golden retriever puppy, was the runt of an otherwise healthy litter of eight born to Nugget, a beautiful creamy golden with the easygoing temperament common to the breed. She'd swallowed a small ball early in her pregnancy that

Harriet had to remove. Thankfully the surgery went well, and the puppies were fine.

Except for Gideon, who was prone to intermittent coughing spells.

Harriet tended to Thomasina, allowing her a few moments of freedom in the recovery room before putting her back into the kennel. The cat protested with a loud yowl but was too polite to scratch or bite.

"I wish I could meet Courtney's grandmother," Harriet said as she latched the door. "You probably wish you were going home to her again. At least you'll be with Polly for the rest of the weekend. She's sure to spoil you rotten."

While Garth and I search the moors for a creature that doesn't want to be found.

Unless the pine marten was spotted again on one of the game cameras, she doubted they'd find him. The stealthy little animal could be anywhere. All she could do was hope and pray he was still alive.

The morning passed quickly as Polly alternated placing the patients in the two examination rooms. Harriet went from one to the other to clean out infected ears, administer vaccinations, answer questions, and offer assurances. No out-of-the ordinary ailments. No mystery illnesses. And the biggest blessing of all—no emergencies.

She marveled once again at how competent and dependable Polly was at her job. Perhaps she should ask Garth about expanding his circle to include Polly in the search for the elusive pine marten. Will and Aunt Jinny too. After all, five sets of eyes were better than two. Especially with a creature known for its skill at hiding.

Harriet entered exam room two for the post-op evaluation of a young herding dog who'd been kicked in the leg by an angry cow. The wound was healing nicely, and Harriet received a grateful lick on the chin from the rambunctious border collie.

"I know it's hard, but do your best to keep him from running for a few more days," Harriet said as she escorted Dale Bugler, a large man with florid cheeks and unruly white hair, to the receptionist area.

"Nigh on impossible," Dale replied with a hearty chuckle. "This one has been going at top speed since he discovered he had legs. So like his grandsire—may that blessed champion rest in peace—that sometimes I can't help wondering if he didn't come back to us again in this one."

"Actually, your theory might not be that far off from a scientific point of view," Harriet said. "Since he has his grandsire's DNA, their temperaments and personalities could be strongly linked. That's why breeders are so careful in their decisions, so that they can nurture and carry on such desirable traits."

When they reached the desk, Harriet handed Polly the dog's file and gave him a goodbye pat. As Polly handled the checkout process, Harriet caught sight of Jack sitting on the floor beside Gideon. Nine-year-old Sarah Jane Philbin sat on the other side of Gideon. The children and the dog seemed oblivious to anyone else, while Janette flipped through a magazine.

Harriet leaned close to Polly. "What is Jack Hunter doing here?"

Polly shifted in her chair for a better view of the waiting area. "I didn't see him come in," she said. "I've been straightening out a billing error with the medical supply company. He can't have been here long, though. At least I hope not. Ms. Hunter will be worried."

"I wish I'd thought to ask for her number," Harriet replied. "I didn't expect to need it." She glanced toward the two examination rooms. One door was closed, which meant a client was waiting for her.

"Maybe Jack has a phone of his own to contact her," Polly suggested. "Do you want me to ask him?"

"I'll do it," Harriet said.

"Who is the lad?" Dale asked.

Harriet paused to consider her answer. The one thing she knew for sure about Elena Hunter was that the woman valued her privacy. Enough so that she'd somehow managed to keep any mention of herself off the internet. Harriet had tried her search again last night after Will left and found nothing.

"A new friend," she finally told Dale with a quick smile before she walked over to Jack.

The boy looked up at her with a huge grin on his face as she knelt beside him. "This is Gideon. He likes me."

"I see that." Harriet scratched Gideon's head and was rewarded by a gaze of pure love from the retriever's dark eyes. He rolled onto his back and waved his paws in the air, causing Jack to giggle.

Harriet grabbed a paw and gently squeezed the pad. "Gideon is a good friend to have. I've known him since he was less than a day old."

Jack's eyes widened as he stared at her. "How big was he when he was born?"

Harriet cupped her free hand. "Not much bigger than this. He was the tiniest puppy in the litter, and we weren't sure he would live. But he's a fighter."

"That's why we named him Gideon." Sarah Jane crossed her arms on her knees and leaned forward. "Do you know that Bible story?"

"I know about Noah's Ark," Jack replied, his boyish face screwed up in concentration. "And how Moses got the Ten Commandments from God. He saw a burning bush too. I can't think of anyone named Gideon though."

"I'll tell you about him," Sarah Jane offered. "Gideon was minding his own business when an angel appeared with a message from God and said he was going to be a mighty warrior. But Gideon didn't believe the angel. He said he was the most unimportant person in his father's house and that their family belonged to the most unimportant tribe in Israel."

"Did the angel believe him?"

Caught up in her story, Sarah Jane leaned forward. "The angel said it didn't matter, because Gideon was the one God chose. It didn't matter that the enemy army was big and scary or that Gideon wasn't a warrior. He obeyed God and won the battle. We named the biggest puppy Samson."

"I know about him," Jack said. "He was the strongest man in the world until some dumb girl cut off his hair." His disgusted expression showed exactly what he thought of Delilah.

Harriet couldn't help chuckling. She placed her hand on Jack's shoulder. "Does your mom know you're here?"

He kept his eyes lowered while he petted Gideon's tummy. "She said I could go outside." His petulant tone gave away the truth.

"But did she expect you to wander so far from home?" Harriet pressed.

He shrugged.

"Maybe we should call her. Do you have a phone?"

He shook his head.

Janette shared a concerned glance with Harriet. "Jack," she said, "I get worried when I don't know where Sarah Jane is. Your mom must be wondering where you are."

"Who's Sarah Jane?" Jack asked.

"I am," Sarah Jane piped up. "I was named for my grandmother, Sarah Philbin, and kind of for my mom. Her name is Janette Philbin."

"I was named for my dad," Jack said. "We have the exact same name except for the number. He was the second, and I'm the third. That's why I'm called Jack."

Was? Once again, Harriet and Janette exchanged a glance. That little word—so tiny yet heavy with meaning—prompted a few puzzle pieces to click into place. If Jack's father had died, maybe his mother had too. Elena could be his aunt, which would explain the family resemblance. If Jack's parents had died when he was quite young, that might be why he thought of Elena as his mother. Which meant she could have custody of him.

"What is your full name?" Harriet asked, doing her best to keep her tone casual. When Jack focused his attention on Gideon, bending to bury his face in the retriever's soft neck, she said, "In a way, I'm named for my grandad. He was Harold Bailey, and I'm Harriet Bailey."

Jack ignored Harriet and raised his eyes to Sarah Jane. "How old are you?"

"Nine. How old are you?"

"Six and three quarters."

Harriet hid a smile at the obvious pride in Jack's tone. So typical of a little boy.

"That's a fine age to be." Janette tugged on Gideon's leash, and the retriever rolled to his feet. She rewarded him with a scratch behind the ears. "This would be a good time to call your mum and tell her where you are." She took her cell phone from her pocket. "Can you tell me her phone number?"

Jack frowned, and Harriet suspected he'd refuse to answer. What would she do then? She couldn't take Jack home when a client was waiting for her in the examination room. Her only option was to ask Polly to drive him to Beckside Croft and pray he'd go without too much fuss.

Janette placed a hand on the little boy's shoulder. "Please, Jack. Like I said, I'd be worried if Sarah Jane came here without telling me."

His frown faded as he lifted his eyes to Janette and recited the number.

"May I?" Harriet asked, and Janette handed her the phone as the call connected.

On the second ring, Elena answered. "Who is this?"

Though Harriet recognized Elena's voice, she was taken aback by her tone. Elena sounded worried, but also wary, as if she was afraid of who the caller might be. "Hello, Ms. Hunter. This is Harriet Bailey. We met yesterday."

"Is Jack with you?" Elena asked.

"He's here at the clinic. Are you able to come for him?"

"I'm already on my way."

"Do you need the address?"

"You're at Cobble Hill Vet Clinic, right? I know where that is."

"Great. We'll see you soon."

The call ended, and Harriet handed the phone back to Janette.

"Jack can stay with us until his mum arrives," Janette said. "That is, if he'd like to spend more time with Gideon."

Jack's face brightened. "Can I, please? My uncle doesn't like dogs, but I love them."

"Then you'd better soak up all the puppy time you can get," Janette told him with a smile.

Polly joined them after ushering Dale out the door. "I'll keep an eye on him," she told Harriet in an undertone, "and let you know when Elena arrives."

"You promise you'll stay right here?" Harriet asked Jack.

"Cross my heart."

"We won't let him out of our sight," Janette added.

Polly handed Harriet the folder for her next patient and shooed her to the exam room. Thankfully, treating the cocker spaniel's infected ear mites didn't take very long.

Harriet was checking on Thomasina in the recovery area when Polly found her.

"Elena's here. I asked her to wait to see you."

"Great." Harriet recorded Thomasina's temperature on her chart then washed her hands. "What about the Philbens? Are they still in the waiting room?"

"I took them to the other exam room as soon as I heard a car in the drive. After what you told me about her yesterday, I wasn't sure Elena would want anyone to see her."

"Probably not." Harried quickly dried her hands and headed for the waiting room.

The *empty* waiting room.

She rushed outside in time to see a late-model luxury sedan pulling onto the main road.

Elena and Jack were gone.

Once the clinic closed for the day, Harriet placed several tins of cat food in a bag while Polly tucked Thomasina into a cat carrier then carried it to her car. As soon as she and Thomasina were headed toward the Thatcher home, Harriet took Maxwell outside for a stroll. While the dachshund sniffed alongside the barn-turned-kennels, Harriet wandered among the flower-beds, admiring the early spring blossoms that brightened the landscape.

A couple of cars were parked near the art gallery that displayed Grandad's paintings. Harriet was about to pop in to visit with gallery manager Ida Winslow when Garth's Land Rover pulled into the parking lot.

Garth slid out of his Yorkshire Coastal Wildlife Centre Landy and waved his electronic tablet. "I got more footage," he said when Harriet and Maxwell joined him. "Our sneaky little pine marten seems to be staying within a relatively small area. Probably because of his injury." His mouth twisted into a grimace. "I think it's worse."

Harriet's heart sank, though she wasn't surprised. Whatever had happened to the pine marten, he had little chance of recuperating on his own. Each passing day meant more pain for him. How much longer could he stay hidden from the predators who staked out the area?

Maxwell let out a sharp bark in an obvious demand for Garth's attention. "I'm sorry, little fella." Garth crouched to scratch the dachshund behind the ears. "I didn't mean to ignore you."

"He really does like you," Harriet said.

"Most animals do," Garth joked. "I think it's my superpower."

"How about using that superpower to get the pine marten to come to you?"

"Wish I could." Garth set the tablet on the hood of the vehicle and tapped the screen. A video showed the pine marten drinking from a stream.

"Is that Restless Beck?"

"That's right. I'm glad I got the camera installed yesterday. It picked up some really good footage."

The pine marten was still dragging his rear leg as he attempted to scamper from beneath a thicket to the shelter of an overhanging rock and then to the stream. He sniffed the air with his pointed nose and scanned the area with his sharp eyes. Apparently confident that no danger threatened him, he lay on his belly and drank from the stream. Then he followed it, stopping every few feet to sniff the air before continuing his journey. Soon he was out of the camera's range.

"I scrounged up a couple more cameras," Garth said. "Can you go with me to set them up? Who knows? We might get lucky enough to find him." Hope was evident in his tone.

Harriet understood how he felt. She wanted to find the wounded pine marten as much as he did. They both hated to see any animal suffer. And the pine marten's endangered status definitely made the situation more urgent. Garth wanted to find the little creature before he died from his injury, but he also appeared driven to find him before anyone else did.

But then what?

The question had been at the back of Harriet's mind since Garth showed her the first video. She doubted that he planned to share his find with any government agencies. She knew he'd been angered at times by their interference in his facility operations. In the few months they'd known each other, they'd had some conversations about the governmental agencies that regulated the Yorkshire Coastal Wildlife Centre. While Garth expressed his support for such agencies on one hand—he had firsthand knowledge of how quickly things could go wrong when a rehabilitation facility slipped below minimum standards of care for the animals it had taken in—he also chafed under the stringency of various requirements that he felt hindered rather than helped his work.

Yet the government was the government. Harriet wasn't sure what obligations she might have, as a vet licensed by the government, to notify authorities of the existence of an endangered animal that hadn't been seen in the area for a decade.

But no matter how conflicted she was, Harriet wasn't about to refuse the opportunity to search for the pine marten with him.

"Can you give me fifteen minutes?" she asked.

Garth's face broke into a huge smile. "No problem."

For hours that afternoon, they combed the moors for signs of the pine marten and set up additional cameras.

But the chocolate-colored creature with the curious black eyes was nowhere to be found.

Though Harriet could have sworn those curious eyes were watching them.

CHAPTER SIX

Before the sun came up on Monday morning, Harriet dressed in heavy-duty jeans, a thick sweatshirt and jacket, and her sturdy hiking boots in preparation to return to the moors. During a moment of sleeplessness, an idea had come to her like a bolt of lightning. Pine martens were mostly active at night. But Garth had texted that only a rabbit and a raccoon had tripped the motion cameras on Saturday night. What if, stressed by his injury, the pine marten was moving around in the early morning hours?

And, obviously, in a different area than where they'd placed the cameras?

Maybe it was time to shift to another area of the moor and go on her own. One person would make less noise than two, and she could go at her own pace.

Maxwell followed her to the door, whining softly as if he understood she was leaving without him on the unusual early morning excursion.

She knelt to caress his ears. "If only you could help me," she murmured. "Though I'm afraid our little friend would get one sniff of you and I'd never find him." To be fair, the same could technically be said of her.

Garth had suggested on Saturday that the marten would become so accustomed to their scent that he'd no longer be wary of them. Maybe that would work to their advantage, but Harriet suspected they'd only find the little creature if he was immobile, which would almost certainly be disastrous for him.

Harriet hadn't been searching for long when the startling crack of a breaking twig caused her to freeze. She hurriedly looked around, all her senses on high alert, but nothing moved in the early morning light. She wanted to laugh at herself for being frightened over nothing.

Except she'd heard *something.*

"Who's there?" she called out. "Garth, is that you?"

A figure moved from behind a tree. "Is that who you were expecting to find?" Elena Hunter asked.

Harriet blew out a relieved breath followed by a self-conscious chuckle. "I didn't expect anyone to be out here, honestly."

Elena stepped closer, moving far enough from the shadows that Harriet could make out her features. Though she wasn't as pale as when they first met, the dark circles under her eyes and the thin line of her lips caused her to appear tired and drawn. She wore a too-large jacket that had seen better days over faded jeans and hiking boots.

"Why are you out here?" Elena asked, a hint of suspicion in her tone. "Searching for one of God's creatures in need of your help?"

Does she know about the wounded marten?

The thought flitted through Harriet's mind unbidden, and she dismissed it immediately. Garth had sworn her to secrecy, so she couldn't believe he'd have told Elena, a stranger, about their mission.

"I couldn't sleep." That much was true. Harriet lowered herself onto a nearby boulder and gazed across the moor. "The sunrises are lovely here, but I sleep through them too often. I decided to take advantage of my sleeplessness today."

Elena tilted her head and eyed Harriet as if she suspected there was something left unsaid. Then her mouth quirked, and she came even closer, her hands in her pockets. "Cobble Hill Farm lies on the cliffs above the North Sea. A few minutes' walk from your front door, you can watch the sun rise over the water, painting the waves and the sky with colors only God can name. Yet here you are, closer to my cottage than your estate, and I have to wonder why."

Though Elena spoke with a matter-of-fact tone, Harriet's cheeks warmed. She couldn't give any other explanation for being on the moor at such an early hour.

"Were you expecting to meet Garth?"

The unexpected question took Harriet aback. "Not particularly."

"My neph—that is, Jack and I have seen him a couple of times on our walks."

Had Elena stopped herself from saying *nephew*? If she was Jack's aunt, maybe he had a different last name than she did.

"Do you come out here often?" Elena asked.

"Am I trespassing?" That was a good possibility. Garth's careful explanation of property lines had made sense at the time, but now everything he'd said was a big muddle. Harriet had no idea how close she might be to Beckside Croft or the size of the property.

Elena didn't bother to answer. "We hear so often about the brashness of Americans," she said instead. "How direct and forthright they are. How rude. Yet you hide your own curiosity and don't ask why I'm exploring the moors this early in the morning."

"I don't suppose it's any of my business."

"And you don't want to tell me why you're really here either."

Harriet responded with a noncommittal shrug.

"Jack likes you. He told me he wants to be an 'animal doctor' when he grows up."

"I was inspired by my grandfather."

"I met your grandfather once. Not far from this very spot, in fact. He was painting *en plein air.*"

Had Elena used the French phrase, which simply meant *outdoors*, in an attempt to impress? To intimidate? Or was it a natural part of her vocabulary? Harriet tended to believe the third option, but Elena's impersonal tone made it impossible to know for sure.

"It was incredible to watch him." Elena's voice became more animated. "He painted with confidence, and yet he had no pretensions."

Harriet gazed over the rolling hills, wishing she could see them as Grandad had. Not for the first time, she wondered how he'd decided what to include in his paintings and what to leave out.

"We have a set of landscapes we call the Moors Collection in the art gallery," Harriet said. "You're welcome to come by anytime to view them and his other work. If the painting you saw him working on is there, I'd love for you to point it out to me."

"It isn't." A genuine smile brightened Elena's features. "He insisted on giving it to me, and it's been hanging above the mantel at Beckside Croft ever since."

"That sounds like something Grandad would do. He loved it when someone truly connected with his work."

Elena settled onto a nearby rock and hunched her shoulders against the morning chill. "I want to believe you're as kind as he was. But…" She paused, taking a moment to seemingly gather her thoughts. "It's not easy for me to trust. Because you're Old Doc Bailey's granddaughter and because Jack likes you, I'll be direct with my question. Maybe you'll even think *I'm* brash and rude."

She stared with such intensity that Harriet found herself leaning away. Her mind swirled as she tried to anticipate what Elena intended to ask. Harriet couldn't come up with even a hint of an idea.

"Please be honest with me." Elena's eyes narrowed, and her voice deepened. "Are you spying on us?"

Harriet almost fell off her rock. Stunned by the unexpected question, she blinked, opened her mouth, then closed it again. Surely she hadn't heard Elena correctly.

"Spying?" she finally managed to eke out. "Me? Why would I do that?"

Elena assessed her for a long time then stood. "You haven't given me a straight answer, but your reaction is better than a denial. I'm glad. I want to like you."

"I want to like you too. I mean, I do like you. And Jack."

Elena's spying suspicion, especially when added to Jack's admission of a secret, prompted Harriet to ask a direct question of her own. "Are you in some kind of trouble?"

A smile tugged at Elena's lips. "There's that American forthrightness I've heard about. Come and go on the Beckside moors as you please, Harriet, but remember that not all strangers are as kind and well-meaning as your grandad."

"I want to help you any way I can—"

Elena waved her hand as if to erase Harriet's offer then disappeared among the trees.

Harriet murmured her interrupted words to herself. "If you'd let me."

Whatever Elena's problems were, she seemed determined to keep them to herself. Harriet involuntarily shivered as another question confronted her.

What might happen to Jack when those problems became too big for Elena to handle alone?

CHAPTER SEVEN

Harriet returned to the clinic after a farm call late that afternoon to an empty reception area. "Polly?" she called.

Polly emerged from the corridor cradling Thomasina, who purred happily in her arms. They'd bonded during their quiet weekend together, and the cat's recovery was coming along nicely.

Harriet glanced at the wall clock behind Polly's desk. Only ten minutes remained until the clinic closed for the day. "Is Courtney on her way?"

"I called her about an hour ago." Polly twisted her features into an exaggerated grimace. "She said she'd be here when she gets here."

"I see." Harriet scratched Thomasina behind the ears, and the cat pressed her head against Harriet's hand. "She's such a lovely cat."

"I can take her home again," Polly offered as she rounded her desk and plopped into her chair. "Dad will grumble for the first five minutes then let her sleep in his lap the rest of the evening. He'll probably even insist on being served supper on a tray so he won't have to get up and disturb her."

Harriet laughed. "That sounds too specific to have been a hypothetical."

"You think?" Polly lowered her voice to mimic her father. "'Can't bother the kitten. She's still recuperating.' He actually said that last night."

Harriet chuckled as she placed her medical bag on the counter. "What about your mom? She might not want a houseguest."

"Mum adores her. Thomasina made herself at home and wasn't a bit of trouble."

"It's too bad you can't keep her. Don't let Courtney know I said that."

"I never would. Especially since I feel the same way." Polly sat in her chair and allowed Thomasina to rest in her lap. "She and Charlie became friends while you were gone. They took a long afternoon nap together until Charlie decided it was time to go outside. She seemed disappointed Thomasina couldn't go with her."

"Charlie gets along with everybody. Two feet, four feet. Fur, feathers, or hair." The gentle calico's loving nature was a wonder.

"Speaking of getting along," Polly said as she pulled a gift bag from the bottom drawer and set it on her desk, "Will stopped by with a surprise for you. He even fixed up the bag all by himself."

Harriet beamed with delight at the playful kittens illustrated on the bag's pale blue background. Blue and yellow tissue paper emerged from the top and hid what was inside.

"Please tell me Ash isn't in there," she joked as she gently lifted the bag. Will had recently adopted an abandoned gray kitten he'd named Ash Wednesday.

Polly chuckled. "If anything alive was in that bag, I wouldn't have shut it up in my desk drawer. Go ahead and open your present."

"Do you know what it is?"

"He told me. You're going to love it."

Harriet slid a DVD from between the folds of the tissue paper. "*The Three Lives of Thomasina*. I can't believe he did this. What a sweet surprise."

"He's a thoughtful one." Polly chuckled again. "Don't watch it without him though. He specifically said he wants to see it with you."

"He's got one week to arrange that, and then it's fair game." Harriet held the DVD in her hands with as much care as if Will had given her one of Queen Elizabeth's tiaras. Over their impromptu supper Friday night, spread out like a picnic on the surgery floor with Thomasina as company, Harriet had told Will about the movie. They'd searched for it on the popular streaming channels, but it wasn't available. Apparently, the fan base for the classic wasn't very big.

"I wish we could watch it tonight," she said. "But he has a missions committee meeting at the church."

"How long will the meeting last? Maybe you could watch it after," Polly suggested.

Harriet was about to reply when the clinic door burst open. Winifred Wilkerson, a ten-year-old with a penchant for finding injured animals, rushed into the area with a small bundle clutched in her arms. To Harriet's surprise, Elena and Jack were right behind her.

Cheeks damp with tears, Winifred made a beeline for Harriet. "Jack and I found him near Beckett Rock," she said between gulps. "You have to fix him. You can, can't you?"

Harriet took the bundle from the girl's shaking hands and carefully pulled back folds of the finely woven fabric. An unconscious fox kit nestled inside a woman's scarf. A bloodstained sock lay against its side.

"That's mine," Jack said, appearing on the verge of tears himself. "We didn't have any bandages."

"Sometimes we have to make do," Harriet reassured him as she felt for a pulse. "This little guy can't be more than a few weeks old. Where did you find him?"

Instead of answering, Winifred gave in to the sobs she'd been trying to contain.

Polly immediately placed Thomasina on her desk and gathered Winifred into her arms while Harriet carefully lifted the sock from the kit's tiny body. Beneath it she found a bad gash that made her breath catch in her throat.

No wonder Winifred was more upset than Harriet had ever seen her before. The young girl usually faced whatever injuries she discovered with the maturity of a future veterinarian. But she'd never brought an animal with such a serious injury to the clinic before.

"Winifred was on a ramble with us when we found it," Elena said quietly. Jack leaned against her for comfort. "I called her mum, and she's on her way."

"Do you know if the den was nearby?" Harriet asked. "Anything about the rest of the litter, or the mother?"

"We didn't take the time to check. Jack pulled off his sock to stop the blood, and I wrapped it in my scarf." Elena cast a maternal glance toward the little girl in Polly's embrace. "Winifred insisted we come straight here."

Harriet nodded as she turned her attention back to the wounded kit. Would she be able to save its life? Or had it already lost too much blood? "I need to get the kit into surgery right away."

"Can I come too?" Winifred asked. "I want to help."

"Not this time, sweetheart. Besides, you've already helped so much." Harriet smiled at the girl, hoping to hide her own concern. "Polly, could you call Garth and tell him what's happened?"

"You got it." Polly clasped Winifred's hands in her own. "Could you watch Thomasina for me while I make that phone call? She had surgery a few days ago, and she's doing much better now. I'm sure she'd love one of your special cuddles. That would be a big help."

Winifred readily agreed, and Polly settled the young girl in a chair with the ginger cat, who purred contentedly. Elena sat beside Winifred while Jack plopped on the floor between them and leaned against Elena's leg.

Harriet breathed a prayer of thanks that Polly knew why the call to Garth needed to be made without that reason being voiced in front of the children. There was nothing he could do for the fox kit at the moment, but if it—she, Harriet learned quickly—survived, he'd certainly find a space for her at the center. What he needed to do now, though, was to go to the scene where this baby had been found, in case any other kits or their mother had also been injured and needed care.

Sometime later, Polly joined Harriet in the surgery as she was settling the sedated fox in a recovery kennel. "That's what I was hoping to see," she said as she stepped closer to take a peek at the baby.

Not that there was much for Polly to see except the little one's mouth and nose. After cleaning and stitching the wound with meticulous care, Harriet had bandaged the kit's abdomen then tucked her into a cozy wrap.

Polly placed a comforting hand on Harriet's back. "The children will be glad."

"She's barely alive," Harriet cautioned, "and I'm not sure she'll survive the night. Though I suppose it wouldn't hurt for them to come back here and see her. At least then, if the worst happens, they'll know I tried."

"They're not here, but Jinny is." Polly led Harriet to the door. "She popped in while I was on the phone with Garth. She's in the kitchen now setting out the tea. We can all have a cuppa while I tell you about the drama you missed while you were saving a life."

"It must have been quiet drama. I didn't hear a thing."

"There wasn't any yelling, but there sure were more than enough 'if looks could kill' moments."

"Between who?" Harriet found it difficult to believe that Elena and Alma Wilkerson, Winifred's mother, would be at odds with each other.

"First, you need to know that Garth came by to pick up the children. He wanted them to take him to the exact spot where they found the kit. Alma arrived right after him, and both she and Elena agreed that they'd all go. I went outside with them as they were making the arrangements."

"Wasn't Garth afraid that five people would be too many?" If the mother was nearby, a crowd might scare her away from her den—and any surviving kits.

"That's what they were talking about. Where to park and where the others could stay while he investigated the scene. That's when Courtney showed up to get Thomasina—fifteen minutes *after* we were supposed to close," Polly added irritably. "If Winifred hadn't brought us that kit, I'd have already taken Thomasina home."

"Maybe that's what Courtney hoped," Harriet suggested.

"That's what I think. Though she made quite a show of concern while Garth was around and wasn't at all happy when Elena and Jack drove off with him."

"She's jealous? Garth and Elena barely know each other." Though Garth had given Elena one or two lingering gazes before she'd disappeared into her cottage the other day. And maybe Elena had hoped to run into him instead of Harriet earlier that morning.

"Maybe. But Garth isn't as adept at hiding his interest as he might think."

Before Harriet could respond, Polly continued. "I can't tell you how much I hated handing Thomasina over to Courtney. Even worse, I had to be polite about it."

"And I'm grateful for that," Harriet said. "Not that I'd expect anything less from the best vet receptionist ever. At least Courtney didn't try to tag along with the others."

"Oh, she tried. But Jinny told her she couldn't go, in that tone she has. You know the one—where she sounds all sweet, but you still wouldn't dream of arguing with her."

"I try to be on the receiving end of that tone as little as possible." Harriet chuckled as she imagined her aunt's pleasant but no-nonsense demeanor besting the former supermodel.

They entered the reception area and headed for the door separating the clinic from the kitchen. Harriet ushered Polly inside and switched off the clinic lights. By the time she entered the kitchen, Polly was already on the floor to greet Maxwell.

Aunt Jinny wiped her hands on a towel and then spread her arms wide to wrap Harriet in a loving embrace. "I made cheese sandwiches. You always loved those as a girl. And the kettle will be whistling any minute now."

"Thank you, Aunt Jinny," Harriet said.

Her aunt leaned back and peered into Harriet's eyes. "Your patient survived the surgery, but you're worried the little tyke won't make it through the night."

Harriet had to give a wry smile. "You know me too well. She's lost a lot of blood, and she'll need constant care. I doubt she's even weaned yet."

"Garth has to bring Elena back here to get her car," Polly said. "Before they left, he said he would run by the center to pick up a care package for the kit. I'll text him an update." She hunched over her phone and laughed as Maxwell maneuvered his long dachshund nose between her and the screen.

The kettle whistled, and Aunt Jinny prepared the tea. The table was already set with cups, plates, napkins, and tableware.

"You go ahead and take a seat," she said to Harriet. "Everything will be ready in no time."

"Isn't there anything I can do to help?"

"Not a thing except relax."

Harriet lowered herself into a chair, suddenly feeling weary and burdened. She almost wished she was ten again and could weep as freely as Winifred had. Feeling the ebb and flow of the tiny fox's life in her hands had unnerved her. Especially when Winifred and Jack depended on her doing everything in her power to save its life.

That life was in God's hands now. In truth, it always had been.

"Harriet? Are you okay?"

Her aunt's compassionate tone brought Harriet from her thoughts. "I'm fine. It's just that some days are extra hard."

"I know they are. I also know you did everything you could. Take comfort in that while we wait to see what happens." Aunt Jinny set the teapot, wrapped in an embroidered cozy, on the table and took a seat. A mischievous glint appeared in her dark blue eyes. "So let's talk about Elena and her son. I can't remember the last time anyone stayed at Beckside Croft. Is she related to the family? What's her last name?"

Harriet grinned at her aunt's blunt curiosity. "Her last name is Hunter. And I strongly suspect Jack isn't her son."

Aunt Jinny's eyes widened. "But he calls her 'Mum.' And the family resemblance between them is strong."

"I have a hunch she might be his aunt."

While Polly extricated herself from Maxwell and joined them at the table, Harriet told Aunt Jinny about the various encounters she'd had with Jack and the comments he'd made about his family. She didn't say anything about her early morning trek to the moors— something she hadn't told Polly either—or the strange chat she'd had with Elena there.

For one thing, Harriet didn't want to slip up and mention her participation in Garth's secret search for the wounded pine marten.

But something else tied her tongue, a reason she couldn't define even to herself. Perhaps it was as simple as wanting to respect Elena's obvious wish for privacy. Or it was the question Elena had asked that sent shivers up Harriet's spine.

"Are you spying on us?"

What—or who—did Elena fear?

As the conversation continued and the women enjoyed their tea, Polly once again mentioned Courtney's after-hours visit to the clinic. She was obviously disappointed not to have had another evening with Thomasina. Polly's natural affinity for animals made itself known every day, but maybe this would inspire her to adopt a cat in the future.

"You wouldn't believe how Courtney fawned over Garth the other day," Polly said to Aunt Jinny as she dropped a sugar cube into her tea. "He did his best to ignore her then like he did today."

"Garth's priority might have been to find the fox den," Aunt Jinny said. "Though you should have seen his expression when he came into the clinic and saw Elena. He obviously finds her attractive."

"He's positively smitten," Polly added. "I'm sure he doesn't want Elena to think he's interested in Courtney."

"Are the two of you matchmaking?" Harriet helped herself to another of the triangular cheese sandwiches.

"Not on purpose," Aunt Jinny said with a good-natured laugh. "Though it did my heart good to see Garth's eyes light up when he looked at Elena. He's been alone for a long time."

Harriet snuck the crust of her sandwich to Maxwell. She'd almost forgotten that Garth had lost his young wife to a rare form of cancer several years before. She hadn't known him then, and he'd never mentioned his marriage to her. In the years since his wife's death, he'd rarely dated, instead devoting his time and energy to the wildlife rehab facility.

"After everyone else left," Polly said, "I invited Courtney into the clinic to get Thomasina. She was nicer to me than she'd ever been before."

Harriet responded with a quizzical look. "You don't say."

"Was she hoping for a discount on her bill?" Aunt Jinny asked with a grin.

"She wanted to talk about Elena. Or, to be more accurate, find out everything I know about Elena."

Harriet's shoulders tensed. "What did you tell her?"

Polly shrugged while she added strawberry jam to a crumpet. "What is there for me to tell? Elena isn't any of Courtney's business. Though she mentioned hearing about an emergency happening at Beckside Croft that turned out not to be an emergency."

"How did she know where Elena is staying?" Harriet asked.

"I think she figured it out when the children were telling Garth where they found the fox kit," Polly replied. "The Wilkersons are close neighbors, so Winifred has been showing Jack all her favorite places."

"Poor Courtney," Aunt Jinny said. "She never sees that she's the cause of her own unhappiness. Sometimes I wonder why she returned to Whitby when her modeling career ended instead of starting over someplace new. Maybe then she wouldn't have this overwhelming need to prove herself."

"Or to be jealous of a stranger," Polly added.

Harriet gave Maxwell another piece of her sandwich while Polly and her aunt's conversation drifted to other topics.

Could it be possible that Courtney was the spy Elena feared?

As much as Harriet didn't want to jump to conclusions, she found that she couldn't rid herself of the horrible feeling that jealousy might not have been Courtney's only reason for asking Polly questions about Elena.

What if she had another, more nefarious, motive?

CHAPTER EIGHT

Harriet placed a portable incubator, about the size of a child's shoebox and equipped with a heating mechanism, on a low table beside her bed. "You'll be snug as a bug in a rug," she murmured to the baby vixen. "And so many people are praying for you. A little girl named Winifred, for sure. And maybe a little boy named Jack. They both want you to be well. So do I."

The kit, who had received a low dosage of a sedative, didn't move except for the slightest rise and fall of her torso.

Harriet rested her fingers on the vixen's side and found comfort in the rhythmic movement. So much so, she soon realized she was matching her own breathing to that of the fox. That wasn't a surprise. She'd caught herself mimicking an animal's breathing pattern before when she was especially concerned about its well-being.

Her text alert sounded, and she picked up her phone to read Will's message.

ANY CHANCE YOU'RE STILL AWAKE?

Instead of sending a reply, she hit the call button. He answered immediately, his tone upbeat yet tired. "Hi there."

"Long meeting?" Harriet asked.

"One of the longest, and with very little to show for it. That's okay, though. This meeting was about being heard. We've gone through that kind of process before."

"You must be exhausted."

"I am. But also energized. When there are so many worthy causes, it's difficult to prioritize one over another. Especially during these times, when the needs are so great. I'm confident that when we meet again, we'll be able to make the hard decisions about what we can support and our budget for each one. Tonight, though, was like herding cats. Everyone has a different priority and a different perspective. But that's good because it means a variety of ideas."

"It's funny hearing you talk about herding cats when you only have one," Harriet joked. "Maybe you should ask Jane Birtwhistle for advice." The retired schoolteacher owned at least a dozen, and Harriet had treated most of them at one time or another. "How's Ash?"

"Cute as a button. And getting mischievous. This morning I found him sound asleep in that brass urn by the hearth. Doesn't seem like the most comfortable place for a nap to me, but Ash apparently loves it. I found him because his purrs echoed in there."

Harriet laughed at the thought.

"Speaking of Jane," Will said, "she stopped in this morning to introduce herself to Ash and give me her blessing, which admittedly was a bit strange, since that's usually my area of expertise. She has a singular gift though. I'm sorry to tell you this, Harriet, but she might speak feline even better than you."

Harriet chuckled at Will's teasing about her ability to connect with the animals she treated. As a young woman, it had often seemed odd to Harriet that others considered her to have a unique talent when she thought her sensitivity to an animal's mood and body language was normal. From her perspective, the odd ones were the people who *couldn't* understand their pet's needs. Years of experience, however, had taught her that God had gifted her with an empathy that was important to her work. The skill was shared by many veterinarians, zookeepers, animal behaviorists—practically anyone who made daily interaction with animals their life work. And people like Jane Birtwhistle and Winifred Wilkerson.

Not to mention the fictional Laurie from *The Three Lives of Thomasina*, the outcast who lived alone in the woods with deer and rabbits, injured badgers and birds. The character had fascinated Harriet when she was a child. She remembered that when she was very young, she'd longed to have wild animals trust her in the same way they did Laurie. When Grandad realized that Harriet's unrealistic longings made her doubt her instincts, he'd explained that Laurie could only do what she did because of the magic of the movies.

Then he'd taken her to a local rescue group where she'd brushed the dogs and played with the cats. One more of the many precious memories Grandad had left her.

"Right now I wish I could speak fox," she said aloud as her gaze fell on the kit.

"Did you say 'fox'?" Will asked.

"Two children found a baby vixen who can't be more than eight or nine weeks old. She has a horrible gash in her side. I'm not sure she's going to make it."

She went on to tell him about the surgery she'd performed while Garth took the kids, Elena, and Alma to the area around Beckett

Rock where they'd found the kit. All the while, her conscience nagged her for not telling Will during their impromptu picnic about Elena and Jack. She had started to more than once, but each time she heard Jack's voice echo within her. *"It's supposed to be a secret that we're there."*

"They didn't find any sign of her mother or littermates," she explained, mentally shushing the nagging voice. "Not even a den. I guess the reason she was alone will remain an unsolved mystery."

"What will happen to her?" Will asked.

"I'm keeping her tonight. Garth stopped by with a formula I can give her when she wakes up." Realistically, she wasn't sure the kit would wake up, but she had decided to be optimistic. "Sometime tomorrow, I'll take her to the center. She'll get round-the-clock care there."

"I'm guessing you won't be sleeping too much tonight."

"My alarm will go off every hour on the hour. It's what I have to do."

"Because of who you are," Will murmured, his voice soft and comforting. "If you need someone to talk to during any of those hours, if you need anything at all, you can call me. I hope you know that."

"I wouldn't want to wake you."

"You can wake me anytime for any reason."

Harriet gave silent thanks for this wonderful man God had brought into her life. When she arrived in England, she'd been understandably reluctant to give a thought to romance after her broken engagement. But over the past year, Will's friendship and steady presence crowded out any lingering hurt, replacing it with joy and contentment. She couldn't be happier about the way her life was turning out. Will was such a kind and thoughtful man.

"Your present," she exclaimed.

Will's chuckle resounded through the phone. "Do you like it?"

"I love it. I should have said so as soon as you called."

"You're concerned about your latest charge. I understand that."

"That doesn't mean you come second in my life," Harriet said.

"I know."

Two little words that spoke volumes. Harriet sensed the warm smile she knew accompanied his assurance.

"The big question now is when we're going to watch it," Will said. "I have huge expectations, you know."

"I still can't believe you'd never even heard of the movie until I told you about it. It's such a mainstay of my childhood."

"I was raised on the classic comedians. Three Stooges. Laurel and Hardy. Jerry Lewis."

Harriet emitted an exaggerated groan, and they both laughed.

"Believe it or not, I'm free on Wednesday. Does that work for you?" Will asked.

"What about your Bible study?" Will was in the midst of teaching a six-week overview of the Gospels.

"The group is going to Whitby that evening. Harvest Community Church is showing a documentary on archaeological finds related to the Gospels. It's very good, but since I've already seen it, I'm free for dinner and a movie. I'll even bring the food."

"That sounds absolutely wonderful." Harriet checked her calendar and found the evening was free. "Is six o'clock too early?"

"I'll be there. How about I pick something up from the Crow's Nest on my drive over?"

"That sounds perfect." The local pub, famous for its hearty comfort foods, was one of their favorite places.

They talked a few minutes longer, with Will promising to stop in at the clinic to see the fox the next day before Harriet took her to the rehab center. After the call ended, Harriet set her alarm and checked on the fox one more time. Her breathing, though shallow, was steady, and Harriet decided to let herself hope that all would be well.

Satisfied she'd done everything she could for the kit, Harriet glanced at Maxwell, who snored softly in his bed without his prosthesis. Walker, Winifred's older brother, had found and brought Maxwell to Grandad after the pup had been hit by a car.

As Harriet drifted off to sleep, she mused on what it would be like to raise the fox and add her to the Cobble Hill Farm menagerie. An impossible dream, of course. The best-case scenario would be for the vixen to recover and be released to the moors where she belonged.

Her thoughts wandered from the fox to Garth to Elena to Courtney. Though Harriet swatted away her earlier conjecture that perhaps Courtney was the spy Elena feared, she was unnerved by all the questions the woman had asked Polly. If she was that jealous because Garth appeared to be attracted to the newcomer, what might she do to her perceived rival?

A scorned woman could be a dangerous woman. An unstable woman like Courtney could be deadly.

CHAPTER NINE

Once the vixen—who'd not only survived the night but had begun to take feedings of Garth's formula—was settled in her incubator next to Polly's desk, Harriet started her workday. Since the incubator was partially concealed behind the office printer, no one who checked in for an appointment noticed it. Yet the arrangement allowed both Polly and Harriet to keep a close eye on their young patient. Though she slept for long stretches at a time, aided by a special sedative, the kit awakened every couple of hours with an empty tummy. After Harriet or Polly fed her, she drifted back to sleep.

Garth stopped in for a brief visit with the kit and a private conversation with Harriet. The pine marten had appeared once again on the video feed from one of the game cameras. Harriet was as surprised as Garth that the sleek-coated animal was still alive. She longed to go with him on another search, but her day was too busy between appointments and caring for the fox kit, so she reluctantly wished him luck and watched him leave.

During a midmorning lull in the schedule, Harriet joined Polly in the reception area for a quick coffee break.

"That's a cute top," Harriet said. "Is it new?"

The paisley design in shades of orange on the lightweight pullover reminded Harriet of Thomasina's ginger coloring.

"It was on display in the window at Corbett's," Polly replied. "A total impulse purchase. It's not really my color, so I don't know why I bought it."

Harriet responded with a skeptical lift of one eyebrow.

"I know what you're thinking. And you're probably right." Polly blew out a deep breath. "I don't understand why Courtney adopted Thomasina in the first place. She obviously doesn't love her."

"I've wondered the same thing." Unfortunately, Harriet didn't have any answers that would give Polly the comfort she needed. Even though Thomasina had never belonged to Polly, she was feeling a sense of loss that was too raw for platitudes. Nor was she in a mood to give Courtney any benefit of the doubt.

People in grief, however, often responded in strange and inexplicable ways. Especially since grief was usually complicated by a swirling mess of other emotions—love, guilt, regret, anger, pain. Perhaps Courtney had taken Thomasina to ease her grandmother's mind then discovered too late she wasn't a cat person. Or perhaps she'd made a careless promise to her grandmother to care for the beloved pet then regretted the promise once she became responsible for Thomasina.

There were as many potential explanations for Courtney's actions as the whiskers sprouting from Thomasina's nose. Harriet doubted their curiosity would ever be satisfied, since it was unlikely Courtney would confide in either her or Polly.

Though perhaps that was exactly what Courtney needed—someone she could confide in.

How do you know she doesn't have that?

Harriet admitted she was being presumptuous. Her sole excuse was that she'd known women like Courtney when she lived in Connecticut. Their relationships often seemed fraught with competition and backstabbing rather than the unconditional love and support that characterized healthy friendships. Harriet felt for those women.

"Someone's awake," Polly announced, a welcome interruption to Harriet's musings.

Polly gently lifted the kit, who was wrapped in a square flannel cloth, and handed her to Harriet. The kit's mouth opened in a wide yawn, and she made a whimpering sound similar to any puppy of the same age as her dark eyes peered into Harriet's.

"Do you want to feed her?" Polly asked. "Next time she wakes up, you might be with a patient."

"I'd love to." Harriet murmured to the kit while Polly warmed the formula and filled the feeding syringe. "After she eats, I'll change her bandage."

"When are you taking her to the wildlife center?"

Harriet grinned. "As late in the day as I can. I'll be glad to get a full night's sleep, but I hate to let her go."

"I'm sure Garth will let you visit as often as you wish," Polly assured her.

As soon as Harriet presented the formula, the kit latched on and drank greedily. Her growing appetite was a good sign.

At that moment, the clinic door opened. Jack rushed inside while Elena paused on the threshold to scan the room.

"We came to see the baby fox," Jack said. "Can we?"

"You're just in time." Harriet bent to show him the kit, who was still wrapped in her cozy blanket. "Would you like to feed her?"

"You'd let me?" His voice was filled with awe.

"If it's okay with your mom." Harriet shifted her gaze to Elena. "Do you mind?"

"As long as you'll stay close and supervise." Elena smiled at Jack. "You must be very gentle. Remember how hurt she was. She may still be in pain."

"Perhaps a little," Harriet said, noting that Elena didn't correct her when she referred to her as Jack's mother. "More than anything, she's hungry."

In less than a minute, Jack and Harriet were sitting side-by-side in the waiting area while the young boy fed the eager kit.

"Wait till I tell Winifred. She'll be so jealous," he said. "She had to go to school, but I'm on holiday, so I don't have to."

Harriet couldn't help but smile at the bragging lilt in his voice. Though in the back of her mind, she questioned why Elena had planned her holiday while school was in session. Another mystery that might never be solved. Unless Elena decided to trust Harriet with her secrets.

As if she'd read Harriet's mind, Elena cleared her throat. "It's an unusual thing to do, I know. But Jack's such a good student, and everyone deserves some fun in their childhood. After all, 'all work and no play makes Jack a dull boy,' and we can't have that, can we?" She tousled the boy's hair.

Her forced gaiety had the opposite of its intended effect. It heightened Harriet's curiosity instead of alleviating it. But she had no right to press Elena for a different explanation.

"We're glad you did," Harriet said. "Especially since Jack and Winifred saved this vixen's life."

"What's a vixen?" Jack asked.

"A female fox," Harriet replied.

Jack's nose scrunched as he frowned. "Why is she called a vixen?"

"I know this one." Polly came around the reception desk. "Or at least I know one theory. The Old English word was spelled f-y-x-e. Over time, it became 'fyxen,' then 'vixen.'"

Elena chuckled, appearing more relaxed than any other time Harriet had seen her. "How do you know that?"

"Old Doc Bailey told me," Polly said. "This isn't the first fox we've treated, and I doubt it'll be the last."

"Does she have a name?" Jack asked.

Harriet hesitated. How could she explain to a six-year-old that naming a wild creature made it even harder to let it go? Though the bitter was laced with sweet. A named animal was a remembered animal.

"Not yet. Would you like to name her?"

Jack frowned. "What about Winifred? She might not like the name I pick."

"I think she'll understand. She chooses names all the time for animals she finds. Now it's your turn."

The boy's frown eased into a smile as he adjusted the feeding syringe. "This is hard. Is she a runt like Gideon?"

"No," Harriet said. "She's the right size for a fox kit her age. Why do you ask?"

"I was thinking she might like a Bible name. Especially if she was a runt too."

"There are a lot of Bible names you could choose from. Mary. Miriam. Abigail. Ruth."

"How about Sarah, Deborah, or Rachel?" Polly suggested.

"You could call her Talitha," Elena said. "It means 'little girl,' so it's not exactly a name. Jesus said the words *Talitha cumi* to Jairus's daughter when He raised her from the dead." She smoothed the back of Jack's hair. "Do you remember that story?"

"Yeah. Jesus told the people who were crying to go away, and they laughed at Him."

"That's right. Then Jesus brought the little girl back to life. In a way, you and Winifred helped bring this baby fox back to life. And so did Dr. Bailey."

"Ta-lith-a," Jack said slowly, emphasizing each syllable. "I like it."

Elena leaned her head against Jack's. "So do I."

The family resemblance between them in that moment was unmistakable, and so was the closeness they shared. It was as if they were alone in the room.

Jack shifted to Harriet. "Do you like the name Talitha?"

"I think it's perfect," she answered while resisting a sudden urge to ruffle his already unruly hair. Her dreams of having children of her own had faded when her engagement ended. But now, an image of Will's handsome face filled her mind. How sweet it would be to see a little boy with his hazel eyes.

She shook her head. Now wasn't the time to daydream about a possible future with the heart-stealing pastor.

Elena pulled Jack into a gentle side hug, and the feeding syringe slipped from the kit's mouth. The formula dribbled from between her tiny lips. When he attempted to give her the syringe again, she yawned, revealing her baby teeth and her long dark tongue without ever opening her eyes, then settled into another deep sleep.

Harriet took the feeding syringe from Jack and eyed the measurement lines on the side. "That's the most she's taken so far. You did a great job."

"Maybe I can be a vet like you when I grow up," Jack said cheerfully. "Or a wildlife man like Mr. Garth. He knows all about foxes and deer and even snakes. He said I could come to his wildlife center anytime I wanted."

"I'm taking Talitha there this afternoon," Harriet said. "I'm sure she'd love for you to visit her."

Jack gazed hopefully at Elena, who smiled indulgently. "We'll see."

The clinic door opened, and a woman entered. She appeared to be in her midtwenties and wore a blazer over matching slacks with sneakers. Gold-rimmed glasses magnified her deep-set eyes, and her ash-blond hair, styled in a pixie cut, framed her round cheeks. A messenger bag with a crossbody strap rested at her hip.

Her smile broadened as her gaze landed on Jack and Talitha.

"This is absolutely perfect," she exclaimed as she pulled the strap over her head and set the messenger bag on a nearby chair. "I must get a photograph. You don't mind, do you?" She didn't wait for an answer but dug through the bag and produced a professional-looking camera.

Elena sprang from her chair and stepped in front of Jack, arms spread wide to hide him from the woman. Harriet and Polly immediately stood on either side of her.

"I mind very much," Elena said, her voice shrill. "I will permit no photographs of my neph—of anyone in my family."

"But he's one of the children who found the baby fox, isn't he? I already took pictures of the young girl while I was at the school." The broad smile, which had faded when confronted with Elena's objection, returned to its full wattage. "I went to get shots of those who'll be in the Spring Festival performance, but all the children were buzzing with the news. The lad there is a sort of local hero. I'm sure he'd love to see his picture in the newspaper, wouldn't you, pet? He's already holding the fox."

"Does the girl's mother know you took her picture?" Elena demanded.

The woman's good-natured smile disappeared. "She signed a release. But I need a few shots of the baby fox. You can be certain I prayed all the way here that the beastie was still breathing. This is my job, you see—writing about the local news."

Harriet understood why Elena might not want her secret holiday to be invaded by a reporter. "Who do you work for?"

"The *Whitby Gazette*, of course." The woman's face twisted into a satisfied smirk. "News like this will go viral. Maybe even get picked up in the London dailies."

The words were barely out of her mouth when Elena, eyes wide with fear, clutched her stomach then collapsed. Thankfully, both Harriet and Polly reacted quickly enough to help break her fall. Together, they lowered Elena to the floor.

"Mum!" Jack's plaintive cry seemed to come from far away as Harriet's mind worked to bring order out of the chaos surrounding her. In a veterinary emergency, she'd have gone on autopilot and seen to her patient first. That was what she needed to do now, except her "patient" was a person instead of an animal.

Well, two persons.

"Everything will be okay," she assured Jack, placing a comforting hand on his knee. "You take care of Talitha, and Polly and I will take care of your mum."

"I'll get your bag." Polly glared at the reporter, who appeared appropriately chastened, before scurrying to the nearest exam room.

"And a blanket," Harriet called after Polly as she checked Elena's pulse and found it to be steady but slow. "And Aunt Jinny, if you can find her."

"On it," Polly called back.

The reporter crept closer, her fingers gripping the camera. "Why was she so upset about a simple picture? It's not like the boy is a member of the royal family." Her tone brightened. "Is he?"

"I don't think so." Harriet rested the back of her fingers against Elena's forehead. Her skin was cool, and her cheeks even paler than the first time they'd met, the day she and Garth had returned Jack to Beckside Croft.

Harriet pointed to the camera. "This is my clinic. You may not take any photographs inside these walls. Do you understand?"

"You're Dr. Bailey," the woman said as she gestured to Harriet's medical jacket. "Of course you are. I have a cousin who lives in Whitby, and her family always brought their bulldog, Neville, to your grandad. It was more of a drive than going to the vet in their town, but they liked the way Old Doc Bailey talked to Neville. As if he and that old dog could have a conversation."

"That sounds like Grandad." Harriet wished the reporter would go away and let her focus on the medical emergency at hand.

Polly returned with a pillow, blanket, and the emergency medical bag. While Harriet tried to revive Elena, Polly covered her with the blanket. "I called Jinny. She'll be here any moment."

Harriet nodded while she patted Elena's cheeks. "Elena? You need to wake up."

Polly, her voice amazingly calm, considering the situation, knelt beside Jack. "You did such a great job feeding Talitha. But now that she's sleeping, we should put her in the recovery kennel where it's quieter. Could you help me?"

A lone tear traced its way down Jack's cheek as he nodded. Polly gently took the kit from him then put her hand on his shoulder to guide him to the surgery area.

"Mum will be okay, won't she?"

The plaintive question tugged at Harriet's heart. Polly's reply was too soft for Harriet to hear, but her reassuring tone surely provided the boy with at least a little bit of comfort.

The door opened, and Will entered the clinic. His customary smile quickly faded as he took in the scene. "What happened? What's going on?"

"She fainted," Harriet said. She patted Elena's cheek again. The woman groaned and moved her head. "You need to wake up, Elena."

Will knelt across from Harriet and placed his hand on Elena's shoulder.

Her eyes fluttered open then darted to Jack's empty chair. "Jack. Where is he?"

The fear in her voice shook Harriet to her core. "He's with Polly. He's fine."

Elena turned her gaze to Harriet. For a moment she seemed to relax. Then she noticed Will, and her body tensed again. "Who are you?"

"He's a friend," Harriet quickly assured her. "And the pastor of our local church."

"I came to see the fox kit that kept Harriet up all night," Will said as if he engaged in small talk with fainting women on a regular basis. "But I'm happy to meet you, even under such strange circumstances."

"You know about me?" Elena cast an accusatory glance at Harriet.

Will frowned in confusion. "Not at all. I always enjoy meeting new people, that's all."

Once more, the door opened, and Aunt Jinny hurried in. Within a few minutes, she and Will were leading Elena into the house, which left Harriet alone with the reporter.

"There's no story here," Harriet said firmly.

The reporter's broad smile and cheerful twinkle returned. "I came to get a photo of the baby fox, not to cause an uproar. Perhaps we could begin again. I'm Amelia Arbuckle, the *Whitby Gazette's* newest reporter." She extended her hand.

A lifetime of behaving in a professional manner no matter the circumstances overcame Harriet's initial hesitation. "Dr. Harriet Bailey."

She shook Amelia's hand and found her grip to be surprisingly normal. Neither weak nor domineering. She'd almost expected the latter, since so many people used a handshake as a show of power.

"As I said, I was at the local school for a different assignment when I heard about the fox kit being found on the moor." Amelia's smile broadened even more. "Don't you see? It's the perfect human interest story for our lifestyle section. Heroic children. A wild baby animal on the brink of death. Even you have a role to play as the lifesaving veterinarian."

"It's not a role," Harriet said.

"No, of course not. I can see you have the same affinity for"—she paused as if wanting to be sure she chose the right words—"the injured and the hurting as your grandfather did. People should know that."

Harriet's usually long fuse was rapidly burning shorter. Her primary goal was to protect Jack and Elena without causing an international incident with the *Whitby Gazette*. She could imagine the headline now: AMERICAN VETERINARIAN REFUSES PHOTOS OF FOX. WHAT IS SHE HIDING?

It was probably best to give Amelia something instead of nothing.

"I'll bring the fox kit out here so you can take her picture," Harriet said. "That's the best I can do at this time." Amelia's face lit up, and Harriet held up her hand. "On one condition."

"Name it."

"Nothing that happened here today is mentioned in the story," Harriet said firmly. "You will not mention my friend or the boy in your story."

"Winifred told me who she was with when she found the kit. I know the boy's name."

"No promise, no photo."

"Loyalty." Amelia nodded her head as if in approval. "I respect that. It's such a rare quality these days."

"It shouldn't be," Harriet said. "I trusted a reporter from the *Whitby Gazette* once before and regretted it. Please don't make me regret trusting you."

"You won't." Amelia sounded so sincere and so eager that Harriet longed to believe her.

Hopefully she wasn't making another big mistake.

CHAPTER TEN

Harriet retrieved Talitha and allowed Amelia to photograph her then saw the reporter off. She joined the others in her living room in time to hear Aunt Jinny offer to drive Elena and Jack home.

"Thank you, but I feel quite well enough to drive the short distance to Beckside Croft," Elena replied.

"Are you sure you should?" Harriet asked. "There's no rush for you to leave. I hope you know that."

"You've already shown me such kindness." Elena nestled in the corner of the upholstered sofa with Jack scrunched beside her. Though a little color had returned to her cheeks, she still appeared pale. "What do you suppose that reporter will write in her article?"

"She agreed not to mention you or Jack in the article if I let her take photos of Talitha. Hopefully she'll keep her promise. If not…" Unsure how to finish the sentence, Harriet lowered her gaze. Elena's protective desire to keep Jack's image off the newspaper's website wasn't that unusual in this day and age, but for her to faint?

Something other than parental privacy had driven Elena's reaction. Not for the first time, Harriet wished she knew what Elena was so afraid of and why her presence in the area was so secretive.

"It means a great deal to me that you tried." Elena scooted forward then slowly stood. She wobbled then sat back down.

"That does it," Aunt Jinny said. "As your physician, I'm declaring you're not ready to drive yourself, no matter how short the distance."

"But you're not my physician." Elena smiled at Aunt Jinny. "Though I do appreciate your concern."

"I'm your physician while you're in White Church Bay." Aunt Jinny returned Elena's smile. "And your chauffeur just this once."

"What about my car? Without it, Jack and I will be stranded at the cottage."

"I can drive it and come back with Jinny," Polly said. "Our next appointment is in about twenty minutes, but it's a routine checkup. It shouldn't be a problem if I'm not back before then." She directed an impish grin toward Harriet. "Right, boss?"

"I think I can manage," Harriet said with a chuckle. Though the days ran more smoothly when Polly was at her desk, it wouldn't be the first time Harriet had handled an appointment on her own.

"I'll stick around here for a while, if that's okay," Will added. "After all, I came to see the kit, and I haven't had the chance yet. I'll make sure Harriet has an extra pair of hands if she needs them."

"Talitha is in her incubator near Polly's desk," Harriet said. "Amelia wasn't happy I insisted the fox stay in the incubator during her photo shoot, but I let Amelia tell me where to position her."

"If this reporter has any skill as a photographer, she should have been able to get at least one good shot," Aunt Jinny said. "I guess we'll see when the *Gazette* comes out. Will her story be in tomorrow's edition?"

"She didn't say. Whether it's in tomorrow's paper or next week's, I'm glad Talitha will be at the center by then instead of here. Otherwise, we might be swarmed with sightseers hoping to get a glimpse of her."

"Like me?" Will joked.

Harriet laughed. "You don't count. Besides, you were invited."

"We should leave before our next client arrives," Polly said, tapping her watch. "They could be here any second."

Once the others were gone, Will settled into Polly's office chair and got his first glimpse of the baby fox. As he cradled her in the crook of his arm, he marveled at her tiny paws and the length of her slender tail.

"What exactly happened before I arrived?" he asked.

"Amelia breezed in, saw Jack holding Talitha, and immediately pulled out her camera. Elena went into mama-bear mode because she didn't want photos of Jack in the paper. Next thing we knew, she'd passed out." Harriet frowned as the scene played itself over again in her mind. "She was hard to wake up. Harder than I would have expected."

"From what I heard in the living room, this is the second time she's fainted."

"That we know about. What if the number is higher, and she's not telling anyone?"

"Maybe that's why she's here. To recover from an illness or something," Will suggested.

"Would she have brought Jack with her for that?" Harriet leaned against the desk. "Elena is afraid of something, but she's not afraid for herself. Whatever is troubling her has to do with Jack."

Whatever that trouble was, Elena seemed determined to keep it to herself even though she obviously needed to confide in someone. If that someone couldn't be Harriet, perhaps it could be Aunt Jinny. The banter about Aunt Jinny being Elena's physician indicated they'd connected. Perhaps merely as doctor and patient, though Harriet prayed the connection went deeper than that.

Suddenly, Harriet smothered a gasp.

What if Aunt Jinny's compassion caused her to get *too* involved in Elena's troubles? Would Elena accuse Aunt Jinny of spying too? It seemed Elena feared the very people who could help her in her determination to hide from those who meant her harm.

If they even existed.

The rest of the day seemed to fly by. Polly had just replaced Will at her desk when an emergency farm call came in. The delayed afternoon appointments stacked up against one another, leaving Harriet and Polly no time for a conversation.

Shortly after school let out for the day, Alma Wilkerson arrived with Winifred and Sarah Jane Philbin. Both girls were so eager to see the baby fox that Alma had driven straight to the clinic from the school. Sarah Jane channeled her father's Scottish roots as she oohed and aahed over the "wee bairn." Winifred, who had more in-depth experience with injured animals, asked pertinent questions about Talitha's feeding schedule and even her vital signs.

Both girls were delighted with the name Jack had chosen.

"We talked about that story a few weeks ago in children's church," Winifred said. "I hope her name helps her stay alive. I know you've done everything you can, but I pray God will be with her too."

Harriet placed her hand on Winifred's thin shoulder. Alma had said once that it didn't matter how many calories she managed to get inside her daughter, all her running around and exploring on the moors burned right through them.

What a wonderful childhood to have, Harriet recalled thinking at the time. So much freedom, with so little fear of harm.

Though that wasn't the case for Jack. Since the day he'd appeared in the clinic with Sarah Jane, Elena rarely let him out of her sight. That tidbit of info came from Polly after Winifred told her that Elena always tagged along with her and Jack on their explorations.

"Every hour Talitha lives gives me hope," Harriet told the girls. "I'm taking her to the wildlife center later this afternoon, where they'll take great care of her. Would you like me to ask Mr. Garth if you can visit tomorrow?"

"Yes, please."

"Me too," Sarah Jane piped up. "I wish we could keep her as a pet, but she probably wouldn't like that. Besides, Mum said no new pets as long as we have Gideon, and she suspects we'll have him for the rest of his life."

The family's popular line of golden retrievers, known for their sweet temperaments and good health, stretched back at least a hundred years. To maintain their stellar reputation, they were particular about placing the right pup with the right family and kept a waiting list of potential customers. Because of their concerns about Gideon's health and development, they'd refused to sell him at the usual age. But of course, the longer they kept him, the more difficult it would be to give him up.

Harriet guessed that Janette was right. Gideon already had his forever home.

"Foxes aren't meant to be pets," Winifred said to Sarah Jane. "I read a story once about a fox who was raised by a boy, but it ended up being a sad story. They're not meant to be domesticated."

Such wise words from one so young.

"We should go now, girls," Alma said. "Dr. Bailey has things to tend to, and so do we." She ushered them out the door with good-natured grace despite their protests and lingering goodbyes.

"I'm going too." Polly shut down her computer and retrieved her bag from the bottom desk drawer. "I promised Mum I'd have the car home as quick as I could." She and her mom shared their vehicle.

"What about you?" Harriet asked in as offhanded a tone as she could manage. "Any special plans?"

"I don't know about that," Polly said. "But Van and I are going to the Crow's Nest. It's Trivia Night, and the winners get tickets to a mystery dinner theater in York."

"That sounds like fun." Harriet tried not to let her tone reveal her excitement about Polly's plans with the detective constable.

"It's a place we wanted to go before, when we were dating. The dinner theater, I mean. It'd be nice to win the tickets."

"I hope you do. Tell Van hi for me."

"I'm sure he'll say hi back." With that, Polly was out the door.

After Harriet locked the clinic door, she checked on Talitha then took Maxwell outside for his usual romp. She was relaxing on a patio glider and enjoying the sweet fragrance of spring blossoms on the sea breeze when Garth's vehicle pulled into the parking area.

Harriet frowned. The plan was for her to take Talitha to him. So why was he here?

"I hope he's not going to ask me to keep Talitha another night," she said to Charlie, who responded with a contented purr. "I'd like to sleep without the alarm going off every hour." Though who was she kidding? She'd sacrifice sleep any night to save an animal's life.

As she walked across the lawn to meet Garth, her phone dinged. Aunt Jinny's text read, I MADE A CASSEROLE TO TAKE TO ELENA. JOIN ME?

Harriet texted back. GARTH IS HERE. WILL LET YOU KNOW PLANS ASAP.

"How's our patient?" Garth asked as soon as Harriet was near enough for conversation.

"Sleeping and eating, which is about as much as we can hope for at this stage," she answered. "She seems to like that formula you gave me. Thanks for that."

"Glad to be of help. Are you ready to let her go?"

"If I must," she said with feigned reluctance. "I thought I was supposed to bring her to you."

Garth's ears grew red. "I was in the area. I thought I'd stop by and save you the trip."

"Still searching for the pine marten?" *Or spending time at a certain seaside cottage?*

"He's an elusive rascal. But I haven't given up yet."

Back inside the clinic, Harriet introduced Garth to Talitha then unwrapped the fox kit so he could examine her wound. "Jack named her."

"He told me." Garth immediately pressed his lips together as if he could take back the words.

"You've seen Jack?" Harriet asked, keeping her tone casual.

"They were out on the moors near where I was searching."

"I see."

"Okay, it wasn't exactly serendipitous. I'm concerned about her. There's all this talk around town about her. Someone even said she fainted again."

"You already heard about that?" Harriet shook her head. "Though I guess I shouldn't be surprised. A reporter was standing right there when it happened."

"Elena insisted she was fine, but something doesn't seem right. Do you have any idea why she's here? Why she seems afraid?"

"I wish I did. But Elena seems determined to keep her personal situation to herself."

While they talked, Harriet changed Talitha's bandage. After the kit was wrapped in her blanket again, Garth carried the portable incubator to his vehicle and slid it into a crate.

"I'll stop by tomorrow to check on her," Harriet promised. "Winifred Wilkerson and Sarah Jane Philbin want to come by too, if that's okay."

"Absolutely. They're welcome anytime."

Knowing Garth had seen Elena made Harriet even more eager to see her again for herself.

As soon as he left, she texted Aunt Jinny. BE THERE IN TEN. She wanted to give herself time to change.

With all the gossip going around town, Harriet imagined all of White Church Bay would know Garth had met Elena on the moors in less time than that. She refused to imagine Courtney's reaction to the news.

Or how the unpleasant woman might retaliate.

CHAPTER ELEVEN

Harriet knocked on the kitchen doorframe and exchanged greetings with her aunt, who was closing the flaps on a wicker basket. Steam rose from the casserole dish on the stovetop, and Harriet breathed in the mouthwatering fragrance of Aunt Jinny's famous rhubarb chicken casserole.

"That smells absolutely delicious," she declared. "And now I'm hungry."

"Then I have good news for you," Aunt Jinny said. "The one on the stove is for you. I split the recipe into two smaller baking dishes instead of a single large one."

"My taste buds and I thank you. And I'm sure Elena and Jack will too."

"I hope so." A frown pulled at Aunt Jinny's lips. "That young woman needs to know that not everyone in White Church Bay is a gossip."

"Especially since Garth has already heard about Elena fainting again."

"I'm not surprised, though I've heard much more than that." Aunt Jinny grabbed her medical bag from a nearby chair. "I'll tell you on the drive over."

"Why are you taking your bag?"

"It's the reason for my visit. I called Elena earlier as a follow-up. She said she was fine, and I said she couldn't fool me. Kindly, of course."

"Of course," Harriet said with a grin.

"I persuaded her to let me pay a house call for a quick checkup. Simply as a precaution."

"Does she know I'm coming? She might not like having another person around for a house call."

"Actually, she asked me to invite you."

Harriet's eyes widened. "Really? She's such a private person."

"Even private people need friends. You gained a bit of her trust when you wouldn't let that reporter take photos of Jack."

"Elena is so protective of him. And scared. I wish I knew why."

"Maybe it's nothing more than not wanting his picture to be publicized," Aunt Jinny said. "Many families are rightfully protective of their children's photos these days."

"For her sake and Jack's, I hope that's all it is," Harriet said. "I don't mean to minimize that as a reason. But if that's her concern, why not simply say so? Her fear does seem to go beyond ordinary caution."

"I'm sure we'll find out what's going on if it ever becomes important for us to know." Aunt Jinny patted Harriet's arm and then pointed to the wicker basket. "Mind toting that for me?"

"Happy to." Harriet cradled the basket in one arm. "I did a quick search of my pantry for something to contribute as soon as I changed clothes. Unfortunately, I didn't have a lot of options."

Aunt Jinny gestured to the cloth shopping bag hanging from Harriet's arm. "Then what's in there?"

"Frozen dinner rolls," Harriet said with a laugh. "They should go well with your casserole, don't you think?"

"Indeed I do." Aunt Jinny made a shooing motion with her free hand. "Now, let's go. Elena is expecting us."

A few minutes later, they were zipping toward Beckside Croft in Aunt Jinny's bright red Renault Clio. As they rolled past the familiar Yorkshire landscape, Harriet shifted to face her aunt. "So, tell me what you've heard about Elena." She was anxious to learn what the grapevine was saying about the secretive woman.

Aunt Jinny huffed. "Only absolutely ridiculous rumors."

"Yes, but what did they say?"

Aunt Jinny darted a playful glance in Harriet's direction then turned her attention back to the road. "When I stopped at Galloway's to pick up a few ingredients for the casserole, I ran into Fern Chapman."

Harriet chuckled. "Then I'm surprised you're not still there. How did you ever manage to get away?"

"It wasn't easy," Aunt Jinny said. "Though I suppose that was partly my fault, since I wanted to hear what she was saying."

"She was talking about Elena?"

"Yes. And Agnes was there, of course, and also Ruby."

"That's an entertaining trio," Harriet mused.

Agnes Galloway and her husband, Gavin, owned Galloway's General Store. Since almost everyone in White Church Bay shopped there, Agnes usually knew what was going on in the village. She rarely engaged in unkind gossip. But, like Aunt Jinny, she must have been interested in whatever Fern was eager to tell about their new neighbor.

Harriet didn't know fabric shop owner Ruby Corbin well enough to say what her motivation might be, but Fern seemed to thrive on rumors and hearsay, no matter how much trouble they produced.

"What did Fern have to say?" Harriet asked, bracing herself.

"That a mysterious woman has taken up residence at Beckside Croft. Fern believes she's in the Protected Persons Service. What you'd know as a witness protection program."

"Maybe she is." Harriet considered that possibility. "Elena would never want Jack's picture in the paper if they were in a program like that."

"I suppose it's possible, though it doesn't seem very likely. On the other hand, Agnes is certain that Elena is an award-winning photographer here to take pictures for one of those high-end nature magazines. Ruby insists that Elena is a famous celebrity caught up in a horrendous scandal. She's hiding out until the media become interested in someone else's troubles."

"Goodness," Harriet said.

Aunt Jinny blew out a breath. "It's so typical of Ruby to go for the celebrity rumor. I didn't dare tell her I'd be seeing Elena today. She'd have pestered me nonstop for details. She might even have stowed away in my boot."

Harriet grinned at her aunt. She and Ruby were opposites in a multitude of ways, and yet they'd been close friends since before Ruby's teen sons were born. Ruby loved popular entertainment magazines and internet sites while Aunt Jinny preferred curling up with a classic novel. She was especially fond of Anne Brontë's *The Tenant of Wildfell Hall*. If Harriet remembered correctly, it was about a young woman living in a country estate under an assumed name with her son, in an effort to hide from her abusive husband.

Before she could check herself, Harriet's imagination took an astonishing leap.

Helen. Elena.

Both with young boys they wanted to protect. One hiding at a neglected estate. The other at a seaside cottage.

Could Elena be hiding from—

"I can't decide which story is more ridiculous." Aunt Jinny's words interrupted Harriet's race down her imaginary rabbit hole, which surely was even more unbelievable than Fern's or Ruby's speculations.

Still, the similarities between the fictional Helen and the very real Elena were striking—including the similarity of their names.

Maybe Harriet should read the novel again—after she and Will had watched the much more uplifting and inspirational story of Thomasina. She so looked forward to sharing such an important movie from her childhood with him.

Aunt Jinny trundled up the lane leading to the cottage, the Clio bumping and bouncing along the rutted lane.

Harriet scanned the surrounding landscape. The icy North Sea stretched eastward to the horizon. The section of land to the west appeared deceptively flat, but the shadows from the late afternoon sun hid dips and ditches. Beyond a gradual rise, hidden behind a stretch of woods that ran north and south, must be the meadow where the antique festival and other special events were held.

"Doesn't Fern live over that way?" Harriet pointed in the general direction of the meadow as she tried to remember what Garth had told her about the area's geography. She'd once followed a faint footpath that led from Cobble Hill Farm to the meadow and found herself behind Fern's property. And interrupting Fern's secret rendezvous with a wealthy widower who didn't want his adult children to know of his romantic pastime.

"Once upon a time all of this land belonged to the Beckett family," Aunt Jinny explained as Beckside Croft came into sight. "Fern's great-grandfather bought what is now the Chapman property when the family was forced to sell after the Great War. So many of the large estates were broken up back then. Other parcels were sold too, and the family relocated to York. All that's left of their original estate is this cottage. Which they've all but abandoned."

"Garth was telling me about the Beckett history last week. Maybe Elena is a relative."

"I suppose it's possible." Aunt Jinny parked beside Elena's sedan. "The Becketts left long ago, and I doubt anyone around here has kept up with their descendants. And yet we're nearly neighbors."

"Only as the crow flies. We take such a roundabout way to get here that I get all confused." Garth's layout made sense to Harriet when they were parked near the location of the game camera but not when she was at the cottage.

"It's not confusing to me, but then again, I'm used to it," Aunt Jinny replied. "Though a brisk walk might have gotten us here sooner than driving this roundabout way."

"Like Jack when he came looking for you the other day."

"And found you and Garth instead." Aunt Jinny shut off the engine. "Should we go inside?"

As the two women followed the paving stones to the cottage's broken gate, Jack rushed out the door toward them.

"Did you bring Talitha?" he asked. "Is she getting better?"

"She seems to be," Harriet said with a reassuring smile. "But I don't have her anymore. Mr. Garth took her to the wildlife center. They can provide better care for her there than I can."

"But you're her doctor." Jack's eyes were wide with concern.

"True. And I'll be checking in on her often. But Mr. Garth has staff and volunteers who can be with her all the time to make sure she eats regularly and has everything she needs. I only have me."

"And Miss Polly. She's nice."

"You're right about that. I couldn't do my job without her."

Elena met them at the front door and ushered them inside. "Thank you for coming."

Wooden tables loaded with an assortment of lamps and knickknacks, upholstered chairs draped with knitted throws, and crammed bookcases crowded the main room. And yet somehow the mishmash of fabrics and colors created a welcoming air instead of overloading the senses. An electric heater, placed on the hearth in front of the stone fireplace, radiated warmth and chased away the damp.

A painting of the moors hung above the mantel.

"This must be the painting that Grandad gave you." Harriet would recognize his style anywhere.

"It is." Elena pointed to a huge boulder in the left foreground. "That's Beckett Rock. Do you know it?"

"I think I do," Aunt Jinny said. "But it's been ages since I've been there."

"It's one of Jack's favorite places, so we walk there often." Elena gestured to the room's interior with an apologetic expression. "Over the years, this place became more of a storage shed than a home, but it's clean and comfortable. We like it here, don't we, Jack?"

"It's fun," he said. "I like my room the best. Mummy used to stay there, and she carved Daddy's initials in the desk. They're my initials too, W.B—"

"You haven't done any schoolwork today," Elena said quickly. "Run along now and see to your studies while I visit with our guests."

"I want to visit with our guests too."

"In a bit you can. Take a scone with you and run along now."

His eyes lit up. "Yes, ma'am."

Once Jack was out of the room, Elena invited Harriet and Aunt Jinny into the kitchen, which was surprisingly modern in comparison to the main room. The walls were painted a pale yellow with sky-blue accents, and the appliances appeared to be relatively new. Crisp yellow curtains hung at the windows, and fresh wildflowers adorned the polished table.

"I can't thank you enough for seeing me here," Elena said as she gestured for them to take a seat. "Tea and scones will be ready in a few minutes."

"Thank you for inviting us," Aunt Jinny said. "Though I didn't expect you to feed us."

"I didn't want this to be purely a medical visit," Elena said. "Besides, sharing tea with company is the neighborly thing to do. Especially when an apology is needed. And perhaps an explanation."

Harriet's nerves tingled as she exchanged a look with her aunt. Did Elena intend to let them in on her secret?

"I don't see any reason for apologies or explanations," Aunt Jinny said. "But being neighborly is always valued."

Harriet placed the wicker basket on the counter near the porcelain sink. "Which is why Aunt Jinny has made her world-famous rhubarb chicken casserole for you and Jack."

"That sounds intriguing," Elena said. "Jack loves rhubarb."

Aunt Jinny pulled out a chair and placed her bag at her feet while giving instructions for reheating the casserole. "Harriet loved it when she was his age. Which gives you an idea how long I've been making it."

When they were settled at the table with cups of fragrant tea and still-warm blueberry scones, Elena directed a hesitant smile at Aunt Jinny. "I suppose we should get this over with." Her voice sounded resigned as she retrieved a medicine bottle from a nearby shelf and handed it to Aunt Jinny.

Harriet resisted the urge to crane her neck so she could read the label too.

"I've been taking these for a few months for a minor heart condition," Elena explained. "I've never had problems with them before, but now I think they might be making me sick. Not every day, mind you. But sometimes."

Aunt Jinny put on her reading glasses and examined the label. "Have you talked to your usual doctor about the reaction?"

"I'd rather not."

Harriet arched an eyebrow at the unexpected answer. But she kept her curiosity to herself. Aunt Jinny apparently had gained Elena's trust and could be counted on to ask the right questions in the right way. Harriet didn't want to interrupt or get in the way of their conversation. She was grateful Elena had even included her, though she wondered what had prompted the invitation.

"Why not?" Aunt Jinny asked. "I'd want to know if one of my patients was reacting badly to a prescription."

"He'd want me to make an appointment," Elena explained. "That would mean going to his office, and I can't do that. Not right now anyway. That's why I asked you to come here." Her voice grew more animated. "I can show you lab results, reports, anything you need, so you can write me a new prescription. Whether you do or not, I can't take any more of those. I have a little boy to care for, so I can't be fainting all the time."

Aunt Jinny appeared puzzled, but a warning went off in Harriet's brain. Whether it was because of all the mysteries she'd read or the ones she'd been involved with since moving to Yorkshire, her suspicions echoed loud and clear.

"You think the pills are poisoned," she blurted.

Elena stared at Harriet, her gaze unwavering and solemn. "It sounds so outlandish when you say it. And yet, it's true. I do think that."

Aunt Jinny fixed Elena with her steadfast gaze. "That's a serious accusation to make against a physician. If there's even the slightest possibility he'd prescribe you something dangerous—but whether he did or not, these came from a chemist. Your doctor didn't have access to the actual pills."

Elena rose from her chair and carried her cup and saucer to the sink even though she hadn't tasted her tea. She placed the items in the basin then rested the palms of her hands on the edge of the sink while keeping her back to Harriet and Aunt Jinny.

"The situation is complicated," she said, obviously struggling to keep her tone even. Her shoulders were bent as if the burden she carried was too heavy to bear. "No one can know where I am. Where Jack is. If I didn't need my medication…"

The sentence was easy to finish. She needed a physician, and she needed people she trusted. But Elena didn't trust them enough to divulge any more information than necessary.

Maybe it was time to take a direct approach.

Harriet took a deep breath and asked the question that had been burning inside her for days. "Elena, how are you related to Jack? The two of you look so much alike that anyone would think you could be mother and son."

"But you don't believe we are?" Elena's tone was more matter-of-fact than defensive.

"The first time Jack came to the clinic, he said you weren't really his mom. And a couple of times, I've heard you start to call him your 'neph' before stopping yourself. I think you were about to say 'nephew' both times."

"He is my nephew." Elena released a deep sigh. "My sister and brother-in-law died in an accident when Jack was barely three. They named me as his guardian."

What a massive responsibility. Harriet had no siblings of her own, but she couldn't imagine losing her cousin, Anthony, and receiving custody of his young twins.

Elena returned to the seat and folded her hands on the table. "He used to call me Auntie Laney," she said with a tender smile. "But when he got a little older, that changed. He so desperately wanted to be like his friends, who all had their mums. I didn't have the heart to correct him, though it pains me that he has only vague memories of my sister. I understand that he needs the comfort of having someone to call that."

"I'm very sorry," Harriet said softly. She'd been devastated when her grandfather died. How much harder must it be to lose a sibling? And she didn't even want to think what it would have been like to grow up without her mother.

"Thankfully, we have lots of photographs and scrapbooks. He enjoys looking at those." Elena's expression brightened. "And he loves to hear my stories about his mum and dad."

"I'm sorry for your loss too." Aunt Jinny held up the prescription bottle. "And I'm concerned about these."

"You're obviously afraid of someone," Harriet added. "If you think your chemist is poisoning you, then we should contact the authorities. Now."

"Mr. Oakden? Impossible." Elena met Harriet's gaze. "But you're right. I am afraid. I came here to hide, and now too many people know where I am. Please. Won't you help me?"

"First, let me do a quick checkup and review your records." Aunt Jinny reached for her medical bag. "Then we'll go to the chemist in White Church Bay together."

In less than an hour, Harriet and Jack were strolling down the sidewalk to the Biscuit Bistro while Aunt Jinny and Elena stopped to pick up the new prescription. Aunt Jinny planned to drop off the current medication at a lab in Whitby for testing the next day. Hopefully she'd get the results back soon.

When they reached the storefront at the bistro, Jack's eyes widened at the large variety of treats displayed in the huge window. "Can I have any one I want?" he asked, his voice filled with awe.

"How about any three?" Harriet replied as she ushered him inside. "As long as you promise not to eat them all at once."

"I promise," Jack agreed as they approached the counter.

Poppy Schofield, the owner, greeted them with a cheery hello and a smile. "Who do you have with you, Harriet? He looks like someone in need of one of my special glazed party rings. On the house."

As she handed Jack the round cookie with its blue glaze, his wide eyes grew even wider.

"Take a bite and let me know what you think," Poppy urged.

Jack glanced at Harriet as if to ask her permission. "Miss Poppy loves to give out samples," she told him. "It whets our appetites so we buy more."

"Now, don't you be giving away my marketing strategy," Poppy playfully protested.

While the women chatted, Jack devoured his party ring. "That was the best biscuit I ever tasted," he declared. "Could I have another, please?"

"Absolutely," Harriet assured him. "We'll count it as one of your three. Now you can choose two more."

He scanned the offerings on the display shelf in front of him. "This is hard."

"Take your time." Harriet turned to Poppy. "Since I'm here, I might as well pick up a dozen to take into the clinic tomorrow."

"Anything in particular?"

"You decide. You know what Polly and I like."

"This is why you're one of my favorite customers." Poppy placed a sheet of parchment paper in a white box emblazoned with the Biscuit Bistro logo. "You're easy to please."

Jack wandered away to view the other offerings.

Poppy leaned closer and lowered her voice. "He's the boy staying out at Beckside Croft, isn't he? With the novelist who has a nasty case of writer's block."

Even though Harriet knew little about the ins and outs of experiencing writer's block—except for what she'd learned from a novelist who'd stayed in White Church Bay a few months before with her African gray parrot—Poppy's characterization of it as some kind of disease struck her funny bone. She hurriedly turned her involuntary giggle into a cough then cleared her throat. She didn't bother to tell Poppy that Elena wasn't a novelist. Nor was she a photographer or a celebrity.

Come to think of it, Harriet still had no idea what Elena did for a living or why she and Jack were staying at the cottage. She could be any one of those things, or maybe even all of them—a celebrity photographer who wanted to write a novel and somehow ended up in England's version of the witness protection program.

What if Poppy was half-right? What if Elena was writing a fictionalized account of a ghastly murder? Perhaps the perpetrator, who had never been caught, would stop at nothing to destroy Elena's manuscript, so she was forced into hiding. Maybe that was why she was in the Protected Persons Service.

Or maybe Harriet was allowing her imagination to get the best of her.

She shifted her gaze to Jack, who couldn't seem to make up his mind which cookies he wanted. With so many tantalizing choices, Harriet often had a hard time too. It was so much easier to ask Poppy to choose for her.

While Jack pressed his fingers against the glass front of the display counter, Harriet studied his reflection.

If she asked his last name, he might tell her. It was almost certainly not Hunter. Even if Elena's real surname was Hunter, her sister would have likely taken Jack's father's last name when they married. But to question him would shatter the shaky trust she was trying to build with Elena. For now, he'd stay simply Jack, and his reason for being at Beckside Croft would remain a mystery.

"There's that man again." Poppy approached the shop's front window, and Harriet followed her. A large man dressed in a black jacket and dark jeans stood in front of the deli across the street. "This is the third or fourth time I've seen him loitering over there in the past two days."

"Maybe he likes the sandwiches," Harriet suggested, even as her pulse quickened. Strangers were common in White Church Bay, which thrived on tourism. What was it about this particular man that made Poppy notice him?

"Then why doesn't he ever buy one?" Poppy glanced in Jack's direction then sidled closer to Harriet. "He was in here the other day, all nice and friendly. Wanted to know about any new families in the area, what the schools were like, and so on. He gave me the creeps, and I was quite glad when he took his biscuits and left."

"Have you told Van?"

"I should, shouldn't I? If he comes in again, I will." Poppy graced Harriet with a smile and gestured to the box. "Let me finish filling your order."

She returned to the trays of assorted cookies and asked Jack if he'd made any decisions. As the two of them discussed various options, Harriet focused her attention on the man across the street.

As if he sensed he was being watched, he suddenly spun on his heel and strode away.

When Harriet had Maxwell and Charlie settled in for the night, she sat at Grandad's desk and booted up her laptop. On the way home from Beckside Croft, she had asked Aunt Jinny to investigate Elena's physician and the chemist who'd filled the prescription that had made her ill. Elena didn't suspect either of them, but she could be wrong. What if the chemist had tampered with the medication? Or given her the wrong prescription? What if human error was making Elena sick?

Aunt Jinny didn't see how the physician could be a suspect, since he didn't have access to the medication. But she promised to make discreet inquiries about him and the chemist if the results of the lab test pointed to either of them. Since she'd kept the label, only Aunt Jinny knew the physician's name, the town where the prescription had been filled, and, most intriguing of all, Elena's legal name. Since Elena hadn't shared any of that information with Harriet, Aunt Jinny didn't either.

But, thanks to Elena, Harriet knew the chemist's name, Mr. Oakden. And she'd picked up another clue—that an accident had taken Jack's parents' lives.

An internet search for *Oakden* and *chemist* brought up a website for a small family-owned company with five locations throughout Yorkshire and the East Midlands. But Elena had said his name almost as if she knew him personally.

Harriet perused the various pages of the website and found three Mr. Oakdens—the founder of the company who was based in York, and his two sons who operated stores in Kingston upon Hull and Lincoln. Which might mean that Elena lived in one of those three towns.

The next search, *Elena Hunter York*, didn't return any helpful results. Neither did Elena's name added to either of the other two towns. The few Elena Hunters in the listings were either too old or too young.

Harriet wasn't ready to give up yet. She searched *fatal car accident* plus the most likely years when it might have occurred. Jack was almost seven, and Elena had mentioned he'd been about three when he lost his parents. Sadly, there were too many results to go through. Harriet tried again, this time limiting the search to the three towns. Nothing.

Disappointed that her sleuthing had been futile, Harriet closed the laptop and readied for bed. As she washed her face and caught her reflection in the bathroom mirror, she jumped with a sudden epiphany.

The deli window reflected the stores across the street, including the Biscuit Bistro. The large man in the dark clothes wasn't interested in the deli. He'd been watching the reflection of the cookie shop.

He'd been watching Jack.

CHAPTER TWELVE

*M*aybe *Fern was right about Elena being in the Protected Persons Service.*

That thought echoed in Harriet's mind as she once more explored the moors while the sun rose above the North Sea on Wednesday morning. Intrigued by how various properties fit together, and especially how Fern's farm shared a property line—and a history—with Beckside Croft, Harriet had decided to search for the pine marten in that area.

First, she followed the footpath that led from Cobble Hill Farm to Fern's property while keeping a sharp eye out for stray tracks or possible places where a small, injured animal might choose to den. After several minutes of hiking, she strayed from the path and headed toward the stream where Garth had set up the additional game cameras. Even though none of the cameras had been activated by the marten in recent days, most animals were creatures of habit. Plus, wounded animals seldom wandered far from water. Harriet's instincts insisted that the pine marten must be somewhere in the general area.

As she searched, Harriet mulled over the events of the previous afternoon with Elena along with Aunt Jinny's conversation at Galloway's General Store. The idea that anyone who lived in or around White Church Bay could be in witness protection seemed as far-fetched as if Harriet herself were in the program.

But wouldn't that be true of any community where such persons were located? The very nature of the UK Protected Persons Service was for authorities to hide their witnesses in the most unlikely places. Why not a small Yorkshire village on the coast? After all, vacationers visited the area even in tourism's offseason. Newcomers weren't viewed with suspicion as they might be in communities where a stranger stood out.

Then again, Elena hadn't quite managed to keep a low profile, despite her best efforts. Maybe the authorities had miscalculated local residents' curiosity about a young woman with a child who'd moved into a rarely inhabited cottage by the sea.

Those kinds of musings took Harriet along other rabbit trails. The longest one had her speculating on what kind of crime Elena, or perhaps Jack, had been involved in that they would need the government's protection. Harriet's curiosity buzzed with anxious excitement about the possibilities, while she also hoped in her heart of hearts that neither one of them had been a witness to anything horrible. Such dramas were entertaining in movies and novels, but not in real life. Especially not for a young boy.

Harriet started to place her hand on a nearby rock to rest a moment then froze while her heartbeat quickened. There, in a thin layer of dirt that had settled in a dip in the stone, was a perfect paw print. And she'd almost obliterated it with a single touch.

She switched on her phone flashlight and bent closer to the print. Her muscles tensed as excitement bubbled within her. Though she was hardly an expert on such things, she was certain that either Garth's pine marten or a close cousin had been on this rock. Maybe a few minutes ago or a few hours, though surely not much longer than that. Not when the track was so pristine and fresh.

She took photos from several angles. If only she had a way to preserve the print. Since that wasn't possible, she texted the photos to Garth with the simplest of messages—a lone question mark. He'd understand the cryptic reference, and no one who accidentally caught a glimpse of the message would learn of the pine marten's existence.

Returning to the flashlight app, Harriet scoured the nearby area and found partial prints leading into an overgrown hedge. Most intriguing of all was a track marred by a long and narrow stripe that could have been made by a creature dragging its hind leg.

Thrilled by her discovery, Harriet took a few more photographs then retraced her steps to the original print she'd found on the boulder. She switched her camera from photo to video, pointed the lens at the track, and pressed record.

"This is the print I sent you earlier," she narrated quietly. "And here's the path our little friend followed." She stopped at each partial print she'd found and pointed it out. "Here's the best part," she said, barely able to contain her excitement when she reached the narrow track that had disturbed the dirt. "It has to be him."

"Who's him?"

Harriet almost dropped her phone at the sound of the unexpected voice but managed to hold on to it as she twirled around to face the interloper.

Fern Chapman. *Of all people.*

Harriet pressed her palm against her rapidly beating heart. "You scared me half to death."

The wiry woman wore her abundant auburn hair in a massive messy bun on top of her head. Her green eyes glistened with amused irritation. In her midfifties and attractive in an eccentric kind of way, she wore a faded flannel shirt over a blue V-neck top and well-worn jeans. Her sturdy hiking boots were scuffed and marred from untold hours of walking the moors and climbing over boulders. She belonged to this land, where she'd lived all of her life, in a way Harriet dreamed of belonging.

"You should pay more attention to what's around you." Fern eyed Harriet's phone. "What are you doing with that?"

Harriet hurriedly stopped the recording and pocketed her phone. "Nothing much. Just exploring."

"This early in the morning? You're trespassing, you know."

"Am I? It's hard to tell the property lines."

"If you're not on Cobble Hill Farm or the public path along the cliff, then you're probably trespassing on someone's land. Lucky for you, we Yorkshire folk enjoy our morning constitutionals enough not to begrudge others of theirs." Her eyes sparkled. "Even when they're Yanks."

"I'm half-British, you know," Harriet countered with a good-natured grin. Anything to keep Fern's focus away from further questions. Though she hated to do it, Harriet slid her foot across the track while pretending to rub something off her boot.

"That's the honorable part of you. It's the across-the-pond bit that's sneaky." Fern wagged her finger at Harriet's feet, her gaze piercing. "What are you trying to cover up in the dirt there? I doubt it's diamonds or any other gems you'd be finding on my land. But it must be worth something for you to be up and about so early this fine morning."

Harriet scrambled for a response. She didn't want to lie to her neighbor, but Garth had asked her to keep the pine marten in strictest confidence.

"I'd say you're tracking an animal of some kind, the way you've been moving about," Fern continued. "Since I know you're busy enough at the clinic, it's a puzzle why you'd be out here searching for more to do. There wouldn't even be a person to pay you for your troubles."

"It's not always about the money."

"You're searching for a wounded animal then. Perhaps the same one Garth Hamblin is seeking." A confident statement spoken without a hint of doubt. Harriet was certain Garth hadn't breathed a word to Fern about his quest. So how did she know?

Because she's observant and astute.

Harriet glanced away as she blew out a breath. And knew without seeing that Fern's self-satisfied stare pointed straight at her.

What could she say that would distract Fern's attention away from its current focus?

"You've seen Garth around here?" she finally asked, doing her best to make her question seem as innocent and disinterested as possible.

"Even more so now that a certain someone and her 'son' have taken up residence at Beckside Croft. Though young Jack is no more her child than you or I."

"Why don't you think so?" Harriet winced at the undertone of defensiveness in her voice.

Fern hesitated a long moment before she answered. "Sometimes folks talk about things when they don't know anyone else is around. Such as a certain someone telling a young boy that his parents stayed at the crofter's hut for part of their honeymoon trip." Fern's voice softened. "Without any of the locals knowing."

The smugness in Fern's tone, as if she were delivering the punch line to a private joke, caused Harriet's pulse to quicken.

"You knew they were here," she said.

"They never knew I knew. Neither did anybody else. Not even Ivy."

"And you were eavesdropping on Elena and Jack."

"You're the only one to know that." Fern shrugged as if her admissions were inconsequential. "She's hiding something. And she's letting her neighbors believe a falsehood."

"Elena never told me Jack was her son," Harriet said.

"He calls her 'Mum,' so those who've heard him assume that's what she is to him. And she's never told them any different."

As much as she'd wanted to take Fern's mind off her tracking the marten, Harriet regretted that Elena was now the topic of their conversation. "Why does that matter?"

"Depends on what her business is here in White Church Bay. And it's not to take any fancy photographs like Agnes Galloway was saying. You can ask your aunt Jinny about that nonsense. She was there at the store, and she heard Agnes go on and on about the photographer who'd come to 'our little corner of the world.' Those were

Agnes's exact words. But I've seen that woman go walking about the moors, and never once has she carried a camera." Fern scowled, folding her arms across her chest. "I don't know where Agnes comes up with such nonsense."

"That story sounds more plausible to me than that she's in the Protected Persons Service," Harriet countered.

Fern's eyes widened. "You've heard that too?"

"Aunt Jinny heard it from you."

"And I heard it from Courtney Millington." Fern's raucous laugh echoed in the still morning air. "Not that a person can trust much that comes from her, though her story is more entertaining than any of the others. That's why I saw fit to help spread it around."

Harriet's jaw dropped though, given Fern's history, she shouldn't have been surprised. "Even though you know the story is false?"

"That's the best kind. Besides, who's to say it isn't true? Courtney's been around, and she knows people. She claims she did her own investigation to be sure there were no squatters staying at Beckside Croft—something all of us should have taken it upon ourselves to do, if you ask me. And that's how she found out."

"Unbelievable," Harriet muttered under her breath.

"No more unbelievable than you rising early in the morning to catch sight of your mystery creature. Maybe I could help you find it. No one knows the nooks and crannies of this land better than me."

Harriet was saved from answering by the vibrating of her phone. She pulled it from her pocket to find a text from Garth. WHERE ARE YOU? HEADED TO CLINIC NOW TO MEET UP.

Though aware of Fern watching her every move, Harriet tapped out a quick reply. SEARCH INTERRUPTED. CAN'T TALK NOW. EXPLAIN LATER.

"I need to get back to the clinic," she told Fern as she once again pocketed her phone.

Fern gave a slight nod of acknowledgment then gazed in the direction of Elena's cottage. As close as they must be, it was hidden by the rise and fall of the landscape. "All this land, from here to the sea, once belonged to the Beckett family," she said, her voice calmer than Harriet had ever heard it. "Over the centuries, it was fought over and divided between sons then sold off piece by piece."

"I heard something like that," Harriet said.

Fern swept her hand in a wide arc that encompassed her own farm and Ivy's inheritance, located on the far side of Fern's. "Our ancestors claimed their acres at least two hundred years ago, during the reign of George III, but we had our own misfortunes, and now all that's left is what belongs to my sister and me. Such a sorry business that neither of us has a child to give it to."

Her tone had become increasingly plaintive and, more importantly, contemplative as she spoke, and Harriet couldn't help empathizing with the tremendous loss of heritage that Fern clearly felt. The property's main house, where the sisters had grown up, was now Ivy's home while Fern had inherited a stone cottage and the majority of the farmland. A neighboring farmer rented most of it except for a few acres that were home to her goats, chickens, guinea fowl, and a large garden.

If Harriet, an only child, didn't have any children of her own, then Aunt Jinny's grandchildren, twins Sebastian and Sophie, would inherit Cobble Hill Farm. Hopefully at least one of them would safeguard the Bailey family heritage. She couldn't bear the thought of Grandad's veterinary practice or his art gallery being lost to time.

Yet Fern and Ivy's legacy faced exactly that kind of loss. In a hundred years, would anyone remember the squabbling Chapman sisters? Their quirks and foibles?

"What would you do if you were in my shoes?" Fern's unexpected question caught Harriet off-guard.

"Is there no one to inherit?" she asked. "Cousins, perhaps?"

"Somewhere, I suppose," Fern said wistfully. "The branches of our family tree that weren't lopped off during the Great War barely survived the second one. I guess Ivy and I shouldn't have been so quick to say no to the offers we received when we were young and popular." An enigmatic smile lifted Fern's cheeks.

Harriet chuckled.

"By the time we were ready to say yes to someone, our favorite beaus had married wiser women. And now, even if Ivy marries that shining knight of hers, it's too late to add another leaf to the Chapman tree."

Harriet inwardly smiled at Fern's reference to Ivy's knight. Sir Halston Dahlbury, an antique collector from Cornwall, was a true knight, though not one who ever wore shining armor. A late monarch had bestowed the honor on Sir Halston many years before in recognition of his academic contributions to Great Britain's seventeenth-century artistic heritage. He and Ivy had maintained a successful long-distance relationship since admitting their feelings for each other a few months ago.

"I wish I had an answer for you," Harriet said. "Though you and Ivy both still have many years ahead of you. Who knows what God will bring to pass?"

"You believe God cares what happens to a sharp-tongued, disgruntled old gossip like me?"

"I know He does."

Fern eyed Harriet, nodding. "I can tell you're one of the few who both talks the talk and walks the walk. That's the reason you and Pastor Will are a mighty fine match. And I'm not alone in that opinion. That's a bit of what I like to call truth-telling gossip."

Harriet's cheeks warmed. Though she wasn't surprised that she and Will were a topic of conversation, Fern's comment touched a deep and tender place in her heart.

A mighty fine match.

Friends and colleagues back home in Connecticut had once said similar things about her and Dustin Stewart, and both of them had happily agreed. But all those people had been wrong. Even worse, Harriet had been wrong.

Could she be wrong about Will too?

"Don't question it." Fern's soft admonition startled Harriet from her descent into the past. "I'm sure the man you left behind was a good one, but he was also a fool."

Harriet quirked her mouth into a half-hearted grin. "He left me first."

"Then I was right about his being a fool. And his shadow shouldn't blot out the sun that's shining on you right here and now. Weren't you the one who just said we never know what God will bring to pass?" Fern raised an eyebrow. "Seems to me like He arranged for Pastor Will to be waiting when you moved here to step into Old Doc Bailey's place."

Harriet made a show of eyeing the woman from the top of her auburn hair to the scuffed toes of her boots. "Who are you, and what have you done with our Fern?" she teased.

Fern let out a hearty laugh. "There's something in the early morning mist that softens a person's rough edges. Besides, I've always been a bit of a romantic." She fixed Harriet with a pretend glare. "Get on back to the clinic with you. But don't think I've forgotten about what brought you out here."

"Can I trust you to keep what you *think* you know about that to yourself?"

"You might not have thought it of me before, but perhaps you do now. I know how to keep the secrets I want to keep." Fern placed her forefinger against her lips as if to emphasize her point. "And I'll keep my eyes open while on my rambles for anything that might be of interest to a veterinarian and a wildlife expert."

Harriet had little choice but to trust the enigmatic woman who'd somehow raised herself in Harriet's estimation despite the gossip she'd purposely spread about Elena.

Since Courtney seemed to have started the Protected Persons rumor, Harriet was now confident it wasn't true. But that didn't change the fact that Elena was afraid of someone to the point that she suspected she was being poisoned.

What if—and Harriet hated herself for even entertaining the unexpected thought that popped into her mind—Elena's fears weren't based in reality?

CHAPTER THIRTEEN

Harriet's hopes for closing the clinic early were dashed when DC Van Worthington and Rand Cromwell, the local dogcatcher, appeared shortly before four with a malnourished spaniel mix. An anonymous caller had notified Rand that the dog had been left behind when the occupants of a rental house moved out. Rand had asked the detective constable to meet him at the address.

"There she was," Rand said to Harriet as he carried the dog to an examination room. "Tied to a doghouse with no food or water. Van here cut the rope with his pocketknife, but we didn't dare try to remove it."

"It's matted in the fur," Van added, his voice shaking with anger. "Instead of a collar, some lowlife just knotted the rope around her neck."

"I see that." Harriet touched the rope but didn't attempt to move it or to slip her fingers underneath it. She didn't want to cause any additional pain or discomfort. She'd seen the result of such neglect on training videos and animal rescue shows but never before in real life. "Have you given her anything to eat?"

"Only a bit of wet kibble." Rand caressed the dog's head with his large hand. "She took a lick as if to show her appreciation but didn't eat anything."

"It's just as well. If she took too much food too fast, it could make her sick." Harriet gently rubbed the spaniel's ear then took in the concerned faces of the men across the table. "I'll need to sedate her to remove the rope."

Rand, with his bald head and long, downcast face, could have stepped out of an old-school horror movie if not for the compassion in his eyes. Van stood beside him, the muscle in his jaw twitching while his fists were clenched at his sides. It was clear that neither man could stand the thought of someone treating an animal so cruelly.

Polly followed them into the room, tears shimmering in her gray eyes.

"I'll start an IV and put her under," Harriet said. "I could use your help, Rand, if you don't mind staying."

"Happy to," he said. "Anything to give her a bit of assurance that her troubles are ending."

Harriet prayed that sentiment proved to be true. "I'll sedate her here, so we don't have to move her again while she's conscious. Then we can take her to surgery and go from there."

"I'll prep the surgery supplies," Polly said. "Is there anything you need besides the usual?"

"We could shave her while she's sedated," Rand suggested. "Get rid of these mats once and for all."

"Agreed." Harriet gazed into the spaniel's large brown eyes. Though in obvious discomfort, her expression was one of trust and gratitude. "Let's have the grooming equipment handy. She'll feel better, and we can check her for any injuries."

"What about me?" Van said. "Is there something I can do?"

"Arrest the scum who did this." Rand's voice shook, and Harriet's heart went out to him. A heart of gold lay beneath his shy exterior. Thankfully, his job usually consisted of rounding up the occasional stray or helping owners find their lost pets. Rarely did an outrage like this occur in White Church Bay.

"Will you be able to find out who did this?" Polly asked.

"It shouldn't be too hard," Van replied. "The man who owns the place is a catering manager for a hotel in Whitby. I'll drive over there to talk to him after I leave here. He should know how to find his former tenants."

"I could go to Whitby with you," Polly said. "That is, if you'd like a bit of company."

Van's ears reddened, and he cleared his throat before answering. "It's kind of you to offer," he said with unusual stiffness, "but I'm meeting DI McCormick there so we can question the tenant together. People who treat a dog like this might be involved in other criminal activity. I can't have a civilian with me, in case there's any trouble. Someone could get hurt."

Harriet had met Detective Inspector Kerry McCormick not long after her move to Cobble Hill Farm. The inspector was an attractive, no-nonsense woman with russet hair, green eyes, and a pale complexion.

"I see," Polly said. Her smile lacked its usual warmth. "I suppose it's best you have another officer with you," she continued, though obviously flustered by Van's refusal of her offer. "In case, as you say, anything happens. Not that anything will. But if it does, you won't be alone. I don't mean you can't handle things on your own. Only that it's nice to have someone else by your side." She snapped her mouth shut and rushed from the room.

Harriet glanced at Van. She wondered what had happened between them to make Polly react that way. Van stared at the doorway as if Polly still stood there then shifted his gaze to Harriet.

"Maybe I could help Polly get things ready," he said.

"Could you also remind her that I need the IV? ASAP?"

Van headed for the door. "Sure thing," he said before he too disappeared from the room.

Harriet turned her attention back to the spaniel mix. Her coat, the color of toffee, might be beautiful after a bath and thorough brushing. Unfortunately, her many mats required a nose-to-tail shave for a new beginning. And the grooming process needed to wait until after the rope was gone from around her neck.

Van soon reappeared with the items Harriet needed to start the IV. Once the dog was sedated, Rand insisted on being the one to carry her to the surgery. While Van and Polly stood on either side of the surgical table to keep an eye on the spaniel, Harriet and Rand donned disposable surgical shirts and pants then scrubbed from their fingertips to their elbows.

Van recorded the procedure. First, Harriet shaved the spaniel's neck so she could see what was going on with the rope. Though the skin had been scraped raw in multiple places, the rope wasn't embedded in the skin. Grateful for small mercies, Harriet carefully cut the rope free. Within a few minutes, the pieces of the rope were sealed in a plastic evidence bag.

With Rand's skillful assistance, Harriet managed to gently remove the matted fur.

"Does she have a name?" she asked Rand.

"The person who called didn't say. If she belonged to me, I'd call her Sahara."

"Like the desert?"

"I was there once a long time ago. She's the color of sand dunes when the sun is at its peak."

Harriet glanced at the dogcatcher with a smile. "It's a lovely name."

"I think so too." Van pointed his camera at her. "Dr. Bailey, how long will you need to keep Sahara here at the clinic?"

"If she had a safe place to go to, I'd release her in a few hours." Harriet removed the last matted section then applied a soothing lotion to the dry skin underneath. "Since she doesn't, I'll keep her overnight and try to find an appropriate foster home for her in the morning."

"I'll take her," a duet of voices chorused.

Harriet stared at Van then Polly.

Polly spoke up first. "Ever since taking care of Thomasina, I've been thinking of getting a pet. But a cat suits me better. Van can take Sahara."

Van paused the recording and faced Polly. "I wouldn't have volunteered if I'd known you wanted her. Besides, you know more about taking care of a pet than I do."

Harriet glanced at Rand. He appeared oblivious to the others as he gently ran his fingers along each of Sahara's prominent ribs. The dog needed more care for the next several days, maybe even for a few weeks, than either Polly or Van could provide given their full-time jobs and other responsibilities.

"I was thinking of Alma Wilkerson or even Clarence Decker," Harriet said, carefully watching Rand's reaction. Clarence, a teenage boy who skipped school more than he should, often took in abandoned and injured animals. Despite his lack of social skills, Harriet trusted him to take care of Sahara.

The corners of Rand's mouth tightened, confirming her suspicion. He wasn't ready to be separated from the sweet dog.

"But," she continued, "perhaps the person who named her is best able to care for her. What do you think, Rand?"

Rand raised his eyes to hers. "It's been almost a year since I lost my Bali. A good little girl she was. Part beagle and part basset hound, if you can picture it. I've got room at my place for Sahara."

"Any objections?" Harriet asked Polly and Van.

Polly shared a smile with Van. "None at all," she said. "I'll put together a care package for you, Mr. Cromwell, and print out information on treating malnutrition."

"Thank you kindly." Rand acknowledged Polly with a nod then turned to Harriet. "When you first came to be the vet here, I couldn't be sure you'd fill Old Doc Bailey's shoes, even though you're his own flesh and blood. But if anyone asks me now, I tell them you've got your own shoes, and you wear them just fine."

Harriet was deeply touched by his words. "You're very kind. Please feel free to call me with any questions. I know Sahara will thrive under your care."

"That she will, Doc. That she will."

A calm contentment descended upon Harriet and seemed to ooze through her pores. Sahara's circumstances were heartbreaking, as were tiny Talitha's. But both animals were being given a second chance to survive because of the good-hearted humans who had found them.

It was too soon to even guess at the fox kit's fate. But Sahara was destined for a happily ever after, and that certainty caused Harriet's heart to sing with praise.

Her euphoric feelings couldn't last forever though. Not when an injured pine marten needed her help and Beckside Croft sheltered a small family in trouble.

Had Elena and Jack left that trouble behind them? Or had it followed them to White Church Bay?

CHAPTER FOURTEEN

Harriet did a final check of the living room. DVD in the player? Check. Coziest blankets and pillows on the couch? Check. Drinks, tableware, and napkins ready for dinner and a movie? Check, check, and check.

Harriet had received a text from Will a few minutes before to let her know the Crow's Nest was closed due to a broken water pipe. Instead, he'd stopped at Cliffside Chippy, a local fish-and-chip restaurant with an amazing view of the North Sea, and was now on his way to the farm.

Their date night would be interrupted when Rand returned to the clinic to pick up Sahara, but such interruptions had become par for the course in their relationship. It often seemed that either Harriet needed to care for an emergency patient or Will faced a pastoral emergency of his own when they made plans.

If their lives were to become intertwined, then this was a fact of their professions that they'd have to learn to accept with grace and good humor instead of disappointment.

Harriet gave Maxwell a treat. "Though it does seem our lives would be simpler—or at least, we'd be able to spend more time together—if we were married."

She immediately reined in her imagination before visions of wedding dresses, bouquets, and honeymoons filled her head. And her heart.

Though her feelings for Will had deepened to an intense level, they hadn't talked about spending the rest of their lives together. Not even in a teasing, casual way. For now, she was content to take their growing relationship one day at a time.

Mostly content, anyway. Once in a while, she indulged in dreams of a future with Will by her side, and then she'd set them aside again. She'd been in love once before with someone she believed had also loved her. She'd been mistaken then. Who was to say she wasn't mistaken now? But that was silly. Dustin and Will couldn't be more different. Knowing both men as she did, there was no doubt in her mind which one she'd choose to stand beside her for the rest of her days.

Her choice would be knocking at her door any minute.

Maxwell suddenly barked and raced to the foyer as fast as his front legs and his back wheels would go. Harriet laughed and followed him.

She opened the front door as Will emerged from his car with the Cliffside Chippy takeaway bag. He was handsome in jeans and an earthy green sweater that complemented his hazel eyes. A broad grin brightened his handsome features as he took long strides toward them.

"What a wonderful greeting," he declared. "Were you watching out the window for me? Or is it the food you're after?"

"You can thank Maxwell," Harriet replied. "I think he knows the sound of your engine."

Will bent to greet the dachshund. "He's a smart pup, aren't you, Maxwell? The smartest dog I know anyway." He straightened and swept his gaze over Harriet. "I've been looking forward to this all day. You look lovely."

She'd changed from clinic clothes into gray slacks and a lavender sweater with a textured design, which he'd told her before that he particularly liked. His appreciative smile let loose the butterflies in her stomach.

But his smile faded the longer he gazed at her. "What happened?" he asked, his voice full of concern.

To Harriet's surprise, her eyes suddenly burned, and she had to blow out a deep breath. She hadn't realized how much pressure she'd been managing on multiple fronts until he'd asked.

"That bad?"

"Not anymore." She managed a weary smile. "At least, I expect things to turn out well." For Sahara and Talitha, anyway. But what about the wounded pine marten? Was he suffering, or had he already succumbed to his injuries? Garth had explored the area where Harriet found the footprints but not until he knew Fern was in Whitby for one of her club meetings and he could avoid her questions. But just as he eluded the curious gossip, the pine marten eluded him.

And what about Elena, whose new neighbors were engaged in concocting, sharing, and believing the most outrageous stories about her? Beyond that nonsense, there was Elena herself, who believed her life was in danger but refused to seek the assistance of law enforcement.

Unfortunately for Harriet, those were two topics she needed to keep to herself, and her promises to keep those secrets were becoming more burdensome with each passing day. Especially when she could share only bits and pieces of those burdens—but not the essence of them—with the man who meant the world to her.

Will rested his palm against Harriet's cheek. "What's bothering you?"

"Rand Cromwell brought in an abandoned dog today. She's little more than skin and bones. We've treated her, but it was really hard to see what someone did to her."

"I'm guessing she's still in the clinic. Can I see her?"

"Let's do that later, if you don't mind." Harriet led the way to the kitchen. "She's peacefully sleeping, and we have a movie to watch."

No matter what was going on in the world around her, she was determined to enjoy every minute of her evening with Will.

They enjoyed their servings of white flaky fish deep-fried in a mouthwatering batter along with the thick chips—or french fries as Harriet still thought of them—sprinkled with vinegar, while getting lost in the mystical story of Thomasina. At the beginning of Thomasina's second life, Harriet's phone rang.

"It's Rand," she said as Will grabbed the remote and paused the movie. She swiped to answer the call. "Hi, Rand."

"Hello, Doc. How's Sahara?"

Harriet motioned for Will to follow her into the clinic while she gave Rand an update. After Sahara had regained consciousness, she'd eaten about half a can of dog food and gotten a gentle bath. Then she'd been placed in a kennel for a much-needed and restful sleep.

When Harriet and Will reached the surgery area where the recovery kennels were located, Sahara raised her head at their approach. She emitted a welcoming whine while pressing one paw against the side of the kennel. She even thumped her tail on the floor.

"How are you, little girl?" Harriet asked as she unlatched the door. "I brought a friend. And your rescuer is on his way to take you home. Maybe even your forever home."

"You weren't kidding about skin and bones," Will said, running gentle hands over the spaniel's head. "Who did this to her?"

"We're not sure, but Van is investigating the people who moved out of the house where she was found." She told Will all the details she knew while she lifted Sahara onto the exam table. She gently rubbed medicated cream into the raw places on the spaniel's neck and changed the bandages on the worst spots, murmuring compliments to the dog the whole time. Sahara held still, as if she understood that Harriet was helping. Obviously, she couldn't wear a collar, but Harriet found a harness for her.

Not that she needed to worry about that. Rand came equipped with a harness and leash of his own, brand-new ones from the look of them.

At the sight of him, Sahara yipped with excitement and wagged her tail so hard her whole back end wiggled.

Harriet beamed. It seemed Sahara and Rand were on the same page about their arrangement.

Rand graciously refused Harriet's offer of a cup of tea, announcing that he wanted to get Sahara home and settled for the night.

Once he was gone, Sahara cradled in his arms and licking his chin, Harriet and Will returned to the movie and its dramatic conclusion.

"What did you think?" Harriet asked him as the movie ended. The magic she'd experienced watching it with Grandad was still with her. How she wished for one of his bear hugs. And though she wouldn't break her confidences even with him, his warmth and comfort would ease her burdens.

"Am I allowed to be honest?" Good-natured humor twinkled in Will's eyes.

"You didn't like it?"

"I'm glad I saw it, but you have to admit, the bit about the cat going through a feline afterlife was a little out there."

"I suppose," Harriet admitted. After all, he wasn't wrong. "But look past that to the intensity of a little girl's love for her pet. And that pet's love for her. And then there's the girl's relationship with the dad, who loses his faith in God when his wife dies, and depends only on his scientific knowledge. He no longer has room in his heart for sentimentality."

"Until he meets Laurie," Will said, "who treats the animals with love instead."

"Which is why I love the movie so much."

Will put his arm around Harriet and drew her close. "And why you're such a skilled veterinarian. You're blessed with an abundance of both knowledge and love. You're a remarkable woman, Harriet Bailey. I thank God every single day that you came to us."

"I thank Him too," Harriet said as she nestled closer to Will and let the warmth of his words surround her.

Suddenly, Charlie sprang on top of their legs, where she proceeded to stretch, yawn, and purr as she wedged her body between them.

Harriet and Will laughed as they shifted apart to give Charlie room. They'd barely settled again when Will's phone rang. "Van," he said after glancing at the screen. "Mind if I take this?"

"Of course not. Should I leave you alone?"

Will shook his head as he accepted the call. "Thanks for returning my call, Van. You're on speaker with Harriet and me."

Van's voice came through loud and clear. "Harriet's there? I was going to call her next. I'm afraid I don't have good news on those tenants."

Disappointment knotted Harriet's stomach. "That's not what I wanted to hear, but I'm not surprised."

"What did you find out?" Will asked.

"They moved in a few months ago but never paid anything beyond the first month and the deposit. The landlord started eviction proceedings a couple weeks ago. He didn't even know they'd left until I told him. He didn't know about the dog either."

Harriet sighed. She was sorry the landlord was out his rent money, but she wouldn't judge the tenants for their nonpayment without knowing more about their circumstances. Sometimes bad things happened to good people.

But good people didn't tie a dog outside and leave it to starve to death. If they didn't have the money to care for Sahara, they should have taken her to a shelter or rescue group.

"Does that mean you're closing the case?" Will asked.

"Not at all," Van said, his tone adamant. "We have a name and a license plate. DI McCormick has already issued an arrest warrant. If they're stopped for a traffic infraction or arrested on any other charge, we'll know about it."

"I guess that's good news," Harriet said. And she hoped they never owned another pet.

"How is Sahara?" Van asked.

"She was well enough to go home with Rand a little while ago."

Van chuckled. "He was pretty smitten with her, wasn't he?"

"Definitely," Harriet agreed. "And in a few months, we probably won't even recognize her as the same dog we treated today."

"I'm sure that's true," Van said. "At least Sahara has a new home now. All's well that ends well and all that. It'll end even better when her former owners are in court."

"You're doing everything you can," Harriet reassured him. "Thanks for the update."

"I'll stay in touch about this. You two enjoy the rest of your evening."

"Don't hang up," Will jumped in. "Do you have a minute to talk about something else?"

"Sorry, Will, it's been such a long day that I forgot I was returning your call. What's on your mind?"

"I had an odd encounter with someone earlier today. There's no crime involved—at least none that I'm aware of. But I'm feeling uneasy enough about it that I thought it best to let you know what happened."

Harriet gave Will a puzzled frown. Obviously, she wasn't the only one with a burden this evening. Why hadn't he said something? Probably because he could tell she was already troubled about Sahara and wanted her to enjoy her nostalgic evening. He was so thoughtful.

"Nothing too serious, I hope." Van no longer sounded quite so tired.

"Did you happen to see the *Whitby Gazette* today?" Will asked.

Harriet's stomach clenched. With everything else going on, she'd totally forgotten the weekly paper came out today. Had Amelia Arbuckle's story about Talitha mentioned Jack after all?

"Yeah, I read it over lunch. Nothing sticks out though."

Will exhaled a deep breath. "Did you read the op-ed about the Protected Persons Service? And the danger it creates for communities?"

"I skimmed it. If you ask me, the writer didn't seem to know what she was talking about."

An op-ed about witness protection? Was it at all possible that the timing was coincidental? Harriet's mind was in a whirl. Courtney must have written it. Or perhaps Fern. Harriet dismissed the latter option as unlikely, especially since Fern didn't believe the story herself, though she was happily passing it on to others. On the other hand, it wouldn't be the first time she'd written a lie. Fern had once written an anonymous note to her sister that had caused all kinds of drama.

But an op-ed wasn't written to an individual. It was meant to be seen by a newspaper's entire readership. Even Fern wouldn't go that far. Would she?

Harriet guessed her copy of the *Whitby Gazette* was on Polly's desk. But she didn't want to miss any of Will's phone call with Van to go get it. If Will's "odd encounter" had anything to do with the witness protection program, then the encounter must have been with Elena. Harriet wanted to hear all the details.

"What you might not know," Will said, "is that the young woman currently staying at Beckside Croft is rumored to be in the program. I didn't think anything of it when it was idle talk at the pub, but in the past couple of days, several members of my congregation have come to me about it. Each story about why she's in the program is more outlandish than the last."

"Is that your odd encounter?" Van asked, seemingly puzzled.

"Not quite. The rumor drove me to go talk to her myself. I wanted to apologize for the gossip and invite her to church. The lane to the cottage is so rough that I parked my car near the main road and walked across Chapman Farm."

Harriet couldn't help chuckling. When she first came to White Church Bay, Will had driven a used hearse that he'd purchased for next to nothing from a local funeral home. Unfortunately, the vehicle hadn't survived an accident. Now he had a zippy Kia Picanto. He sometimes admitted to being more attached to the nifty little hatchback than a pastor should be to a material object. She wasn't at all surprised that he'd chosen to walk rather than drive his precious car along a rutted lane.

"Elena wasn't home," Will continued. "That's what I get for not calling ahead, but I didn't want to take a chance she'd tell me to stay away."

"If Elena wasn't there," Harriet piped up, "then who did you encounter? Fern?"

"Courtney Millington." Will said the name as if he was still surprised that she'd been the one he met. "I found her going through the rubbish bin."

"Why was she doing that?" Van asked.

"Truth be told, I think I was more embarrassed at catching her than she was at getting caught. She didn't even attempt to make an excuse. She told me she was doing her 'civic duty.' I asked her to put back the papers she'd taken, but she ignored me and left."

"Does Elena know?" Van asked.

"I doubt it. I waited around for a while but never saw her." Will let out a frustrated sigh. "Garth Hamblin showed up though. Said he was tracking an injured animal."

Harriet widened her eyes at the exact moment Will turned to her. His eyes narrowed as he tilted his head in a silent question.

Harriet smiled at him, and he returned to his conversation. "It might not be against the law to go through someone's trash," he said, "but it's an invasion of privacy. If Courtney can't be stopped from her brazen snooping, then someone should warn Elena."

"I'll do that," Harriet quickly volunteered.

She welcomed any excuse to have another conversation with Elena, especially since her fears of being spied on had come true. Maybe now that Harriet could tell Elena *who* was spying on her, Elena would trust Harriet enough to tell her *why*.

CHAPTER FIFTEEN

Harriet spent most of the night tossing and turning, her thoughts a muddled whirlwind of pine martens digging through trash cans, Aunt Jinny ordering Elena to swallow a pill the size of a meatball, and Polly chasing Courtney's cat through a thunderstorm. Though still caught within the restlessness of her dream, Harriet somehow sensed that lightning split the dark skies and thunder echoed across the moors. The rhythmic pounding of rain against the mullioned windows lulled her into a restful sleep as the sun ascended behind dark clouds.

Over an hour after her alarm was set to go off, she awoke to Maxwell's desperate whimpering and groaned as she checked the time.

"I'm coming," she said to Maxwell as she pushed back the covers and slid her bare feet into fleece-lined slippers. He responded with a sharp bark. "I turned off my alarm instead of snoozing it."

Maxwell was more interested in getting outside for his morning romp than in Harriet's excuses. She attached his prosthetic wheels then carried him outside to the patio. A brisk wind swept around the corners of the house and caused her to shiver. At least the downpour was over, and patches of blue appeared in the gray skies.

Harriet groaned again when she spotted Polly pedaling her bicycle toward the barn where she stored it during the day. She herself was still in her pajamas and hadn't had her coffee yet, and the clinic was about to open. Not a great start to her Thursday.

She left Maxwell outdoors and hurried to the kitchen to insert a pod into the single-serve coffeemaker. While the coffee brewed, she raced upstairs for a quick makeover. Within seconds, she'd swept her hair into a bun that definitely earned the "messy" moniker. How had Fern made her messy bun look so intentional?

Harriet pushed her way from the kitchen to the clinic, coffee mug in one hand and a banana in the other, then made her way to the reception area. Polly sat at her desk, springtime fresh in a pink-and-white top while she opened the mail.

"It's not fair," Harriet said. "You shouldn't be so cute when I'm this frazzled because I overslept. Have the decency to be developing a massive pimple on your nose or something."

"Did Will stay past curfew?" Polly teased.

"He stayed late for a weeknight, but then I had trouble sleeping." Harriet told Polly how Rand had picked up Sahara, followed by Van's phone call. "He said the landlord didn't know his tenants had moved out and he doesn't have any idea where they might be."

"Can this landlord be trusted? Maybe he's covering for them."

"Van seemed to believe him." Harriet took a sip of her coffee and spied the *Whitby Gazette* on a table next to a few pet-centric magazines. "Did you read that yesterday? Was there anything about Talitha?"

"Not a word. According to my anonymous sources, who we'll call Mum and Dad, the story will appear next week."

"How do they know that?" As far as Harriet knew, neither of Polly's parents had a connection to the newspaper.

"They bumped into Alma Wilkerson at the bookstore yesterday, and she told them. The editor wanted to get photos of Talitha at Garth's rehab facility to go along with the ones Amelia Arbuckle took here. He called Alma to tell her about the delay so she could tell Winifred."

"Did Alma say anything to your parents about Jack?"

"Only that it was a shame he couldn't have gotten a bit of the credit. Apparently, Winifred isn't comfortable with all the kudos coming her way. She doesn't think it's fair for her to have her picture in the paper, but Jack can't."

"I'd like to know the real reason for that myself," Harriet said. "But all we can do is speculate."

"Like that ridiculous op-ed? Did you read it?"

"No, but Will and Van were talking about it." Harriet went on to tell Polly about Will's reason for visiting Elena and instead finding Courtney going through her trash. She left out the part that Will had also seen Garth at Beckside Croft, to avoid any conversational paths leading to the pine marten.

Polly was as shocked by Courtney's behavior as Harriet had been. "Maybe we should invite Elena to lunch or even to a movie," Polly said. "I agree with Will. She needs to know that not everyone in the village thinks she's a criminal seeking a plea deal in exchange for her testimony. Or that she saw something that put her life in danger. I mean, of all the ridiculous things."

"I talked to Fern yesterday, and she said that Courtney started that rumor. But even if Elena is in witness protection, I'm not sure she's the one being protected."

"You think it's Jack." Polly's tone was as solemn as her expression. "I totally agree. Though I also wonder if we've been watching too many crime shows."

Harriet laughed. "You're probably right about that."

The phone rang at the same moment the front door opened. An older man Harriet didn't recognize entered the reception area carrying a covered bird cage.

"The day begins," Harriet said to Polly in a conspiratorial whisper. She stepped forward to greet her first appointment while Polly scooped up the phone's receiver.

The cage held a beautiful parakeet that needed its beak trimmed. While she worked, she listened to the bird's owner in fascination.

The man, a literature professor from Nottingham, was on a road trip throughout the United Kingdom. He planned to stay the night in each county of the four countries of England, Scotland, Wales, and Northern Ireland during the summer holiday. "I'm blessed to have former colleagues and former students scattered around the UK who've agreed to put me up and show me around," he said in his jolly voice. "A perk of long years in academia."

Harriet wished him well on his journey as he went to settle his bill with Polly. Then she tended to the next patient on her roster.

A gap between appointments that afternoon gave her and Maxwell the opportunity to retreat to the reading nook for a short respite. The tiny room, which adjoined the entryway, was the coziest room in the spacious house with its bow window alcove and fireplace. There was enough space for the comfortable wingback chair and its matching ottoman, a standing lamp, and a side table. Harriet leaned her head against the pillowed back, folded her hands across her abdomen, and closed her eyes.

She was glad the morning storm had prevented her from getting up at the crack of dawn to embark on another futile search for the elusive pine marten. If not for the freshness of the tracks she'd found the day before, she'd have given up the search by now. But the tracks had convinced Garth, and he'd convinced her—not that she needed much convincing—that they couldn't give up hope. Not yet.

All too soon, Polly whispered Harriet's name and nudged her arm. "Wake up," Polly urged. "Jack and Winifred are back with another injured animal. And you'll never guess who's with them."

Harriet sat up and rubbed the sleep from her eyes. "I'm guessing it's not Alma or Elena."

"Fern Chapman," Polly said. "What is she doing with those children?"

"I haven't a clue. What kind of animal do they have? Another fox kit?"

Polly folded her arms and frowned. "They won't tell me, and it's inside a wooden crate that I'm not allowed to open. Apparently, what they found is a 'classified secret'—Winifred's words—and you're the only one who can know. Oh, and 'Mr. Garth.' Jack said they already called him, and he's on his way."

Harriet's heart leaped in her chest. Suddenly wide awake, she hurried toward the kitchen. "Where are they?" she called over her shoulder.

"Exam room two," Polly replied as she started after her.

"Could you please see to Maxwell?" Harriet asked as she pushed open the door that led to the clinic. "I removed his wheels so he could sleep better."

She hated leaving Polly out of the secret and wasn't sure how much longer she could. Especially if… No. She refused to entertain the hope surging inside her. Otherwise, she'd be opening herself up to devastating disappointment.

When Harriet reached the door to exam room two, she paused and smoothed the front of her medical jacket while taking a couple deep breaths. Since Fern Chapman was in that room, Harriet needed all her wits about her.

She twisted the knob and opened the door. Winifred and Jack stood on one side of the exam table while Fern stood behind them with a cat-who-swallowed-the-canary smile on her face. The wooden crate, long enough to hold a pine marten, rested on the table.

"First things first," Harriet said, directing her words to Fern. "Do Alma and Elena know the children are here?"

"Of course they do." Fern did her best to sound offended at the question, but her eyes sparkled. "We've been on an expedition."

"What did you find?"

"Open the box and see for yourself."

The children were clearly trying to suppress their excitement as they shifted from one foot to another, barely able to stand still. But beneath the fun of having a secret, Harriet sensed their anxiety.

"Will what you found bite me?" she asked.

"It's sleeping," Fern assured her. "And in desperate need of your help."

Harriet slowly lifted the lid to reveal a chocolate-brown creature with a daffodil-yellow bib lying in the folds of a blanket that rested on a layer of fresh hay. A white bandage was wrapped around his hind leg and also a thick twig, about the circumference of Harriet's little finger, that acted as a splint. A tiny muzzle on his nose would prevent any bites, though not any attempts to bite once he was awake.

"How in the world?" Harriet could hear the awe in her own voice. After all the days she and Garth had spent searching for the pine marten, Fern and two children had found him.

"We'll tell you our story once Garth arrives," Fern said. "Alma and Elena are on their way too. No need for us to tell our story more than once. Isn't that right, children?"

Both Winifred and Jack readily agreed.

"Though I'll tell you that he'll need a top-up of something if you want him to stay asleep," Fern added.

Harriet replaced the lid on the box. "Is his leg broken?"

"I'm not sure if it's broken, but it's in bad shape. I thought a splint might help keep it immobile at least until you saw it."

"That was the right call. Thank you. I'll take him to surgery and start an IV. When Garth comes, we'll examine him together."

"What about us?" Winifred asked. "We want to see the examination. He's a very special creature. Miss Fern said so."

"I wish I could allow that, but this isn't a routine surgery," Harriet told her. "I need to focus so I don't make any mistakes."

"Dr. Bailey is right," Fern chimed in. "But we can stay in the waiting area as long as the operation takes. That is, if your mums say it's okay."

Tension coiled a knot in Harriet's stomach. Garth's circle was widening beyond her control. Even so, at least one more person needed to be included in it. "I'll need Polly's help. Even if I didn't, I can't keep her out of this any longer."

Fern's lips pressed into a thin line. "If too many people get wind of what's in that box, their existence won't be a secret much longer."

"'Their'?" Harriet echoed.

"This one isn't alone. You must have known that."

"I certainly hoped it." Harriet stepped into the hallway and glanced at the waiting area. Thankfully, no clients waited for her. She gestured for Polly to join them.

"What's going on?" Polly asked as she entered the room and peeked inside the box. "Is that a weasel? What happened to it?"

"It's a pine marten," Winifred whispered. "But you can't tell anybody."

Polly shot a quizzical glance at Harriet.

"Okay, everybody. Here's what we're going to do." Harriet doled out assignments. "Polly, I need you to cancel the rest of today's appointments and lock the door. Then join me in surgery. Fern, you contact Garth, Alma, and Elena. Tell them to enter through the patio door into the kitchen. I need Garth in surgery, but everyone else needs to stay in the kitchen until I say otherwise. I'm closing the clinic for the rest of the day, and none of you should be seen."

"You're closing the clinic? Are you sure you want to do that?" Polly asked, her expression a mixture of surprise and *have you lost your mind?* "Won't that raise even more questions and get tongues wagging?"

"Maybe," Harriet conceded. "We'll have to come up with an acceptable explanation in case anyone asks. But we can't worry about that right now. Our main concern is to save this pine marten's life and then to keep him safe."

Though how they were going to do that, she had no idea.

While they set out the needed supplies, Harriet filled Polly in on the search for the elusive pine marten and apologized for the secrecy. Polly assured her that no apologies were necessary, gave her a hug, and joined the others in the kitchen.

After Garth arrived—and spent a few seconds staring in awe at the sedated creature—Harriet reviewed the surgical plan with him. A short time later, they were scrubbed, gloved, masked, and ready to operate.

During the surgery, Garth monitored the little creature's vital signs and the anesthesia while Harriet focused on setting the injured leg and doing everything in her skill set to repair the damaged skin and muscle. After that, whether he lived or died was up to God.

"He's going to need round-the-clock care like Talitha," Garth said. "I wish I could take him to the center, but I can't keep his presence a secret there. Our duo of people in the know has already spread like pancake batter on a hot griddle."

"Fern already knew, or at least guessed," Harriet said. "We just didn't know it."

"That may be a blessing in disguise. If he survives, she might also know the best place to release him."

"I think we can trust everyone else too. Polly understands client confidentiality and upholds it with a vengeance. And Elena has a secret of her own that she's not telling anyone."

Unless she's told you.

It wasn't the time to ask if he and Elena were spending time together. Fern had said Garth was spending more time on the moors since Elena had arrived. To search for the pine marten or to spend time with Elena? Harriet hoped the answer was "both."

She covered the stitched incision with a bandage and refocused her thoughts on their conversation. "I'm concerned the children might let something slip, but I trust Alma."

"So do I," Garth agreed.

"One could almost say the circle is exactly as big as it needs to be and has the right people in it. As if God Himself drew it."

"Do you suppose He left enough room for one more person?"

"You mean Will?" Harriet asked as relief flowed through her. "I don't like keeping a secret like this from him."

Garth chuckled. "Do you suppose God left enough room for *two* more people?"

Harriet would have smacked herself in the forehead if she weren't wearing surgical gloves. "Martha Banks. Why didn't I think of her?"

"I believe she represents the perfect solution," Garth said. "She doesn't face the same scrutiny and bureaucracy I do. No one will know she's fostering this little guy. We've worked together for a long time. I trust her."

Harriet did too. She'd met the sweet woman when she and Will had taken an orphaned fawn to Martha's hobby farm.

"Let's wait to talk to her until we see how he does tonight," Harriet suggested. "For now, I guess I'll be setting my alarm every hour on the hour."

"Nope," Garth declared. "I'll take the night shift. Already have a sleeping bag in my Landy for such emergencies."

Harriet started to argue with him then changed her mind. "I have a cot we can set up in the recovery area. But promise to wake me if there's any change."

"I can do that. Are you about finished?"

"Last bandage."

In less than twenty minutes, the pine marten was settled in a kennel and being stared at by several pairs of eyes.

Please save him, Harriet silently prayed. *And help us all to keep his secret.*

CHAPTER SIXTEEN

Not long after the children's guardians picked them up, Will arrived. Harriet took him to the surgery where Fern, Garth, and Polly sat at a card table playing a board game.

"Is this what you wanted to show me?" Will teased. "Some kind of twenty-first-century backroom gambling parlor with lettered tiles instead of cards? Maybe I should call Van and leave an anonymous tip about this den of iniquity."

At the mention of Van's name, Harriet glanced at Polly, whose features momentarily brightened. She'd told Harriet that she'd had a great time at Trivia Night, though she and Van had come in third place, winning a gift certificate to the Crow's Nest. Hopefully their recovering friendship would lead to something permanent, since it was obvious—at least to Harriet—that they still cared deeply about each other.

"Actually, I wanted to introduce you to our new temporary resident." Harriet led Will to the heavy-duty glass cage, similar to a fish tank, that Garth had provided.

Will peered at the sleeping creature, his brows knit in puzzlement. "I mean, it's cute and all, but what's so special about a weasel?"

"This is a pine marten," Harriet replied. "Not a weasel, though they're related."

"I don't think I've heard of them before."

"Pine martens are an endangered species. Garth saw him on a video feed from a game camera about a week ago and asked me to help find him. But he didn't want anyone to know, and I promised to keep his secret."

Will glanced toward the others and stage-whispered, "Seems like the secret isn't much of a secret anymore."

"Except it is," Harriet insisted. "Everyone who knows the pine marten is here—including Winifred and Jack—also know the importance of never talking about him to anyone else."

"Winifred and Jack know?"

"They were the ones who found him. With Fern's help."

Will raised an eyebrow in surprise.

"She has apparently known all along that a small colony still existed in the area."

"And I never told a soul," Fern piped up. "Not in years, even though I spot two or three of the lovely creatures every spring."

Harriet was about to fill Will in on the rest of the details when her phone buzzed. Puzzled, she answered the call.

"Someone broke into my house," Elena said, her voice quivering. "I don't know what to do."

"Stay on the line with me and take deep breaths. I'll have someone here call the police." All eyes turned to Harriet, and the room fell silent. She placed the call on speaker.

"No police," Elena squeaked. "I can't get involved with law enforcement. I simply can't."

"Elena, please. What if the intruder is still nearby? Or still in your house?"

Garth quickly rose, his face drawn tight. For a moment, Harriet thought he meant to take the phone from her, but he clenched his fists at his side instead.

"We're back in the car," Elena said. "With the doors locked. But I left the keys in the house, so we can't go anywhere."

"I'm on my way," Garth said.

"I'll come with you." Will grasped Harriet's arm. "Keep her on the phone until we get there."

"But I should go too," Harriet protested.

"Not this time," Fern said firmly as she stood. "You have a patient to watch over. Polly and I will go."

In less than a minute, Harriet was alone in the surgery with the sedated pine marten and Maxwell, who dozed in a dog bed that Polly had tucked into a corner.

"Are you still with me, Elena?" she asked.

"I'm here."

Jack's little voice came through the speaker. "So am I."

"I'm glad to hear both of your voices," Harriet said, and she meant it. Elena's and Jack's welfare was more important to her than any animal, even one on the endangered list. But as much as her heart protested, reason insisted she was where she needed to be. Will and Garth would scout around the cottage while Polly and Fern gave Elena the emotional support she so desperately needed.

Until they arrived, that was Harriet's role. Perhaps the best way she could help Elena in this moment was to focus on Jack.

"You're quite the hero, Jack," she began. "Two of God's precious animals are alive thanks to you and Winifred."

"I guess Winifred can name that one," Jack said. "Or maybe Miss Fern should name him. She knew the best places to look."

"I'm sure Miss Fern would be honored to choose the pine marten's name." At least this version of Miss Fern might be. Harriet would never have thought that of the Miss Fern she'd known before their encounter on the moors.

The conversation continued until Elena announced that Garth's vehicle was approaching. Her voice sounded calmer, even relieved, though she didn't end the call until Garth and Will emerged from Garth's Land Rover.

Harriet regretted losing the connection, even though it was completely unnecessary for her to stay on the line when Elena was no longer alone. "Except now I'm the one who's alone," she said when the call ended.

Maxwell whimpered in his sleep, causing Harriet to smile.

"Though not completely." She busied herself with tidying up the already immaculate room and keeping a close eye on the pine marten, whose chances of survival had risen considerably.

When her phone buzzed again, Harriet answered it without even checking the screen. "Hello?"

"Whoever was here is gone now," Will said. "Elena doesn't think anything is missing, though she can't be totally sure."

"Do you think Courtney came back? Maybe she decided going through the trash wasn't enough."

"Enough how? What do you think she was trying to accomplish?"

"I think she's searching for information about Elena."

Will lowered his voice. "Courtney is my number one suspect too, though I'm loath to accuse someone without evidence."

"I didn't have a chance to tell Elena about Courtney. Did you?"

"No, but one of us needs to. I wish I could talk her into letting me call Van. At least he already knows about Courtney. But Elena is adamant about no police."

"Maybe I could persuade her. We've become friends. In a way."

"That's why I'm calling. Elena is putting on a brave face, but I don't think she wants to spend the night here."

"She's more than welcome to come here."

"That invitation might be best coming straight from you."

"I'll text her now." Harriet switched to the text app and fired off a message to Elena. I HAVE PLENTY OF ROOM HERE FOR YOU AND JACK. PLEASE SAY YOU'LL COME. "Message sent," she said to Will.

"Garth is talking to her at the moment. If you ask me, that man is smitten."

Harriet let out a soft chuckle. "I think so too."

A few moments after Will ended the call, Elena responded to Harriet's text. IF YOU'RE SURE WE WON'T BE A BOTHER. I'M HAPPY TO HAVE YOU!

As soon as she sent the text, Harriet raced upstairs to ensure the extra bedrooms, each with its own bathroom, were ready for her guests. She spritzed the linens with a floral scent and laid out fresh towels. Elena and Jack could use both rooms or share the larger one—whichever option they preferred. After the day they'd had, first with the excitement of finding the endangered pine marten and then the horror of the break-in, they might want to be together.

Harriet paused on the landing and stared out the window before going downstairs. One part of her mind mulled over her hostess duties not only for Garth, Elena, and Jack, but also for Will, Polly, and Fern if they wanted to linger with the others for a while.

But mostly she gazed at the vast North Sea, where long shadows cast by the lowering sun darkened the rolling waves. From her vantage point, the world appeared peaceful and still. And yet a nearby cottage had been ransacked by an unknown intruder. To what purpose?

Jealousy? Nosiness?

If Courtney had broken into the cottage, those could be her motives. But what if Courtney had a more nefarious reason? Fern had mentioned that Courtney "knew people." Was it possible she was somehow connected to the shadowy people who'd compelled Elena to hide in an isolated cottage under an assumed name?

And if so, was she working on their behalf?

CHAPTER SEVENTEEN

The good news was that the pine marten, under Garth's watchful care, survived the night. The not-so-good news was that, as a mature male, he wasn't as docile as the fox kit, even when he was still slightly sedated.

"He's got plenty of fight," Garth said to Jack and Harriet as they stood in front of the thick glass cage early Friday morning. "That means he's a survivor."

"When can he go home?" Jack asked.

"Do you want to take that one, Doc?"

"It's difficult to say," Harriet replied. "It depends on how soon he heals. How well he gets around. We want to make sure he's healthy and strong enough to protect himself."

Jack tentatively touched the glass with the tips of his fingers. "Do you think he misses his home?"

Harriet and Garth exchanged glances over the little boy's head. The question obviously went deeper than perhaps even Jack himself knew, and needed to be answered with care.

"I'm sure he does," Harriet said, her tone soft and soothing. "He probably lives in a colony with others like him."

"Are they his family? Does he have a mom and dad?"

"Probably. And brothers and sisters and cousins."

"I'm an only child."

Harriet couldn't tell from Jack's tone if he was happy or sad that he didn't have siblings. But she guessed he missed home—wherever that might be.

"I am too," she said brightly.

"Did you ever want a brother and a sister?"

"Sometimes I did. But other times I was glad there was only me." She refrained from stating the obvious benefit of having her parents all to herself. Jack didn't even have them. "What about you?"

"Nah," he drawled, though without much conviction. But as he continued talking, his little face hardened. "Mum and I stick together, and I won't leave her, no matter what Uncle Timothy or anyone else says. Not even for all the crown jewels in the Tower of London."

Harriet tensed with the possible implications of Jack's uncompromising vow, especially in connection with his uncle. Was "Uncle Timothy" the same family member who didn't like dogs? Were Elena and Jack hiding from him?

This conversation had entered rocky waters. Though tempted to dig for more details, she loathed the idea of using a child to gain information. That would be worse than Courtney going through Elena's rubbish.

"How would you like to help me feed Maxwell and Charlie?" Harriet asked. Jack had been fascinated with the dachshund's wheeled prosthesis the night before, and Maxwell seemed to be fascinated with Jack. They'd curled up in front of the television together until both were sound asleep. "You probably want a bit of breakfast yourself, don't you?"

"Mum said she'd make pancakes. Hers are the *best.*" Jack emphasized his point by practically shouting the last word.

"Quiet there, buddy." Garth took Jack by the shoulders and propelled him toward the kitchen. "This room is a hospital for animals. They need quiet so they can rest and get better. Save the noise for outside, okay?"

"Okay, Mr. Garth," Jack replied, lowering his voice to a near-whisper.

Harriet followed them. A busy day was before her, since Polly had sandwiched a couple of yesterday's appointments in between the ones already scheduled for today. She prayed there would be no farm calls or any other emergencies.

The morning schedule ran like clockwork, thanks to Garth taking Jack to the wildlife center and Elena volunteering to give Polly a hand in the office. She answered the phone, greeted patients as they came in, kept the files straight, and even entertained a delightful toddler during Harriet's appointment with the harried young mom and the family's six-month-old Great Pyrenees puppy.

Harriet welcomed the break late in the afternoon when she received a text. Aunt Jinny had noticed Elena's vehicle in the parking lot and was extending an invitation for tea at the dower cottage.

A pot of chamomile tea was already brewing when they arrived and gathered around the kitchen table. Harriet inhaled the soothing fragrance as she took her seat.

"Forgive my nosiness," Aunt Jinny said to Elena. "Are you and Jack staying with Harriet now?"

"We did last night." Elena cupped her hands around her cup. "While we were away yesterday, someone broke into the cottage."

Aunt Jinny's mouth dropped. "Why on earth?"

Elena's cheeks paled. "I wish I knew. You saw all the items in the living room. Without an inventory list, which I'm sure doesn't exist, I can't even know if anything was taken. At least I know they didn't take any personal items that Jack and I brought with us."

"Do the police have any leads?"

Elena lifted her cup to her lips and took a long sip of her tea.

Harriet answered for her. "Elena didn't want to call the police. Not even Van. Though he already knows about Courtney."

"Courtney?" Aunt Jinny said, her tone indicating her confusion.

"Who's Courtney?" Elena asked.

Harriet blew out a frustrated breath. She'd intended to tell Elena about Courtney last night and again this morning. But there hadn't been an opportunity, and she hadn't gone out of her way to create one. The young woman had already experienced the horror of a home invasion. Harriet hadn't wanted to pile on.

"Courtney Millington is the woman who came into the clinic shortly before you and Garth and the others left to search for the fox den."

"Oh, yes. I remember her." Elena's eyes flashed with mischief. "She's a little obsessed with Garth, isn't she?"

"More than a little." Harriet grimaced as she recalled Courtney's unseemly behavior the day of Thomasina's surgery. "This past Wednesday, Will went to the cottage to pay you a visit. You were gone, but Courtney was there, going through your trash. She took a pile of papers with her, but he didn't know what they were. Van Worthington, our local detective constable, said you could file a complaint, but there wasn't much he could do."

"Because going through someone's trash isn't a crime," Aunt Jinny added, her tone indicating it should be. "Such an invasion of privacy."

"But trespassing is a crime," Elena said. "Though I doubt she found anything of value. I've been going through files and papers. Most of what I threw away were old invoices, livestock records, and outdated how-to manuals. Why would she want any of that?"

"Was your name, your legal name, on anything you threw away?" Aunt Jinny asked.

"I don't see how. I'm not receiving any mail here, and I didn't bring anything with me only to toss it out."

"But it can't be a coincidence," Harriet said. "Courtney steals papers on Wednesday. Your home is broken into on Thursday. What might happen today or tomorrow?"

"Harriet," Aunt Jinny said gently.

Realizing her voice had risen and that her previous train of thought wasn't helpful, Harriet paused to take a calming breath. "I've seen how scared you get anytime law enforcement is suggested. But you can trust Van. He's a dear friend and one of the most upstanding and honorable men I know."

"I'm sure he is." Elena set her jaw. "But I have my reasons."

"You may change your mind when you hear what I have to say." Aunt Jinny's somber tone captured both Harriet's and Elena's attention. She retrieved a folder from the counter and opened it.

"Is that the lab report about my prescription?" Elena asked, her voice shaking.

Aunt Jinny nodded. "The lab determined that a certain drug was added to the bottle. Most of your pills were fine, but traces of the substance were found on a few others. As if someone added the tiniest amount of the substance then shook the bottle. Some pills are more tainted than others. Some not at all."

Elena stared at Grandad's painting of some German shorthaired pointers, which hung on the kitchen wall opposite her, but Harriet doubted she even saw it.

"Someone is trying to kill me." Her voice, deathly quiet, caused shivers to race up Harriet's spine. "I wondered if it was my imagination playing tricks on me."

"The drug that was introduced does present a danger to your health," Aunt Jinny said. "Jack couldn't even wake you up, and that's dangerous. But the amount was too small to be fatal except in very rare circumstances. In other words, whoever did this doesn't necessarily want you dead. That individual wants you to be sick."

Harriet was horrified by the idea. What kind of person went to so much trouble to make someone else sick? "Now will you talk to Van?" she asked Elena.

"It wouldn't do any good." Elena appeared to come to a decision. "Though perhaps a little scare will teach this Courtney a much-needed lesson. I'll talk to your DC about her trespassing. About her theft of papers from my property. Maybe even accuse her of the break-in." She placed her hand on the lab report. "But I will not talk about this. You must promise me, both of you, that you won't mention it either."

"I don't know if I can promise that," Harriet said. "If something happens to you or Jack because we didn't speak up—"

"Nothing will happen to Jack." The strength in Elena's tone practically dared either of them to contradict her.

Her tough demeanor startled Harriet, who'd often thought the fearful young woman was on the verge of a breakdown.

"As much as I wish it weren't so, Jack is a pawn in all of this," Elena continued, her voice softer now. "But the two of us stick together."

"He told me as much earlier," Harriet murmured.

Suspicion flashed in Elena's eyes. "What else did he say?"

"That he's an only child, which I had already guessed. That he doesn't need siblings because he has you. He loves you very much."

Elena smiled. "I love him too." She shifted her gaze from Harriet to Aunt Jinny and back again. "Well, ladies? Do I have your promise?"

Both women nodded reluctantly, and Harriet dug her phone from her pocket. "I'll call Van right now."

Van agreed to meet with Elena at Aunt Jinny's home to take her statement and begin the investigation into the break-in. After the call, Harriet returned to the clinic, leaving Elena behind.

By the end of the day, Harriet was the last witness Van still needed to interview. She invited him to join her in the cushioned chairs on the covered patio outside the dining room. Maxwell had enjoyed a long romp before coming to rest at Harriet's feet, while Charlie lounged on top of a cat tree that Will had made for her out of scrap lumber and carpet samples.

"Can I offer you tea or anything?" Harriet asked.

"No thank you," Van replied. "But you can tell me what everyone was doing here when Elena called you about the break-in last night."

"Fern had brought me an injured animal," Harriet said. Since she wasn't sure whether Garth had included or wanted to include

Van in the pine marten case, she didn't give specifics. "She stayed to make sure he was doing okay. Polly and Garth helped me perform emergency surgery. I think Will was here for a social call and simply happened to turn up in the middle of everything else."

Van nodded as he wrote on his notepad. "That tracks with what the others said. Do you know why Elena called you instead of the station? Or why no one else called?"

"Elena has come to know me and perhaps trust me a little. I think she panicked and wanted a familiar voice at the time. I can't answer why she didn't want your department involved, because I don't know myself, but the rest of us respected her wishes and didn't inform you."

"I suppose, but I'd have thought Polly would have called," Van said. "Even if no one else did."

"I'm sure she wanted to."

Van stopped writing and met her gaze. "Do you really think so?"

"I do," Harriet replied. "But if Polly had called you about the break-in, she'd be calling you as a friend and not as a detective constable. She understands you can't ignore your duty as a DC any more than I can stop being a veterinarian or Will can stop being a pastor. My guess is that she didn't want to put you in that kind of dilemma."

As Van mulled over Harriet's words, his expression eased into understanding. "That was thoughtful of her. Though I do wish she'd been able to call me as a friend."

"Polly respects your commitment to your job. We all do." Harriet gave him an encouraging smile. "Don't you want to know about Elena's phone call?"

"That is why we're here."

Within a few minutes, she'd given him the gist of her phone calls with Elena and Will. In less than a minute, she'd confirmed the times and lengths of both phone calls from her call log.

Van scribbled the information in his notepad, asked a couple clarifying questions, then stood. "I guess that's everything."

"I'll walk you to your cruiser." Harriet gestured to the end of the patio. "What happens now?"

"Like I told the others, Courtney Millington is being held for questioning and, from what I've been told, threatening to sue everyone at headquarters from the janitor all the way up the ladder." Van rolled his eyes. "She's making a fool of herself with her threats and pouting."

"Do you think she had anything to do with the break-in?"

"Too soon to know. Right now, DI McCormick is at Beckside Croft with Elena, searching for clues to the intruder's identity. We're not holding out much hope for that, though, considering all the traipsing around there by your bunch."

"I doubt there was much 'traipsing,'" Harriet protested as they rounded the corner of the house and headed toward the cruiser, which was parked on the other side of Harriet's Beast. "Will and Garth know the importance of preserving evidence, and so does Polly. I imagine Fern has watched enough crime shows that she does too."

"We'll see," Van grumbled.

As they neared the cruiser, everyone Van had interviewed except for Elena came toward them. Alma and Winifred were there too, even though they'd left before Elena had called the night before.

Jack was at Garth's side, and as they approached, the boy slipped his small hand into Garth's big one. The man glanced down at him, startled, then quirked the corners of his lips in a small smile.

"What's all this?" Van asked.

Garth extended his free hand to Van. "Congratulations, DC Worthington. You're now a member of the in-the-know circle. But seriously, folks, we can't tell another soul."

"What about my husband?" Alma asked. "Shouldn't he be included? I don't feel right about keeping anything from him."

Garth rolled his eyes skyward as if seeking patience from above. "I suppose. But seriously, no one beyond that. No best friends or cousins or neighbors. I don't even want you telling your pets."

Amidst the good-natured laughter, Van's voice rose above the others. "Hold on a second. What is it I'm supposed to know?"

"If you have a minute," Polly said to Van, "I'll tell you."

"I have plenty of time," Van assured her.

"Come into the clinic. I have something to show you." Polly led him away.

"You know, we really should tell Aunt Jinny," Harriet said to the remaining group.

Garth groaned, making Jack laugh. "I told one person my secret. Only one. And now look how many people know. What did I just say, Harriet?"

She directed a sheepish smile at him. "Fern already knew," she reminded him. "And the children found the pine marten, not us. If I know my aunt, she's already figured out that something is going on, if for no other reason than all the people who are here right now."

Garth good-naturedly threw up his hands. "Who's hungry? Pizza's on me."

Harriet pulled out her phone and sent a text to Aunt Jinny. PIZZA PARTY AT MY PLACE. I HAVE A SECRET TO TELL YOU.

I LOVE A SECRET. BE THERE IN A FEW.

The impromptu dinner quickly took on the air of a celebration. Yet Harriet's buoyant mood was dampened when she recalled something Elena had said when they were at Aunt Jinny's house.

If Jack wasn't in danger because he was merely a pawn, then who was the chess master?

CHAPTER EIGHTEEN

T his farm is one of my favorites in Yorkshire," Harriet told Garth as he pulled into Martha Banks's driveway the next day. "I don't know how Martha manages to care for so many animals and maintain such a tranquil atmosphere at the same time."

"That's the magic of Martha." Garth drove past the two-story farmhouse to park beside the long barn with its red-tiled roof, crimson door, and bright blue window frames. As usual on a clear day like today, the windows were wide open to the sunlight.

Not long after her first visit to the Banks farm, Harriet had joked to Aunt Jinny that Martha must spend every morning brushing the cobwebs from the barn's rafters, since there were none to be found. That wasn't true of most barns in the area.

Garth shut off the engine and shifted in his seat to face Harriet. "Are you ready to let Beckett go?"

"Truthfully? No." After a couple days in recovery, the injured pine marten checked off all the necessary boxes to leave the clinic. No fever, steady heartbeat, good appetite. Harriet worried about a potential infection, but Garth believed that Beckett—the name given to him by his young rescuers—needed more space to move about than the heavy glass cage allowed. Otherwise, his leg might never recover its former strength. Harriet couldn't disagree. Once she'd stopped sedating him, he had taken to constant pacing. That behavior alone told her he needed more room to heal well.

Though she was loath to admit it, Harriet's reluctance was due to pure selfishness. She'd spent hours researching pine martens, both online and in her grandfather's ample library of veterinary manuals and his personal journals, to be sure she was providing Beckett with the best possible care. After reading an article on environmental enrichment, she'd put a flat stone, a leafy tree branch, and brand-new toys into his cage.

The pacing had lessened, but not enough for Garth to change his mind.

"He's such a joy to watch," she said. "The way he moves, even with his bandaged leg, is adorable. He's intelligent too, and so curious. When I talk to him, I almost feel as if he can understand me with his bright little eyes."

Garth chuckled. "And he's a wild animal, not a pet. The point of rescuing him was so we could release him safely, remember?"

"I know." Harriet didn't dare tell Garth that in a moment of total self-delusion she'd considered turning a section of the barn into a pine marten playhouse. She'd quickly come to her senses though. No matter how well-intentioned, confining Beckett for the rest of his life was an act of cruelty. He deserved to roam free and be with his family.

A knock sounded on Harriet's window, and she turned to see Martha grinning in at them. She wore a plaid shirt and her typical overalls. Her gorgeous silver hair hung in a long braid over her shoulder.

Harriet sheepishly rolled down her window.

"Will you be staying inside there?" Martha asked, her eyes twinkling. "Or would you like to see Beckett's temporary home?"

Harriet opened her door and slid out. "It's good to see you again, Martha. How have you been?"

"Busy with this, that, and the other thing, as usual," she said. "Though not as busy as you've been, I hear."

Garth rounded his vehicle to join them. "I told Martha all about your recent patients—at least, the ones I know about—while I was thanking her for agreeing to help us with the latest."

Martha patted Harriet's arm. "Some of us old-timers were worried about what would happen to Old Doc Bailey's practice," she said. "You've proven to be an answer to our prayers."

"You're the answer to mine," Harriet replied. "I wish I could keep Beckett until he's fully recovered, but that's neither possible nor practical. Thank you for taking him in, especially under such unique circumstances."

"I'm happy to do it. And eager to meet my newest guest."

Garth opened the back hatch and unlocked one of the temperature-regulated transport boxes that were specially constructed to fit inside the space. "We gave him a sedative for the drive, so he may be a little woozy," he explained to Martha as he slid the metal crate out and placed it on the ground.

"Such a beauty," Martha marveled as she knelt beside the crate. "Isn't God a wonder to have created such a creature?"

The pine marten peered at them through half-closed eyes as he rested on a thick towel. Seemingly satisfied that no danger existed, he curled into a ball and flicked his long tail over his eyes.

Martha laughed in delight. "We know what he thinks of us now, don't we? Bring him on inside, will you, Garth?"

They followed her into the airy, well-lit barn to a renovated horse stall. A fine mesh stretched from the top of the stall's wooden boards to the ceiling, which allowed Martha to observe any animal housed inside. The trunk and branches of a dead tree provided hiding places. A rock fountain offered fresh water.

"This will be his home when he's recovered from his injuries enough that he doesn't need daily attention," Martha explained. She led the way to a large room at the opposite end. "Until then, he'll be in a smaller habitat. He won't have quite as much fun, but I'll have a much easier time getting hold of him when I need to."

The space reminded Harriet of an exhibit she'd seen in a zoo once. Three wide boxes with wooden sides, thick glass doors, and mesh tops and bottoms rested on a slatted platform. Like the larger habitat, these boxes were outfitted with tree branches and a water source.

Since he'd done this before, Garth knew exactly how to situate the door of the crate against a panel located in the wooden side of one of the boxes. When the panel was raised, Beckett could walk through the open door of his crate into his new home.

"He seems to be enjoying his nap," Harriet observed.

"Which is a good sign," Martha replied. "It means he feels safe and comfortable. But let's give him a little enticement."

She went to a nearby refrigerator and retrieved a container of apple slices. Garth piled the slices a short distance away in the first box. Beckett raised his head and sniffed the air. Though his bandaged back leg made it awkward for him to walk, he managed to follow his nose through his open cage door and to the apple slices. While he enjoyed his treat, Garth removed the cage and secured him inside the habitat.

"I call that a success," Martha said, beaming. "You don't need to worry about him, Harriet dear. He'll do fine here."

"I'm sure of it." Harriet used her phone to snap a photo of Beckett then caught sight of Garth's annoyed expression. "Don't worry. I'll print it at home then delete the original so that no hackers get it from my phone. I promise."

Garth scowled then muttered, "Print me a copy too."

"Will do." Harriet placed her hand flat against the glass door. "Bye, Beckett. Get well."

"Where did his name come from?" Martha asked as they retraced their steps to the Landy.

"Fern Chapman and the two children who found him chose his name," Harriet replied. When she'd asked them about it, Fern had merely smiled, while Jack and Winifred giggled.

"They told me it was because of all the things named Beck in the area. Beckside Croft, Restless Beck, Beckett Rock." Garth frowned and shook his head. "I think there's more to it than that, but they're having fun with their secrets, so I let it go."

"The Beckett family used to own much of the land in that area a few hundred years ago," Martha said. "I don't know of any Becketts who live around here anymore. Not that it matters. The name is a fine one."

When they reached Garth's vehicle, Harriet thanked Martha again for taking in the wounded pine marten and keeping his existence a secret.

"It's no trouble at all. And I'll contact you when he's ready to be released," she replied.

Garth put the metal crate back in the Land Rover. "We'll invite everyone who knows about him to join us," he said.

"And both of you are welcome to come visit whenever you wish," Martha added.

After receiving assurances that Martha would call at the first sign of an infection or any other difficulties, Harriet gave her a hug and climbed into the Landy for the drive back to the clinic.

With the morning appointments out of the way and no more animals in the recovery kennels, the afternoon beckoned Harriet with the promise of rest and relaxation. She was free to start a new novel—though not *The Tenant of Wildfell Hall*. She didn't feel like dealing with heavy themes and depressing storylines.

A long and peaceful nap also sounded like a great option, especially with the lack of sleep she'd experienced over the last week.

If Will was free, perhaps they could drive into Whitby and catch a matinee at that dinner-and-a-movie place. Polly had mentioned that she and her girlfriends enjoyed the experience and that their specialty cheeseburger was delicious.

So many options for a lovely, lazy day.

Garth dropped Harriet off near her front door with a cheery goodbye. As he drove away, Harriet noticed the first three letters on his personalized license plate and smiled in delight.

GBH.

Garth B-something Hamblin.

B for Beckett, maybe? Doubtful, or he probably would have said so when Martha asked about the pine marten's name.

Harriet stopped in her tracks as a faint memory poked her mind. Jack had said that his mom carved his dad's initials into a desk at the cottage. That his dad's initials were WB. He'd started to add another letter when Elena interrupted him. Could the B of Jack's middle initial stand for Beckett?

As Harriet entered her house and greeted Maxwell, her phone buzzed. The text from Elena simply read, CAN YOU COME OVER? I NEED YOUR HELP.

Slightly alarmed, Harriet tapped out her response. ARE YOU OKAY? IS JACK?

I'LL EXPLAIN WHEN YOU GET HERE. COME ALONE.

CHAPTER NINETEEN

Yellow crime scene tape flapped against both sides of the cottage doorframe while the door itself stood wide open. Puzzled by the broken tape and mindful of Van's comment about "traipsing" at a crime scene, Harriet stayed on the porch and peered inside. Books and papers littered the floor along with the contents of overturned drawers. An ornate vase she'd admired previously lay in shards on the floor. The bowl of a vintage lamp had been shattered into thousands of pieces.

"Elena," Harriet called. "Are you here?"

"Be right with you." The voice came from the kitchen, and a moment later Elena appeared on the threshold between the two rooms with a dish towel in her hands. "Don't mind that tape. Come on in."

"Are we allowed to be in here?"

Elena shrugged. "What does it matter? Courtney denied making this mess, and now she's free to make it again."

"They let her go?"

"They had no choice. Your friend, Van, called and told me all about it. When he questioned her about going through the trash, she claimed Will was snooping around when *she* stopped by to visit."

Harriet gasped.

"Naturally, no one believes her story," Elena assured Harriet. "Will is too well respected in this community, and his word is trusted."

"As it should be."

"When that ridiculous ploy didn't work, Courtney cast suspicion on Garth for the break-in."

"That doesn't even make sense. He was with us when this happened." Harriet waved her hand to indicate the mayhem. "Does he know she tried to accuse him? We took the pine marten to Martha shortly after lunch, and he didn't mention it."

"Van already had our statements. He knows it couldn't have been Garth. And even though she doesn't have an alibi, I don't believe Courtney did this." Elena appeared to retreat within herself, her eyes sad. "Unfortunately, DI McCormick could find no physical evidence that would help identify the intruder. Not that she didn't try. I was here with her when she dusted all around the doors and windows for prints and searched the ground for footprints. She tried so hard to find a clue. There's nothing."

"She's a competent investigator. If she didn't find anything, there's nothing to find." Harriet studied the wooden frame of the door and then the door handle. The locking mechanism appeared intact. "How did the intruder get in?"

"Very carefully." Elena flapped the dish towel then folded it in half as she regarded Harriet, who still stood on the porch side of the threshold. Her face broke into a smile. "Please come in and stop loitering in the doorway. No one from the police will be coming back here. Not even to remove their silly tape."

"If you insist." Harriet removed the tape herself and entered the room, taking care where she stepped. "You'd think with all the things that were thrown on the floor and broken, there'd be at least one fingerprint. Though I suppose the intruder wore gloves."

"Oh, there are tons of fingerprints. Years' worth. But this county doesn't have the resources to process them all. Even if they did, it'd be a herculean task to match them."

"I'm so sorry this happened." Harriet checked the spot above the mantel and was relieved to see that Grandad's painting remained intact. "Is Jack in his room?"

"He's staying with the Wilkersons. I didn't want him to see this. Thanks to your and Alma's hospitality, he hasn't been here since the break-in."

"I hope you know you can stay with me as many nights as you need to. I'm enjoying your company. And Maxwell definitely enjoys Jack's."

Elena chuckled. "Jack loves Maxwell too. If I get the worst of this mess cleaned up, then we can come back here."

"Only if you think it's safe."

Instead of answering, Elena pressed her lips together in a stubborn scowl and averted her gaze. She was no longer the trembling, standoffish woman she'd been when they first met. Had the break-in somehow transformed her into an angry mama bear? Perhaps knowing she had friends gave her courage.

That was fine, as long as she didn't put herself and Jack into unnecessary danger. Harriet would prefer them to stay at Cobble Hill Farm until the intruder was identified. But she'd save that conversation until later. Now it was time to get to work.

She pushed the long sleeves of her T-shirt up past her elbows. "Where do you want me to begin?"

A small smile tugged the corners of Elena's mouth. "I didn't ask you here to clean. I need help with something else."

"But I want to help. And I'm free the rest of the day."

"Let's sit first." Elena made her way to a short sofa with thick patterned cushions and moved an electronic gaming device out of the way.

Harriet guessed that the device had been left there by Jack. How intriguing that it hadn't been stolen.

"I have a story to tell you," Elena said when they were seated. "One that I can't tell Van or DI McCormick, much as I respect both of them. That is, if you want to hear it."

"Of course I do." Though Harriet's assurance was sincere, as soon as the words were out of her mouth, she second-guessed whether she should have said them. Someone had gone to a great deal of effort to poison Elena's prescription. Someone with resources and no regard for others—a dangerous combination. Would learning Elena's story put Harriet herself in that person's crosshairs?

She straightened her shoulders. Whoever it was, they needed to be stopped, so that Elena no longer had to hide. So that she no longer needed to fear for Jack.

"You already know," Elena began, "that I have legal guardianship of Jack because my sister and her husband were killed in an accident when he was three." She paused for a moment and seemed to gather herself. "Their fishing boat capsized during a sudden storm in the North Sea."

A boating accident. Harriet had assumed it was a car accident when she'd conducted her online search for information. "I'm so sorry," she said. "How heartbreaking for all of you."

Elena gave her a grateful smile. "My sister and brother-in-law—everyone called him Beck—left everything they had in trust to Jack except an amount set aside for me. Not that I needed a financial incentive. I would have taken him in a heartbeat with or without that. But it was enough that I was able to quit my job at an actuary firm to be a full-time mum to Jack."

Another Beck, Harriet noted as Elena told her story. Then she remembered Jack saying he was the third person in his family to have the same name. Which meant his dad had been the second. Three generations, each with the initials WB something. B for Beckett? It must be, and Jack's dad was called Beck to differentiate him from his father.

"Jack and I were doing great together." Tears welled in Elena's eyes. "And then Jack's grandfather died. His will divided his estate between his two sons, with Beck's share going into Jack's trust fund. He also left a generous stipend for me, an annual allowance for our living expenses. Timothy, the younger son, took over the family business."

"Jack mentioned Timothy once or twice. Is this the same uncle that doesn't like dogs?"

Elena snorted. "He's Jack's only uncle. No, he doesn't like dogs. Or cats or guinea pigs or goldfish. Honestly, I think he only likes himself."

While Harriet listened, Elena told her a story of family tensions, sibling rivalry, and Timothy's greed. At the same time, she studiously avoided mentioning any details that could identify them, such as Beck's surname and the nature of the family business.

Timothy had been livid that Jack's stake in the business equaled his own. Jack was a child now, but eventually he'd be an equal partner. Which meant, in Timothy's twisted mind, that Jack needed to be molded in his image—a ruthless, unscrupulous petty tyrant who cared for nothing but money and power.

"He wants sole control of the trust, so he's demanding custody of Jack," Elena said, her voice trembling. "He threatened to fight his own father's will in court if I didn't willingly give up my guardianship."

"I assume he wants the money too."

"He wants everything. Even the allowance stipulated by Jack's grandfather, plus what Beck left to me." She closed her eyes then met Harriet's gaze. "I know no one believes it when someone says the money isn't important. But for me, it's true. I'll go back to actuary work if I have to and be fine. But people who loved Jack gave me that money so I can raise him the way they would have wanted. I've put more than half of it into a separate trust that he can have when he's an adult." Elena raised an eyebrow with a slight smile. "Timothy doesn't know about that one."

"Surely no court would go against the provisions of two wills without evidence of some kind of fraud," Harriet said. "How can Timothy win?"

"I don't know, but he's confident he can. And I can't take any chances." Tears trickled down Elena's cheeks. "I offered to give him all the money that comes to me if he'd agree not to challenge the guardianship. He laughed in my face and called me a naive simpleton. I've been so frightened about how far he'll go to get what he wants."

"The pills," Harriet exclaimed suddenly. "He wanted to make you sick—too sick to care for an active little boy."

"That's why I refused emergency services. Timothy would love to get ahold of that kind of report." Elena scooted from the couch to sit cross-legged on the floor. She placed one of the overturned drawers on her lap and arranged items that were scattered on the floor inside of it.

Harriet immediately joined her. "Does it matter which drawer I put these things in?"

"Not really. Organization isn't my priority right now."

"What is?"

Elena slowly gazed around the crowded room as if taking it all in. Maybe even memorizing all its nooks and crannies. "Do you know anything about the history of this place?"

"Garth told me about the Beckett brothers and their feuding centuries ago. I'm guessing that's where your brother-in-law got his name. Does Beckside Croft belong to Jack now?"

"I can see why you'd think that, but the truth is more complicated. And it'll explain what I'm doing here."

Harriet settled into the task of righting the mess in the room while Elena talked.

The Beckett family had kept Beckside Croft, containing the cottage and its surrounding acreage, even after they moved to York. Jack's great-grandmother wasn't a Beckett herself, but rather a childhood friend of a Beckett girl. Despite the difference in their social classes, the girls grew up together and remained best friends throughout their lives. The great-grandmother chose Beckett as her son's middle name in honor of her friend. The name was then given to that son's son, Jack's father, and then to Jack.

"But as you can see," Elena said, "they aren't the Becketts of Beckside Croft and Beckett Rock."

"But you are," Harriet burst out with sudden insight. "Am I right?"

"A branch of it, yes." Elena went on to explain that Jack's great-grandmother and her Beckett friend both had sons, and the boys were as close as brothers. "He's my great-uncle, and this place is his. He worked most of his life for Jack's grandfather as a kind of adviser and manager, but then he moved a few years ago to be closer to his own grandchildren."

"Makes sense," Harriet murmured, enjoying the tale of two families intertwined across generations.

"Since the remaining Becketts rarely visited the cottage anymore, they gave permission for Jack's grandfather to use it as an escape, especially when he needed time away from Timothy's attempts to take over the family business," Elena said with a note of bitterness. "He'd spend a few days alone with his thoughts, without anyone knowing he was here unless he met someone while he was walking across the moors."

Harriet idly wondered whether he'd ever encountered Fern Chapman that way but kept the thought to herself.

"My great-uncle is too frail to travel and probably won't live much longer," Elena said sadly. "But after Jack's grandfather died, I got a letter from my great-uncle, likely written in one of his last moments of clarity. The last time Jack's grandfather came here, he wrote to my uncle about Timothy's latest schemes. He said he was going to write a new will before he returned to York that would name Jack as his beneficiary—for everything. Timothy was to get nothing."

"Wow. It sounds like his father got sick of his scheming and didn't intend to reward him for it."

Elena paused to take a deep breath. "I didn't think much of it at the time, but now that Timothy is threatening a lawsuit, I have to take it seriously. If Jack's grandfather did write such a will, then I need to find it. That's why I'm here."

"Is a handwritten will even legal?" Harriet asked.

"I wondered that too, so I looked it up. A will is legal here as long as it has been witnessed by two other adults. You don't even need a solicitor."

"I had no idea," Harriet said. Then she paused to consider the situation. "He wanted to change his will, so he wrote it himself. But even if he wrote it here, that doesn't mean it's still here. Wouldn't he have given it to his solicitors in York? You know, to be filed through the proper channels?"

"I don't think he trusted them anymore. It seems they were already working for Timothy by that point, so they probably would have 'lost' a new will that didn't benefit him." She reached for her phone. "I can show you his letter. I took a picture of it and put the original in my safety deposit box." She scrolled and tapped her screen then handed the phone to Harriet.

My Dearest Elena,

The news of Winston's death has saddened me beyond words. I am certain his loss is keenly felt by both you, whom he had come to love as a daughter, and young Jack. Both of you have already suffered so much after losing Beck and Elspeth.

In addition to my condolences, I wanted to share with you that Winston wrote me a few months ago during his short stay at Beckside Croft. Perhaps he didn't confide in you the horrible news of Timothy's treachery. I won't go into the details here, but the betrayal was enough for Winston to disinherit him of all but what he called a "living allowance."

If you've not already done so, you can find Winston's handwritten will, his last will and testament, hidden behind the Rock.

My apologies for not writing sooner. My mind takes me to strange places at times, so I'm writing this today on what my family euphemistically calls one of my "good days." All my love and prayers to you, sweet Elena, and to young Jack.

Yours always,
Great-Uncle Tobias

Elena took back her phone when Harriet held it out. "Uncle Tobias said that Gramps planned to hide the will 'behind the Rock.' I thought he meant Beckett Rock, but nothing's there. One of my cousins tried to find out more details, but my uncle is too far gone mentally now."

Harriet furrowed her brows. "Perhaps he meant to hide it at Beckett Rock, but for some unknown reason couldn't. He might have hidden it here in the cottage for safekeeping until he could hide it there."

"That's what I think happened."

"So the person who broke in here is searching for the will too." Harriet frowned as another thought came to her. "But how would anyone else know about it?"

"My cousin," Elena said flatly. "The cell service out here and on the moors isn't all that dependable. When she couldn't get in touch with me, she called Timothy and said more than I wished she had. It wasn't her fault. She didn't know what he was up to."

"So he came and did this."

"More likely, he sent one of his minions." Elena released a heavy sigh. "I thought I could come here in secret and he wouldn't know where to find me." She gave Harriet a wry grin. "We can all see how that worked out, but I'm not sorry. Not when there were such good friends to be made."

"And a quest to be undertaken." Harriet rose and brushed off her hands. "Let's find that will."

CHAPTER TWENTY

H arriet took the final scrumptious bite of the last of the rhubarb, chicken, and rice casserole, feeling satisfied with the comfort-food warmth in her stomach. As in many dishes, the longer the casserole ingredients had to combine, the more satisfying it became. Aunt Jinny's dish was especially perfect for a Monday that had arrived with a thunderstorm. Thankfully, the sun had chased away the clouds a couple of hours before.

While rinsing her dish and fork, Harriet glanced at the clock. "Lunchtime is almost over," she said to Maxwell, who responded with a furious wagging of his tail and a happy bark. "But I think we can fit in a quick stroll before Rand brings in Sahara for her checkup. I can't wait to see her again. How about you?"

This time, Maxwell barked twice in quick succession, which Harriet interpreted as agreement.

It had been nearly a week since Rand and Van first arrived at the clinic with the abandoned spaniel mix. Under the dog catcher's expert care, she'd already gained a little weight. Every day since he'd taken her home, Rand had texted one or more photos of her to Harriet.

She opened the kitchen door that led out to the patio for Maxwell then followed him outside. Charlie immediately appeared and rubbed against Harriet's legs. She scooped up the calico, relishing her contented purrs. Then she wandered into the garden, breathing in the fragrant, sun-kissed breezes.

To her left was the old barn that was now used as a boarding kennel. It had been empty for a couple of weeks, but Harriet didn't mind. Especially not with the busy schedule she'd had last week.

"A fox baby, an emaciated spaniel, and a wounded pine marten," she murmured to Charlie. Three major cases in the space of a few days. "I'm happy to tell you that, according to my sources, each one is improving beyond all expectations. You'll see for yourself when Sahara gets here, but you'll have to stay home when I leave to check on Talitha and Beckett."

Polly had posted a couple of appointments besides Sahara on the afternoon schedule. Barring any emergencies, Harriet planned to leave early so she could visit Talitha at the Yorkshire Coast Wildlife Centre and Beckett at Martha Banks's farm before joining Elena at Beckside Croft for supper.

And another round of their new favorite game, Where's the Will?

They'd had no luck finding it on Saturday, though they'd managed to clear away the mess left by the intruder. After church on Sunday, Harriet and Will drove to the cottage in the Beast, which he'd insisted could handle the bumps and ruts better than his little Kia Picanto. Garth joined them too, and after a meal of deli sandwiches, coleslaw, and potato salad, they'd once again set to work.

Each book was taken from the shelf and flipped through. They checked for hidden pockets in the furniture upholstery and secret compartments in an old secretary desk. Will and Garth examined the floor for any loose boards.

They'd found nothing but a scattering of coins, lost buttons, and dust bunnies.

When everyone was ready for a break, they'd rambled to Beckett Rock, a large boulder that stood like a sentry along the coast. Elena had told them that, according to family lore, a fire was lit on top of the rock whenever a new Beckett baby was born into the world, as an invitation for the neighboring families to celebrate. Whether true or not, Harriet thought it was a sweet story.

For the evening's search, Harriet and Elena planned to sort through more piles of ephemera that had accumulated over the decades. After all, where better to hide a piece of paper than in a stack of paper? A perfect example of the old "hiding in plain sight" cliché.

Harriet had asked Elena about the papers that Courtney might have found when she went through the trash. Though Elena's facial expression made obvious her scorn for Courtney's brazen behavior, she couldn't imagine she'd tossed anything of importance. She certainly hadn't thrown away any legal documents.

Maxwell's low yip at a lizard sunning itself on a border stone brought Harriet's attention back to the present. She kissed the top of Charlie's head then released her.

"Come along, Max," Harriet called to the dachshund. "That lizard is minding its own business, so you need to tend to yours."

Maxwell hurried to catch up with her as she continued her stroll.

The art gallery that displayed Grandad's paintings was situated beyond the low stone wall that surrounded the patio gardens. The thatch-roofed building, constructed of local stone, looked even more like a fairy-tale cottage than Beckside Croft. Harriet loved the multitude of windows, each with panes of hand-blown glass. Even more, she loved that visitors came almost every day to admire her grandfather's landscapes and animals.

The tranquility of the moment was broken by the roar of a speeding engine and a blaring horn. Harriet rushed to the front of the house as Elena's car sped past and jerked to a stop in front of Aunt Jinny's medical office. Elena popped out of the driver's seat and opened the back door.

Harriet raced toward the vehicle, arms pumping and heart pounding.

Not Jack! Please don't let it be Jack.

She arrived at the scene moments behind Aunt Jinny, who was already halfway into the back seat. Elena, eyes wide and with all the blood drained from her face, caught sight of Harriet.

"He tried to hit me," she babbled. "And there was Polly, and the next thing I knew, he hit her bike." Elena's words ended in a gasping gulp, but Harriet barely heard anything after Polly's name.

Harriet sprinted around to the other side of the car and peered in the window. Polly sprawled across the back seat, her eyes closed and her face muddy. Her helmet rested on the floor.

Elena had followed Harriet. "I called emergency services and told them I was coming here. Polly managed to crawl into the car—I helped her as much as I could. What else can I do?"

Harriet clasped Elena's shoulders and forced her to make eye contact. "You need to be calm. Aunt Jinny and I will take care of Polly until the ambulance arrives. Sometimes it helps to count your breaths. Inhale to a count of seven, hold to a count of four, and exhale to a count of eight. Slow and easy. Can you do that?"

"I can, yes." Elena immediately started the breathing.

"That's good." Suddenly, Harriet's heart clenched, and her gaze darted to the front seat. It was empty. "Where's Jack?"

"With Garth at the wildlife center. He's been there all morning. I was on my way to pick him up when..." She gestured helplessly at Polly's prone form.

Harriet pulled her into a hug. "All that matters is that he wasn't with you. Call Garth and tell him what happened while I help Polly. I'm sure he'll be happy to keep Jack a little longer."

Elena nodded and pulled her phone from her back pocket.

Harriet cautiously opened the door and stooped to gaze into the car. "What can I do?"

Aunt Jinny had her fingers on Polly's pulse. "Elena said Polly was still conscious when she got into the car. Nothing seems to be broken, but I'm concerned about a concussion."

"Should we try to wake her?"

"I already have." Aunt Jinny carefully moved aside the torn fabric from the arm of Polly's shirt. The exposed skin was raw and gritty with dirt. "Run inside and get a blanket so she doesn't go into shock. Hurry."

As Harriet retrieved the blanket, she debated calling Van. Since Elena had already called emergency services, it was likely he'd heard about the incident. But did he know Polly had been involved?

When she returned to the car, Ida Winslow, the manager of the art gallery, stood beside Elena. "I heard the commotion," she said to Harriet. "How can I help?"

"We're waiting for the ambulance." Bending into the car's back seat once more, Harriet tossed one end of the blanket to Aunt Jinny.

Together, the two women gently tucked the ends around Polly's legs and arms.

Talking to Garth and having Ida by her side seemed to steady Elena's nerves. By the time the ambulance arrived, she was able to tell a more coherent story about what had happened.

As she'd said earlier, she'd been on her way to pick up Jack at the wildlife center when she came up behind Polly, who was riding her bicycle to the clinic. Elena stopped for a quick chat then continued on her way. Seconds later, a huge black vehicle raced toward her. Thankfully, the road was lined with hedges instead of a stone wall. Elena steered into a break in the hedge as the black car careened past her and smacked her rear bumper with enough impact to push her car deeper into the hedge.

In a state of disbelief, Elena looked into her rearview mirror in time to see the out-of-control driver fishtail on the rain-slick road and clip the back tire of Polly's bike as he sailed past.

Van arrived as the emergency medical staff finished moving Polly onto a gurney and started an IV. He went straight to the gurney and touched Polly's hand, staring worriedly into her face. "Will she be all right?"

Aunt Jinny rested a comforting hand on his arm. "She needs time. And you need to do your job." Her tone was gentle but firm.

Suddenly, Polly groaned and moved her head.

Aunt Jinny laid a hand on her shoulder. "Stay still. We're taking you to the hospital."

Polly's eyes flickered open, and her gaze landed on Van. The uninjured corner of her mouth crooked upward. "Ye seventy-three," she mumbled. "Four to two." Her eyes fluttered shut again.

Harriet shared a puzzled glance with Aunt Jinny. Then she turned to Van. "What does that mean?"

"Polly?" Aunt Jinny said. "Can you stay awake, honey?"

Polly grunted but seemed unable to say anything else.

"What did she say?" Harriet asked. "Maybe it was important. Ye seventy-something. Four to two?"

"I thought she said forty-two," Elena said, and Ida agreed.

One of the EMTs gestured for them to stand back. "We need to go now. Dr. Garret, are you going with us?"

"I am." Aunt Jinny gave Harriet a quick hug. "Try not to worry. I'll be in touch." She squeezed Van's hand. "The same goes for you."

Harriet stood with the others in a tight group as Aunt Jinny was assisted into the ambulance after the gurney. As soon as the doors were closed, the vehicle sped away with its siren screaming.

"I wish I knew what Polly was trying to say." Harriet glanced at Van, who was scribbling on his notepad.

When he finished, he held up the page. The block writing read: YE73 422

Elena was the first to respond, and awe lifted her voice. "It's a license plate number. Can you believe Polly got that?"

"She sure did," Van said with obvious pride despite the shakiness in his voice. "I need to call this in."

"The car was registered here in Yorkshire," Ida said as Van headed toward his cruiser.

"How do you know that?" Harriet asked.

"It's the license plate code," Ida explained. "YE is one of the letter combinations for Yorkshire."

Harriet could hardly believe she was engaged in a conversation about the meaning of license plate numbers right after her closest friend had been carted away in an ambulance. On the other hand, Polly had provided vital information in her moment of coherency.

Harriet scanned for Elena and found her standing beside her car. The rear side panel and bumper bore deep dents from the accident.

Except this wasn't any accident. The driver had purposely targeted Elena, though Polly had taken the brunt of his aggression.

"Someone's coming," Ida announced. A dusty cargo van with the Yorkshire County Animal Control logo displayed prominently on the side entered the clinic's parking area. "Must be Rand Cromwell."

"He's my next appointment." Harriet darted another glance at Elena. She hated to leave the young woman alone, but as Aunt Jinny had reminded her, she had a job to do.

The shattered expression on Elena's face changed her mind. In this instance, friendship won out over responsibility.

"Ida, could you please tell Rand I'll be with him in a moment? He can wait in an exam room until I get there."

"I'd be happy to. You'll let me know about Polly, won't you?"

"Of course I will," Harriet promised. The she joined Elena. "Are you okay?"

"This is all my fault," Elena replied, her eyes downcast. "I should have been honest with you, with Van, with everyone, from the beginning."

"I'm not sure that would have changed what happened today."

"I'd change places with Polly if I could. When I swerved out of the way, I never imagined—"

Her voice broke, and Harriet wrapped an arm around her shoulders.

Elena took a couple of deep breaths then continued. "Timothy is a vindictive man. He must know I'll never willingly give up guardianship of Jack. So now he's coming up with these horrible schemes to wreck my life so I *can't* take care of Jack."

"Who's Timothy?" asked a familiar voice, making both women jump. How long had Van been standing there?

"He's Jack's uncle," Harriet explained. "He's trying to take him from Elena."

Van raised his eyebrows at Elena. "But aren't you Jack's mum?"

Elena swiped her cheeks and shook her head.

Harriet gently squeezed her arm. "Tell him," she urged. "He'll be able to help you better if he knows the truth."

After taking a deep breath, Elena straightened her shoulders and lifted her chin. "First, you should know that my last name is Hazeldine. Hunter was my mother's maiden name. I'm Jack's aunt and legal guardian since his parents—my sister and her husband— died. Timothy is Timothy Paul Lancaster. He's Jack's paternal uncle, and he controls Lancaster Enterprises, at least until Jack becomes an adult."

"You mean the Winston Lancaster Enterprises?" Van interrupted Elena. "Little Jack is one of *those* Lancasters?"

"Jack's full name is Winston Beckett Lancaster III. He's always been called Jack to avoid confusion. He inherited his father's share of the company when his grandfather died." Elena took another deep breath. "I know Timothy. Even when Jack is old enough to claim his inheritance, Timothy will want to stay in control of the company. That means he needs to control Jack. Starting now."

"Timothy is trying to intimidate Elena into surrendering Jack's guardianship to him," Harriet added.

"Was he driving the car that hit Polly?" Van demanded.

Elena shook her head. "I doubt it. Timothy has other people do his dirty work for him."

Van glanced at the open page in his notebook. "Is one of those people named Roscoe Rafferty?"

"I don't know their names."

"That's who the car is registered to. Here's his driver's license photo." Van held out his phone. "Do you recognize him?"

"I do recognize him," Elena replied, "but I'm not sure why."

Harriet peered at the photo over Elena's shoulder and gasped. "That's the man from the deli."

"The one Poppy Schofield called me about?" Van appeared as amazed as Harriet.

"Probably. I took Jack to the Biscuit Bistro last week, and this man was across the street, staring at the deli window. I don't think he was window-shopping though. Later that night, it struck me that he was probably using the reflection from the window to watch us."

"I'll show this to Poppy when I get back to town. Meanwhile, we've already got an alert out for the vehicle and arranged for road-blocks." Van's features hardened with determination. "We'll find him. I promise you that."

"Timothy isn't going to get away with this—any of it," Harriet told Elena as Van returned to his cruiser. "Soon this nightmare will be over."

"Will it?" Elena asked, her tone without hope. "It's more likely that this Roscoe Rafferty will take the blame and Timothy won't even get a slap on the wrist. I don't know how to keep Jack from being raised by his uncle while also protecting his inheritance. What if I can't do both?"

"Where there's a will, there's a way," Harriet reminded her. "We're going to find that new will. I promise."

As soon as she said the words, Harriet prayed that, despite all the odds against them, she could keep that promise. For Elena. For Jack. And even for Polly, who'd been the innocent victim of a cruel man's greed.

If the will existed, they'd find it.

If it didn't, Harriet was afraid to think what that might mean for Elena and Jack.

CHAPTER TWENTY-ONE

The moment the last appointment walked out of the clinic, Harriet locked the door, flipped the Open sign to Closed, and hightailed it to her bedroom suite. The spacious room was furnished with polished antiques, and a gorgeous needlepoint rug covered the wooden floor. Thanks to the fireplace's cast-iron insert, she'd enjoyed many late nights with a cozy fire during the bitter winter months. An en suite bathroom and large dressing area added to the room's comfort and luxury.

She showered then dressed in jeans and a light pullover sweater, which the locals would call a jumper. Since her hair was still slightly damp, she wore it loose and occasionally ruffled the strands near her scalp with her fingertips as she drove to the hospital.

Aunt Jinny had telephoned a couple of hours before with the wonderful news that Polly was awake, drowsy from the pain medication, and eager to go home. The head physician wanted her to stay for observation until they were certain she didn't have a concussion.

Harriet stopped at the gift shop for flowers and a balloon then made her way to Polly's room. As she passed a nearby waiting area, Aunt Jinny called her name. She took Harriet's arm and led her to a quiet nook in the corridor.

"Did you see all those people in there?" she asked.

"I didn't really notice. Who are they?"

"Polly's brothers and two or three close friends. You missed Will by about five minutes."

"That's disappointing." Harriet hadn't exactly expected to see him, but she never liked to miss him. "Are her parents with her?"

"They haven't left her side."

"Has Van stopped in?"

"I've talked to him a couple of times, but he's been too busy to come. Police found the hit-and-run car in an alley, and then they caught the driver at the bus station."

"That was fast." Harriet brought her aunt up to speed on what she'd learned from Elena about Jack's uncle Timothy. "Hopefully this nightmare will be over soon. Not that I'm in a hurry for Elena and Jack to return to York. I feel like they belong with us now."

"I feel the same way," Aunt Jinny agreed. "Come along now. Let's see if we can get you in to see Polly."

In a stroke of good fortune, the door to Polly's room opened as they approached, and her parents, Crispin and Tracy Thatcher, emerged into the corridor. Both smiled at the sight of Harriet and Aunt Jinny.

"I'm so glad you came." Tracy gripped Harriet's free hand. "You go right on in. I know Polly wants to see you."

Harriet entered the room and found Polly reclining in the hospital bed with her hands in her lap. A large bandage covered one side of her face from her temple to her chin. Another bandage extended from the short sleeve of her gown and ended at her wrist. Her lips and chin were bruised, and her knuckles were scraped.

"That was a nasty spill," Harriet said as she added her vase of flowers and balloon to the multitude of others in the room. "I'm so sorry."

"There's no one to blame but the man who hit me." Polly's voice sounded weak and tired. "Dad said he's been arrested."

"I heard that too." An unsettling helplessness swept over Harriet. She wanted to do something, anything, to make Polly more comfortable. But her friend wasn't a baby fox who could be cuddled or a pine marten in need of environmental enrichment.

"I'm glad you came." Polly nestled deeper into the bed. "I can rest with you."

Unexpected tears sprang to Harriet's eyes at the compliment. "That's one of the sweetest things anyone has ever said to me."

"I mean it." Polly's eyes closed. "Tell me about today's appointments. Has Sahara gained weight?"

"Yes, and at a healthy rate. Rand is so good to her, and Sahara openly adores him." For the next few minutes, Harriet described the patients she had seen that afternoon. Polly seemed content to listen except for the occasional question or comment. Before long, she was sound asleep.

Harriet closed her own eyes and said a prayer for her friend, as well as for Van, Elena, and Jack. When she left the room, she found Polly's mom outside the door with Aunt Jinny.

"Oh, Harriet," Tracy exclaimed, "I truly am glad you came to see our Polly. I thank the Good Lord she wasn't injured more than she was, though her entire left side from her head to her toes is all scraped and bruised. I told Pastor Will I need to pray that God forgives me for the thoughts I had about the man who hit her. How's she doing in there?"

Harriet smiled. "She fell asleep while we were talking."

"That's good. She needs her rest." Tracy dabbed at her eyes with a tissue. "There's a few here who want to see for themselves that she'll be fine, but I want her to myself for a bit. I never tired of watching her sleep when she was a baby, and I don't mind watching her again and remembering those days."

"I think that sounds wonderful," Aunt Jinny said with a compassionate smile. "Her friends will understand."

Harriet accompanied her aunt to the waiting room so they could chat with Polly's brothers and friends before they left. Harriet's heart warmed to know how much love and support the Thatcher family was receiving in their time of need.

Not that she was surprised. She'd witnessed many examples of such generous outpourings since her move to White Church Bay.

I never want to leave.

The conviction of the thought from the very depths of her heart simultaneously surprised and delighted her. She'd known for a long time that she loved it in White Church Bay. Now she knew that she belonged there as much as Elena and Jack did. Her future was there, with the clinic, Aunt Jinny, her cousin and his family, Polly, and the other friends she'd made.

And Will. When she pictured her future, she realized that the future she wanted was one that featured him prominently.

More than that, she knew with every fiber of her being that she not only loved Will—she was *in* love with him. If only she could find the courage to tell him.

She sighed and whispered, "'Perfect love drives out fear.'" She'd learned the words from 1 John 4:18 when she was a child in Sunday school. In that moment, Harriet prayed for God's perfect love to drive out her fear of being wrong again.

Aunt Jinny touched her arm. "You're looking exceptionally thoughtful. Are you worried about Elena and Jack?"

Harriet made the mental shift from her prayers to the present situation. "I am now. Elena told me that Timothy is vindictive. I'm afraid of what he might do next."

And who else might get caught in the crossfire, as Polly had.

Since Harriet had missed Will at the hospital, she decided to stop at the village church on her way home. If he wasn't too busy, perhaps they could go out for fish and chips or pizza. She parked the Beast beside his Kia hatchback then paused a moment to gaze at the charming old stone building with its steeply pitched roof. Though some claimed that it reminded them of an aged mariner gazing out to sea, Harriet had always loved the church's soaring design, including its narrow windows with their tall arches. To her, it felt as if every part of the church was reaching to heaven.

She stepped inside the foyer, surprising Will and Courtney, who stood near the sanctuary doors. "Oh, forgive me. I didn't mean to interrupt."

"You're not," Courtney rushed to say. Then she paused to take a deep breath. "That is, I can't believe you're here. I was going to call you later to see if we could get together and talk."

"You want to talk to me?" Harriet repeated, certain she'd misheard.

Instead of answering, Courtney lowered her gaze. Harriet could hardly believe that the quiet woman standing in front of her was the same diva who enjoyed creating chaos wherever she went.

Will stepped closer to Harriet and touched her arm. "Courtney and I have been talking. She heard about the hit-and-run, and after being a suspect—"

"I didn't break into Elena's cottage," Courtney interrupted. "But people are blaming me for that. I can't stand the idea that they might blame me for what happened to Polly after she was so kind to Thomasina."

"Would people really think that?" Harriet asked.

"They already do. People I thought were my friends asked me if it was me. They were laughing, and suddenly I realized that I didn't want to be *me* anymore. And I don't want friends who believe I'm capable of doing anything like that."

"Courtney wants to make amends," Will said. "To you for her behavior at the clinic. To Elena for going through her trash. And to a few others."

"You were marvelous with Thomasina," Courtney said. "And I didn't appreciate it. At the time, I thought she was a nuisance. But the truth is that I missed her the whole weekend she stayed with Polly. I came home to an empty house, and the place felt so cold without her there to greet me. Will you forgive me for behaving so badly?"

"Absolutely," Harriet assured her. Then she grinned. "And if you'd like some new friends, give me a call."

Courtney returned the smile. "Thank you, Harriet. I'm not surprised people around here think so highly of you. I'd like to give friendship with you a go."

She left shortly thereafter with plans to connect with Elena and return the papers she'd taken from her rubbish. As she left, she paraphrased Ephesians 4:28. "Let those who steal, steal no more but do something useful with their hands. That's what I hope to do."

"You are amazing," Harriet told Will when they were alone.

"Not me," Will replied as he drew her into a hug and pointed heavenward. "Him."

CHAPTER TWENTY-TWO

Unlike many of their neighbors, the Philbins weren't professional farmers even though there'd been Philbins at Green Grove for a hundred years or more. After Garth's geography lesson and Harriet's own rambles where she'd paid more attention to the geography, she realized that the farm's acreage was another parcel of land that had been part of the Beckett brothers' vast holding three centuries before.

Mr. Philbin worked at a bank in Whitby while Janette managed the daily farm chores. She kept two dairy cattle, five sheep, and a flock of assorted chickens because she delighted in finding different colors and sizes of eggs in the nest boxes.

The sheep provided a bit of income when the lambs were sold, but Janette primarily raised them for their wool. What she didn't spin herself was sold to other spinners. What she spun she dyed, using colors made from wildflowers she gathered on the moors. Over the years, she'd established an online business selling her custom-dyed yarns and handcrafted creations.

In recent days, four of her ewes had given birth to a total of six lambs without any difficulty. The fifth was in trouble. Early Thursday morning, Harriet and Janette worked together to get the lamb into the correct position and ease his entrance into the world.

They celebrated the mom-and-baby bonding with mugs of fresh coffee poured from a thermos and laced with cream from milk that had been procured earlier that morning.

"Can you come to the house for blackberry muffins?" Janette asked. "The pan is ready, so I only have to pop it into the oven. You can say hello to Nugget and Gideon too."

"I'd love to. There isn't much going on at the clinic this morning. I've got time for a visit."

"You must be thankful for the lull, since Polly is still recuperating. I saw her mum at Galloway's yesterday, and she gave me an update. Such a nasty business." Janette held open the screen door to the mudroom so Harriet could enter first. "Everyone is proud of our DC Worthington and how fast that hit-and-run driver was arrested."

Harriet had heard similar praise for Van, along with a few comments that he'd found the driver so quickly either to impress Polly or because of his anger that she'd been hurt. Only a handful of people seemed to know that the driver had also intentionally forced Elena off the road. While photos of Elena's damaged car and Polly's mangled bike had appeared in yesterday's edition of the *Whitby Gazette*, Amelia Arbuckle's story omitted the driver's deliberate action.

Neither did it mention the most galling aspect of the case, which was Roscoe Rafferty's refusal to accept any responsibility or to admit even knowing Timothy Lancaster. He pleaded not guilty to all hit-and-run charges and tried to shift the blame to Elena, despite Polly's sworn testimony.

Harriet suspected that the *Gazette*'s chief editor was holding back information at the request of local law enforcement, but she didn't know that for a fact.

While the muffins baked, Janette showed Harriet a few skeins of yarn she'd recently dyed using black-eyed Susans. She planned to sell the golden yarn at local craft shows later in the spring and summer. Nugget joined them in the kitchen and gave Harriet a warm welcome.

"I'm surprised Gideon hasn't shown his face," Janette said. "He loves company. I'll go see if he's in the backyard."

Before Janette returned, the timer sounded on the stove. Harriet removed the piping-hot muffins, inhaling their fragrant blackberry aroma as she did so. A moment later, Janette came back, her features twisted with worry.

"I can't find him in the yard," she said. "Maybe he followed me to the barn and I didn't notice."

"Does that happen often?"

"Never," Janette said. "As little as he is, he usually makes his presence known in a big way."

"We'll find him," Harriet reassured her as they pulled their boots back on.

When they stepped outside, Harriet's phone buzzed with a call from Elena. "By any chance is Jack with you?" she asked, her voice on the edge of panic.

"No, I haven't seen him at all."

"I can't find him anywhere. Why can't he stay close to the cottage like I tell him to?"

Because he's an adventurous little boy. And a bit of a rascal.

Harriet kept those sentiments to herself. With everything that had happened the past few weeks, Elena had every reason to be fearful for Jack.

"He probably wandered farther than he meant to, and maybe now he isn't sure how to find his way back. I'll call Van and come help you look. We'll find him, Elena."

"Thank you."

When Harriet ended the call, Janette gave her a relieved smile. "Don't tell me. Jack is missing too."

"Do you think he's with Gideon?"

"He's been here a couple of times to play with Sarah Jane and the dogs. They could both be in the barn."

"Let's check before I call Van."

"Good idea," Janette said as they headed out the door. "Jack is especially fond of Gideon. So much so that I've considered asking Elena if she'd take him."

Harriet's eyes widened. "That's generous of you. I thought you meant to keep him."

"I trust Elena to do right by him. Truthfully, she'd be doing us a favor. Nugget will be retiring from puppy duty in a couple of years, so we need to keep a female from her next litter to keep our line going. I know from experience that two dogs are a blessing, but three is one too many for the Philbin household."

Harriet chuckled. "You're wise to know your limits." She wished more of her clients did. Too often some of them didn't realize they'd taken on more responsibility than they should have until it was too late.

Except for Jane Birtwhistle. No matter how many cats she adopted, she always had the time, patience, and resources for another one. She was definitely the exception to the rule.

"It was a hard lesson learned," Janette replied. "Right now, I have all my species and their numbers exactly where they need to be."

They passed the sheepfold and checked inside in case Jack had spotted the newborn lamb. When they didn't find him there, they continued to the barn where the children had played with the dogs before.

Harriet fully expected to find Jack and Gideon among the bales of hay or playing in one of the wagons. But they weren't there either, and now she was worried.

"Beckside Croft is that way, right?" Harriet asked. "As the crow flies."

"If you cut across that field, you'll reach a stream—"

"You mean Restless Beck."

"That's right. It'll lead you close to Beckett Rock. Do you know it?"

"I've been there." Harriet reached for her phone and searched for Van's number. "I'll head across the moors—"

"And I'll go to the cottage via the roads." Janette clasped Harriet's arm. "Don't worry. We'll find him. He's not the first Yorkshire child to lose his bearings on the moors, and he won't be the last."

Harriet phoned Van while following the directions Janette had given her. He promised to organize a search party right away. As Harriet crossed the field and followed the stream, she called Jack's and Gideon's names. She was on the most likely path Jack would have taken to get to the Philbins' home. Maybe he was following it back again to the cottage.

At a curve in the stream at the top of a gentle rise, Harriet stopped and looked around to get her bearings. On the next rise over, she could barely make out a rutted lane that stopped at a stone wall.

That was where Garth had taken her after their first encounter with Elena. Harriet shaded her eyes to see better. Was a vehicle parked by the wall?

An inexplicable fear chilled her bones, but she knew what she had to do. She also knew she didn't have to do it alone. Van would be busy putting together the search party, but she had someone else to call. As she headed down one rise and up the next, she got Will on the phone and told him what was going on.

"Wait to approach the car until I get there," he said.

"You know I can't do that." She had to find out if Jack was in or around the car—immediately. He might be hurt.

"Then stay on the line with me. I'm on my way."

To both her relief and disappointment, neither Jack nor Gideon were in, under, or near the big black SUV. After peering through the back window to check the cargo space one more time, she noticed the tag number.

"This is interesting," she said to Will. "The tag is YE73 423."

"Isn't that similar to the license plate on the car that hit Polly?" Earlier in the week, Harriet had told him how Polly recited the tag number.

"That one was 422. Only one number off."

"We need to let Van know."

Harriet stared in the direction of the cottage. If the car belonged to another of Timothy's henchmen, then Elena should be warned. "Why don't you do that," she said. "I'm going to the cottage."

Before Will could protest, Harriet hung up and dialed Elena's number. The call went straight to voice mail. Without taking the time to try again, Harriet climbed over the stone wall and jogged along a faint track. Her phone buzzed, but she didn't stop to answer. All that mattered was that she got to Beckside Croft. Fast.

Before the cottage came into view, Harriet noticed smoke curling into the sky. Though her leg muscles burned and her lungs screamed, she pushed herself even harder.

One more rise, and the cottage came into view. Smoke poured from the chimney but also from beside the chimney and out two of the front windows.

Practically in tears and fearful of what she'd find inside, Harriet dialed emergency services.

"What is your emergency?" a voice asked.

"I'm at Beckside Croft. The cottage is on fire. There may be people inside." *Please, God, don't let Elena or Jack be trapped in there.*

"Do you have an address?"

"No, I don't know it." Despair threatened to paralyze her. She couldn't give in to it. Not now. Not yet.

"Are you nearby?"

"Yes." Harriet's voice wavered.

"Can you give me your coordinates from the location app on your phone?"

A glimmer of hope eased her panic as she found the app and recited the numbers.

"Thank you. I see your location." A pause. "Emergency services are on the way. Please stay on the line with me till they arrive."

"Okay." *But don't expect me to wait on them.*

Harriet cautiously approached the back door, since that end of the cottage didn't seem to be on fire. Yet.

"Elena, are you in here?" she called. "Jack?"

Was it her imagination, or did a groan answer her from the main room? Smoke billowed through the kitchen door, causing her to cough. In the distance, she thought she heard the faint sound of a siren.

She cleared her throat and shouted, "Elena? Jack?"

There it was again. A definite moan.

She started forward, but the billowing smoke burned her eyes and forced her backward. She bumped into the sink then grabbed a dish towel. She soaked it and wrapped it around her nose and mouth. Slowly, keeping her eyes slitted open, she made her way into the living room.

A stranger sprawled on the floor near a pile of burning papers. His legs were trapped beneath the antique secretary desk that had apparently collapsed on top of him. Harriet tried to push the heavy piece of furniture off the man with all her remaining strength. But it wouldn't budge.

She sank to her knees beside him.

A ghostly shadow loomed over her, said her name.

She couldn't speak. Couldn't breathe. She was vaguely aware that she lay on the floor.

The shadow lifted her, arms like iron under her back and knees. It deposited her in a less-smoky place and ordered, "Go, Harriet. Get out of here. Hurry."

No longer able to breathe, barely able to think, she staggered out the door...and into Will's outstretched arms.

CHAPTER TWENTY-THREE

Harriet lay on the gurney with an oxygen mask over her nose and mouth while sunshine warmed her skin. Her groggy mind could make little sense of the bustling activity around her. Firefighters in their heavy coats and protective helmets pointed thick hoses at dancing flames. Paramedics hurried from gurneys to ambulances and back again. She closed her eyes, wanting to sleep and wake up in her own bed, where dancing flames stayed in a cast-iron insert. Where they didn't eat up the last will and testament of a benevolent grandfather or turn a centuries-old cottage into ashes.

When Harriet opened her eyes again, the sun was gone, and an overhead light had taken its place. The oxygen mask was gone too, replaced by tiny nozzles shooting air into her nostrils.

"You're awake." Will's voice washed over her, and he caressed the loose strands of hair along her temple. "How do you feel?"

"I don't—" She pressed her fingers against her aching throat.

"Maybe you shouldn't try to talk. Not yet. You inhaled a lot of smoke."

She caught his hand and stared into his hazel eyes, which were full of worry. Memory assaulted her. "Jack?"

"He's fine. Gideon too. They always were." Will lifted her fingers to his lips. "The little rapscallion made his way to Green Groves to play with Gideon. His story is that Gideon followed him when he left. Instead of going home, he went to the Wilkersons' farm. Alma was in town running errands, and naturally Winifred was in school. Jack decided to wait for her to come home."

Harriet had to smile.

Will gave a slight chuckle and shook his head. "The lad had no understanding of how many hours he'd have to wait. Elena found him sound asleep under a maple tree with Gideon curled up against his side."

He was safe. Harriet released a pent-up sigh that grated her throat. God had watched over him.

"Elena sent me a photo of it." Will let go of her hand to find the image on his phone. "She said that she probably should have been furious with him for scaring her, but when she found him safe and sound, she had to take a picture."

Harriet gazed at Will's face before looking at the phone. He was trying so hard to make this nightmare feel like a normal moment, but it just couldn't be. He said the right words in the right way, but fear of what could have been tempered his tone. He smiled and chuckled, seemingly amused at the antics that made so much sense in a little boy's mind. But fear deepened the worry lines around his mouth and his eyes.

She loved him for trying. She loved him for being with her. She loved that he was the one who had met her at the burning cottage's back door.

He tapped the image so the photo filled the screen then showed it to her. Jack and Gideon, peacefully asleep in the midst of the storm they'd created. The photo tugged her lips into a smile.

Will set aside his phone and took Harriet's hand once more. His familiar touch worked like a soothing balm and seemed to connect her to the world outside of herself when weakness and discomfort defined her entire being.

"It looks like Jack's uncle started the fire," Will said. "He was the man in the cottage."

Timothy himself? Not one of his henchmen?

"I...tried..."

"Yes, of course you tried to help him," Will assured her. "We know."

Such a needless tragedy and an outlandish scheme. Who burned an entire house to destroy a piece of paper? Timothy was the perfect example of the wicked falling into their own nets. If only he'd heeded the biblical warning instead of being consumed by greed and ambition.

"They transported him to a hospital in London that specializes in long-term burn treatment," Will continued. "He's expected to live, but he's got a long and painful recovery ahead of him. Elena thinks he tried to burn down the cottage to destroy his dad's final will then somehow got trapped by that desk. It sounds like a plausible explanation to me, but we'll know more once the arson investigation is complete."

Harriet nodded.

Will's pleasant smile faded. He clutched her hand in both of his. "There's more news. I'm afraid it's not very good."

She gestured for him to go on.

"After getting you to the kitchen, Van went back for Timothy."

Van? Harriet squeezed Will's hand. *Van was the ghostly shadow?*

"I wouldn't have believed it if I hadn't seen it with my own eyes. Van walked right out the front door, past all the flames, carrying Timothy across his shoulders. It was like something you'd see in a movie." Will shook his head, as if still battling with disbelief. "It was the only way out by then. Part of the ceiling had collapsed in the kitchen."

She closed her eyes, bracing herself for whatever the bad news was.

"He breathed in a lot of smoke. Much more than you did." Will rubbed her hand between his. Harriet couldn't decide whether it was for her comfort or his own. "He's in the next room over. The doctor says it's touch-and-go."

Harriet's cheeks dampened, and it took a moment for her to realize she was crying. How did it make sense that Timothy was expected to survive despite his burns, but Van, who had saved him even though he was so selfish and did such awful things, could die?

"I know." Will lowered his voice to a whisper. "It's not fair. All we can do is pray."

A knock sounded on the door a moment before it opened. Aunt Jinny entered and directed her loving smile toward Harriet. "How lovely to see you awake, dear. Am I interrupting?"

Will shook his head as he stood. "I just finished telling her about Van."

"He's getting excellent care," Aunt Jinny said firmly, as if saying the words was enough to make them true. Not that Harriet doubted her. But sometimes even the most excellent care wasn't enough. "As are you. I'm here to take you to get a chest X-ray so we can see if there's smoke in your lungs. The good news is that your oxygen levels are satisfactory. Not quite where we want them to be, but given the circumstances..."

Her composure broke, and she raced to the bed. She cupped Harriet's face in her hands while her tears fell. "I may never let you out of my sight again. I don't care how old you are."

Aunt Jinny kissed Harriet's forehead, enveloping her in the best medicine of all.

Love.

The rest of Harriet's day was taken up with more tests, examinations, and intermittent naps. Aunt Jinny arranged a video call with Harriet's parents, who wanted to catch the next flight to Yorkshire. Harriet's throat still ached too much to talk, but with Aunt Jinny's assistance, she managed to persuade them to wait a few weeks. She'd much prefer spending a few days with them when she could fully enjoy their time together.

As news of the tragedy spread through the local community, Harriet's room filled with flowers, balloons, stuffed toys, and treats from her neighbors and clients. A few stopped by to deliver their gifts personally—Doreen Danby arrived with a huge batch of her famous apricot scones—and to share words of comfort with Will and Aunt Jinny, who proved to be fierce guardians of Harriet's need for peace and quiet.

Will made an exception for Elena and Garth, sensing Harriet's concern about how her new friend was handling the loss of the cottage and Timothy's actions.

"Remember," Will said to Harriet as he let them in, "no unnecessary talking. Which means no talking, since there's no such thing as necessary talking. Not today." He smiled to soften the words, but Harriet knew he meant them.

Harriet nodded agreement and pressed her lips shut. Now that a few hours had passed, Will's fears for her seemed to have eased. She was noticeably stronger than when she'd arrived at the hospital. He'd spent a while in the chapel earlier, while Aunt Jinny stayed with Harriet. When he returned, his entire demeanor was much calmer.

Elena, wearing a lightweight sweatshirt with the Yorkshire Coast Wildlife Centre logo on the front, tentatively approached Harriet's side. "First Polly, now you and Van. I'm so sorry for all the trouble I've caused. You must wish I'd never come here."

Harriet opened her mouth, but Will stopped her. "You promised, and I know what you would say anyway." He faced Elena. "You're wrong about that. We want you and Jack to make your home here. We're the ones who are sorry for what you've lost."

Harriet applauded then gestured for a pen and paper. *What will you do now?* she wrote.

"That depends on Timothy. With the kind of recovery he's facing, I hope he'll stop threatening to take Jack. But if he doesn't, I'll fight him every step of the way. He's caused too much pain to people I care about, and I won't let him win. Not now. Not ever."

Garth wrapped his arm around Elena's shoulders. "You won't be fighting alone."

Harriet and Will exchanged a glance. Who could have guessed that a frightened little boy, a wounded fox kit, and an elusive pine marten could unwittingly team up together to play Cupid for the unexpected pair? In springtime on the moors, it seemed love flourished in unexpected places.

Later in the day, Aunt Jinny entered Harriet's room with a wheelchair. Harriet's eyes brightened, and she pushed back the bedcovers.

"Not so fast, young lady," Aunt Jinny scolded. "You need a robe and slippers. Which I have." She picked up a bag from the wheelchair seat.

Will stepped out of the room while Aunt Jinny helped Harriet get clothed and situated in the chair.

"Polly is with Van," Aunt Jinny said softly, "and she's inconsolable."

Harriet fixed her aunt with a questioning gaze.

"She's been in a state ever since the news got out, demanding to be allowed to see him. Her parents finally decided it would be better for her to visit him than to imagine the worst." Aunt Jinny placed a partially folded blanket over Harriet's lap. "I assume you want to join them. Please don't use your voice, no matter how much you want to. It'll be enough for you to simply be with her."

Harriet gave her a thumbs-up.

Aunt Jinny smiled and patted her shoulder. "Let's go then."

Van's room, like Harriet's, was filled with flowers and other tokens from well-wishers. Will had told Harriet about a couple of the gifts earlier, so she knew that the oversize teddy bear perched in the corner was a gift from DI McCormick and others at the county headquarters. Harriet had nearly laughed at the idea of the stern inspector ordering the giant stuffed bear. The local firefighters, who'd arrived at the fire as Van emerged from the burning building with Timothy, had brought him a large stuffed Dalmatian wearing a red fireman's helmet. The badge around the dog's neck was engraved with the words HONORARY FIREFIGHTER.

Polly sat in a chair beside Van's bed, a cane propped beside her. Harriet wasn't surprised to see that her friend had left the wheelchair behind as soon as she was able. The bruising and cuts on her face were healing, though still noticeable through the tears falling down her cheeks. She moved stiffly, as if her entire body ached, as she shifted toward Harriet. A few pink strands brought a pop of spring color to her dark hair, as if she was determined to be a cheerful presence despite the dismal circumstances.

"Hi, Harriet. It's good to see you."

Harriet, mindful of her standing orders not to speak, smiled.

Aunt Jinny wheeled Harriet's chair into position next to Polly's then walked around to the other side of Van's bed. "I think he'd want you both to know he's improving. His family will be here tomorrow, and it will be up to them how much they want to share about his medical condition."

"Thank you," Polly murmured. "He's so pale. And I've never seen him so still."

"His stillness is good. It means he's resting, which is what his body needs." Aunt Jinny adjusted Van's blanket. "I'll be right outside the door if you need me."

Once she'd gone, Polly took Harriet's hand. "Are you all right? Don't say anything. I know you're not allowed to talk."

Harriet nodded and squeezed Polly's hand. Her gaze slid from Polly to Van. After carrying Harriet into the kitchen, where had he found the courage to return to the inferno in the main room? How had he summoned the strength to single-handedly move the heavy secretary desk off Timothy's legs and carry him from the danger?

"Everyone is talking about him," Polly murmured. "They're calling him a hero and talking about awards and a banquet and a big write-up in the *Gazette*."

Harriet pointed to Van, cupped her hand as if she were carrying an object, then rested her palm against her chest.

"He saved your life," Polly said, interpreting Harriet's motions. "That's why I'm glad he was there. But this?" She gestured to the bed. "Forgive me, Harriet, but I also wish he'd been anywhere else."

Harriet patted Polly's arm to show her that she understood.

No doubt Van had harbored similar thoughts when he'd heard that Polly had been hit while riding her bicycle. If she hadn't been in that spot at that moment, she wouldn't be bruised and battered now. So many things in life happened that way. Ordinary decisions resulting in tragic consequences. A man penned his last will and testament, and a cottage burned, and lives were changed.

Though the reverse was also true. A beloved grandad left his home, vet clinic, and art gallery to his granddaughter, and her life was changed. A frightened boy sought help for the only mum he knew, and their lives were changed.

"I love him," Polly suddenly blurted. "Truly and deeply and with all my being. What if I never get the chance to tell him?" She laid her head on Harriet's shoulder as fresh tears streamed down her cheeks. "Why didn't I say yes when I had the chance?"

As Harriet tried to comfort Polly, she glanced at Van—and was surprised to see his eyes half-open, fixed on Polly, and shining with joy.

"Did…," he rasped, the word barely audible. He paused then tried again, apparently intent on speaking no matter how much it hurt. "I hear you right?"

Polly stared at him as she swiped the tears from her face. "Yes."

Van closed his eyes and breathed a sigh of peace. "I love you too."

CHAPTER TWENTY-FOUR

No matter how long Harriet lived in Yorkshire, American lemonade and homemade cookies was still one of her favorite combinations to enjoy on the patio on a sun-kissed Sunday afternoon. She liked the fizzy British version of lemonade well enough, but sometimes nothing would do for her but the smooth, tangy sweetness of the drink she'd grown up with.

She inhaled a deep breath of the passing breeze, scented with the fragrance of the moors' wildflowers, and gave thanks that she could do so in relative comfort. She would never again take something as simple as breathing fresh air for granted.

"I'd ask you if you're glad to be home," Elena said with a chuckle, "but the answer is pretty obvious." She lifted her hands, palms up, as if they were scales. "Between the hospital and Cobble Hill Farm, no one in their right mind would choose the hospital."

"I hope Van gets to leave soon." Harriet's voice still rasped, but at least she could talk.

According to Aunt Jinny, it could be another week before Van was released even though his oxygen levels were almost normal. His medical team wanted to be sure the local hero was as healthy as possible before they discharged him.

Charlie appeared out of nowhere, climbed over Maxwell, and vaulted into Harriet's lap. Her purrs grew louder as she settled in for a nap. Sunday afternoons were made for such moments. Harriet felt rested, content, and thankful for all those who'd helped her the past few days.

The Old Boys Club, three area veterinarians who'd been colleagues of her grandfather and served as references for Harriet, had taken shifts at the clinic on Friday and Saturday, with Elena doing what she could to maintain the office.

At Harriet's invitation, Elena and Jack were staying at Cobble Hill Farm, and they had cared for Maxwell and Charlie in her absence. Neighbors brought more casseroles and desserts than Harriet, Elena, and Jack could possibly eat, which meant Will and Garth were frequent mealtime visitors.

The two men were with Jack now at a secret fishing hole somewhere along Restless Beck. They'd been aghast to learn, during after-church dinner, that the little boy had never been fishing, and made immediate plans to rectify that situation.

"My cousin called me last night to talk about Beckside Croft," Elena said. "They're offering it to me for good. Jack and I will be your neighbors. Permanently."

"That's terrific news," Harriet exclaimed. "How long will it take to rebuild?"

"I can't even guess, but I'm meeting with an estate agent on Monday so we can find a rental," Elena said. "Jack doesn't want to leave here, and neither do I."

"I'm so glad," Harriet said, and she meant it from the bottom of her heart. "I hope you'll find something close. At least as the crow flies."

"Close to you, the Wilkersons, and the Philbins," Elena said, laughing. "Once we get settled, Janette is giving Gideon to Jack. But it's a secret, so don't tell him."

"I won't. Cross my heart," Harriet promised.

It was great news, especially since she knew Elena was devastated about the damage to the cottage at Beckside Croft. The preliminary arson investigation surmised that Timothy had first burned papers and books in the fireplace. When the flame was large enough, he'd dragged the fire out onto the hearth and added more books. At some point, he'd poured an accelerant on the couch—too much accelerant. The investigators could only speculate how he ended up on the floor beneath the antique desk, but he was certainly paying a high price for his folly.

"I also need to enroll Jack in school," Elena said. "He won't like that as much as wandering the moors all day, but it won't be long till summer."

Maxwell stirred, and his ears perked up. He scampered to the end of the patio and barked.

"Oh, hush," a familiar voice told him with a chuckle. "You know who we are."

A moment later, Ivy Chapman and Sir Halston Dahlbury stepped onto the patio and joined Harriet and Elena. Maxwell wagged his tail in welcome.

"I leave for a few weeks, and all kinds of mayhem ensues," Ivy said to Harriet. "You must be exhausted."

"I'm feeling much better," she assured the older woman. "And you look beautiful."

"That Cornwall air is good for whatever ails you," Ivy said as she and Sir Halston sat together in a gliding love seat.

Harriet made introductions.

"I'm pleased to meet you both," Elena said. "I've become a little acquainted with Fern since I arrived here."

"She's told me all about you," Ivy replied. "Don't worry. I never believe more than half of what Fern tells me. It's true that you're Jack Lancaster's guardian?"

"I am."

"And Jack is Winston Lancaster's grandson?"

"He is."

"Well, she got those things right at least. Winston must be rolling over in his grave at what Timothy has done. He did spoil the boy, but that's no excuse for his atrocious behavior."

"You knew the Lancasters?" Harriet asked.

"For ages. Winston and I even went on a few dates." Ivy's cheeks flushed. "That was before I met Halston."

Ever the gentleman, Halston gave her a besotted smile and patted her hand.

"Then I'm even more pleased to meet you," Elena said. "Jack adored his grandfather, and he was very generous to me after my sister and brother-in-law died."

"Possibly more generous than you can know," Ivy said. She and Halston shared a glance, then Ivy took a deep breath. "Fern told us you were searching for Winston's final will. One that he wrote while staying at Beckside Croft."

"That's why I came here, but I couldn't find it. The sole clue I had was that it was 'behind the Rock.'"

"Even though it's too late," Ivy continued in an apologetic tone, "you should know that Halston and I were witnesses to his signature and signed the will ourselves. We're willing to testify to that in court."

"That's incredible," Harriet exclaimed while Elena seemed to be in momentary shock. "Do you know where he hid it?"

"Just where he said. 'Behind the Rock.'"

"We looked all around Beckett Rock," Harriet said. "We didn't find anything."

"Winston didn't mean the rock itself," Ivy said. "He meant the rock in the painting over the fireplace." Her gaze shifted to Harriet. "The one painted by your grandfather."

"He hid it there?" Elena's voice trembled with excitement.

"He'd fashioned a little slot in the canvas that he could slip papers into—between the canvas and the frame," Halston explained. "It's barely visible if you don't know what you're looking for. Not as easy to get the papers out though."

"It doesn't matter now," Harriet said. "The painting must have been destroyed in the fire." She faced Elena, whose eyes were large and bright. "I'm so sorry. It never occurred to me to think of the painting."

Elena jumped up. "The painting wasn't destroyed."

"It must have been," Harriet protested.

"It's in the art gallery."

"How? Why?"

Elena perched on the edge of her seat. "The day Polly got hit, Ida showed me around the art gallery. I told her about the painting Dr. Bailey had given me, and naturally she was interested in seeing it. I ended up loaning it to her for a special display."

"But that means…" Harriet trailed off.

Elena finished the sentence for her. "It means the will is in the art gallery."

CHAPTER TWENTY-FIVE

The sun had barely risen, spreading its warmth slowly across the moors, when Harriet slid into the driver's seat of the Beast with Fern in the passenger seat. Will shut her door then piled in the back seat with Elena and Jack.

Over two weeks had passed since the fire, and this was her first official outing though she'd returned to work in the clinic after a few days of rest. Harriet maneuvered her vehicle out of the clinic parking lot then followed the map Garth had sketched for them.

Fern thought that was totally unnecessary. "I know exactly where we're going," she said. "Wasn't I the one who suggested the spot?"

"You walk across the moors to get there," Will reminded her. "We're driving. There's a difference."

Fern snorted.

Once they turned off the main road, they followed first one lane then another deep into the moors until they reached their destination. Garth, Alma, and Winifred waited at the spot along with Martha Banks and the guest of honor—Beckett, the pine marten.

The others who knew about Beckett had opted not to come. Both Aunt Jinny and Mr. Wilkerson had prior obligations.

Though Van had been released from the hospital, he was still on medical leave with orders to recuperate at home. Polly spent as much time with him as possible—cooking meals, chauffeuring him to appointments, and keeping things tidy. Plus playing games, putting together puzzles, and watching movies. They'd borrowed *The Three Lives of Thomasina* from Harriet, and Polly had loved it.

After Harriet parked behind Garth's Land Rover and everyone exchanged greetings, Garth carried the cloth-covered crate with its precious cargo to the top of a knoll. The downward slope was dotted with boulders and trees, providing enough hiding spots and food for any small creature to live out its life in relative obscurity.

Garth set the crate on the ground then looked at the others. "I don't really have a speech prepared, but I do want to say thank you. And to assure you that we're doing the right thing by keeping Beckett—and the rest of his colony—a secret. Fern has done so for years. We honor her discretion by being discreet ourselves."

Fern nodded her approval of his words.

Garth stooped so he was at eye-level with Jack and Winifred. "Secrets can be hard to keep. We feel special when we know something no one else does. We might want someone to feel jealous because they don't know our secret. Or we might want to make ourselves feel more important by letting others know we have a secret. But for a secret this big, do you know what the best thing to do is?"

Winifred piped up. "You keep your secret a secret. So no one even knows you have one."

"That's right," Garth said, obviously pleased at her response. "Can you do that, Winifred?"

"Yes, Mr. Garth. I would tell my mum, but she already knows."

"How about you, Jack?"

"I won't tell anyone. I promise."

"Then let's do this." Garth removed the cloth to reveal the pine marten. Beckett didn't appear frightened or nervous. He sniffed the air and stretched his long, sleek body. He no longer wore a splint or a bandage, and his wound had healed nicely. The only sign that he'd ever been injured was his slight limp. Harriet hoped that it would become even less noticeable in time.

"I'm going to open the crate door so it faces downhill," Garth explained. "We all need to stand behind it. Actually, it might be better if we sit. Can you all do that?" He waited till they'd formed a rough semicircle behind the crate. "Okay, then. Let's do a quiet countdown together. Five."

Everyone joined in, saying the numbers in hushed tones. "Four. Three. Two. One."

Garth opened the crate door then stepped back beside Elena, who was recording the venture for Garth's personal records.

Beckett approached the opening and peered out onto the landscape, his head held high and his tail twitching. Then he suddenly darted out of the crate and raced for the trees as fast as his little legs could carry him. Harriet was glad to see that his speed seemed unhindered. His chances of survival were very good now.

Unable to be still a second longer, the children broke out in cheers while the adults clapped and congratulated Garth, Harriet, and Martha. All but Fern, who wandered a little away from the group and dabbed at her eyes.

Fern Chapman, sentimental? Would wonders never cease?

"Winifred and I baked a cake," Alma announced. "For a bit of a celebration on this momentous day."

There was a bustle of activity as the group gathered around the back hatch of her vehicle to ooh and aah over the cake's design, which closely resembled a pine marten. Everyone enjoyed a piece of the chocolate cake with its creamy daffodil-yellow frosting while Martha and Garth shared stories of other animals they'd rescued and released.

Not everyone was ready to leave the knoll at the same time. Fern left with Alma and Winifred while the others stayed behind.

Garth led Elena and Jack to a place where climbing roses grew free, their vines cascading along a series of boulders, and Will and Harriet, hand in hand, headed toward a nearby rise with a gorgeous view of the North Sea.

"Take care you don't overexert yourself," Will said as they rested on a moss-covered boulder that formed a natural bench. Salty breezes from the sea cooled Harriet's face while the sun warmed her again.

"I feel great," Harriet assured him as she gazed toward the horizon. Tiny boats bobbed in the distance. "This view is rejuvenating."

"Definitely worth the long and winding road to get here."

"That's an interesting choice of words."

"Why?" Will asked as he placed his arm around her shoulders.

She nestled closer to him, delighting in the woodsy scent of his aftershave, which blended so naturally with the floral scents from the moors. "I was thinking of our own long and winding roads. A woman from Connecticut and a man who grew up on the moors meet in White Church Bay."

Will chuckled. "That sounds like a trailer for a happily-ever-after romance."

Harriet flushed at his words. "As difficult as this month has been, we've had a few happy endings. Like Winston Lancaster's last will and testament."

The document had been found exactly where Ivy and Sir Halston had said it would be. Having uncovered indisputable evidence that Timothy was embezzling funds and engaging in other unethical practices, Winston had left the bulk of the family fortune in a trust for Jack. He'd bequeathed a generous allowance to Elena, along with two seats on the Winston Lancaster Enterprises board of directors so she could protect her nephew's interests until he reached adulthood. In a final blow, he'd reduced Timothy's inheritance to a pittance.

"And Beckett the pine marten," Will said. "He's free again too." He squeezed her shoulders. "And Garth says Talitha is getting stronger every day."

"Rand still sends me photos of Sahara from time to time. She's a lovely dog, and I think she's bringing him as much healing as he is to her, though it's emotional healing rather than physical. I'm so glad Rand was able to open his heart again after the loss of his dog, and just when he and Sahara needed each other the most."

Will pressed his temple against Harriet's. "You and me? Do we count as a happy ending?"

Her pulse quickened as contentment filled her heart. "We certainly do."

His fingers brushed her jawline, and his gaze met hers. "I hope you know that I'm in love with you, Harriet."

She placed her palm against his cheek, beaming. "I'm in love with you too."

His gentle kiss held the promise of a wonderful future.

FROM THE AUTHOR

Dear Reader,

Two of my favorite four-letter words are *love* and *home.*

These words were especially on my mind as I was completing this story. In an incredibly strange set of circumstances that could have only been orchestrated by God, my son-in-law was offered a job in Orlando. And his new employer wanted him in the office in less than three weeks.

Exciting news, right? Except that we—my son-in-law, my daughter, their two daughters, and I—lived in Tulsa, over a thousand miles away. Needless to say, we were overwhelmed with the challenges of finding a place to live with three dogs and a cat, plus all the other logistics of a major move.

But here's the best part, and where God's gracious love shone upon us. My children were raised in the Orlando area. We found a house on the outskirts of the same small town, though it isn't quite as small as it used to be, where we lived before.

We arrived with all our belongings less than two weeks ago.

But we are already *home!*

The Florida sun shines upon us. We're spending time with life-long friends. We already know how to get to the grocery store, the post office, and other important places.

Long-legged sand cranes amble around the neighborhood. Ducks wander the bank of the pond behind our house where ibises and egrets perch among the reeds and an alligator resides. Around here, a gator in the pond is the norm.

In the story you just read, Elena and her nephew come to White Church Bay to hide from the world. Instead, they meet neighbors who care about them and their troubles. Elena and Jack sought a temporary respite from the world but instead found a new home.

Love, another important theme in this story, revealed itself in several relationships. Though my personal favorites are Rand with Sahara and Jack with Gideon, I am honored to have written the scene where Harriet and Will say those three precious words to each other: *I love you.*

My prayer is that, no matter your personal circumstances, you bask in the security of God's steadfast love for you. And that wherever you live, you are *home.*

Signed,
Johnnie Alexander

ABOUT THE AUTHOR

Johnnie Alexander is an award-winning, bestselling novelist of more than thirty works of fiction in a variety of genres. She is on the executive boards of Serious Writer, Inc. and Mid-South Christian Writers Conference, co-hosts an online show called Writers Chat, and is board secretary for the Mosaic Collection, LLC, a select group of international award-winning indie authors.

A fan of classic movies, stacks of books, and road trips, Johnnie shares a life of quiet adventure with Griff, her happy-go-lucky collie, and Rugby, her raccoon-treeing papillon.

TRUTH BEHIND THE FICTION

Anne Brontë and *The Tenant of Wildfell Hall*

Elena and Jack's circumstances were *sparked*, though not truly *inspired*, by Anne Brontë's second and last novel. The distinction is important because Anne's protagonist, Helen, was embroiled in circumstances much more dire than Elena's during a historic period when women rarely made the choices that Helen did. Society did not allow it.

While Elena and Jack, like Helen, are hiding from a relative, the stories have few other similarities.

Still, I am fascinated by Anne's novel and how she—the youngest daughter of a clergyman living in an isolated part of England— came to write such a controversial story with such extraordinary themes for the time. These included husband-wife relationships, women's property rights, and theology.

Anne's reply to such a question is that she simply wanted to tell the truth about the world she occupied. During her brief life, she endured harsh conditions at a boarding school and as a governess.

You may be familiar with the story of how Anne and two of her sisters, Charlotte and Emily, wrote and published their poems and novels under the pen names of Acton (Anne), Currer (Charlotte) and Ellis (Emily) Bell. They submitted their first manuscripts to the

London publishers as a package, which no doubt contributed to the rumor that Acton, Currer, and Ellis Bell were one author writing under the three names.

Eventually, the identities of the three literary geniuses were revealed. And society gasped to discover they were three sisters.

Jane Eyre, Charlotte's classic novel, was the first to be published, in 1847. Because of its success, a different publisher released *Wuthering Heights*, Emily's classic, and *Agnes Grey*, Anne's first novel, in 1848 as a three-volume set. *Wuthering Heights*, my favorite Brontë novel, made up two of the volumes with Anne's novel as the third.

Anne, the youngest of six children, was born in 1820, and died when she was only twenty-nine years old. One wonders what other amazing stories she might have gifted us with had she lived on.

YORKSHIRE YUMMIES

Aunt Jinny's Rhubarb Chicken Extra-Special Casserole

April in Yorkshire means three things: flowers galore, gamboling lambs, and…rhubarb!

For 4 to 6 servings.

Ingredients:

½ cup jasmine rice

1 tablespoon butter

1 large onion, diced

6 stalks rhubarb, diced

1 red pepper, diced

4–6 raw chicken thighs, diced or shredded

1½ tablespoons flour

½ cup milk

2 cups shredded cheese (your choice)

Salt and pepper to taste

Fresh chives to taste

Directions:

1. Preheat oven to 350 degrees.
2. Cook rice and set aside.
3. Melt butter in large skillet.
4. Sauté onion and rhubarb for about 5 minutes.

5. Add red pepper and chicken to skillet. Sauté until chicken is nearly cooked through.
6. Add flour and stir. Simmer for two to three minutes.
7. Add cooked rice to skillet and stir.
8. Add milk and simmer until sauce thickens.
9. Transfer to lightly oiled casserole dish (8x8 or 9x9).
10. Sprinkle shredded cheese on top.
11. Garnish with chives and season with salt and pepper.
12. Bake for 15 to 20 minutes or until cheese is melted.

*Read on for a sneak peek of another exciting book
in the* Mysteries of Cobble Hill Farm *series!*

Caught in a Trap

By Beth Adams

Harriet Bailey patted Hercules, the young Portuguese water dog who'd gotten sick after eating some of Madison Tyler's leftover Easter chocolate, before she headed for the door.

"He'll be back to normal soon," Harriet promised Meredith, Madison's mother.

Meredith pressed her lips together then said, "I'll make sure the rest of the candy is where he can't get into it. I didn't realize Madison had put it on the bottom shelf." She stroked the dog's head, and he leaned against her.

"These things happen," Harriet said. "He's still a puppy, so he's going to get into everything. You did the right thing bringing him in."

"Thank you, Harriet. I appreciate your kindness." Meredith's tired face betrayed the smallest hint of a smile. "You're just like your grandfather that way."

Harriet thanked her and walked out into the hall, smiling. She couldn't think of a better compliment than being compared to her grandfather, Harold Bailey, who had run the clinic before her. Now she made her way up front and saw that the waiting room was empty except for her receptionist and friend, Polly Thatcher.

"Was Hercules the last one for the day?" Harriet was scheduled to have dinner with Will Knight, the minister of White Church. They'd been steadily dating for a few months and she was eager to get going.

"Er—sort of." Polly tugged at a loose thread on the cuff of her sweater.

"What do you mean, 'sort of'?"

"It's a bit strange," Polly said. "We just got a phone call from Van. He's at the marina in Whitby."

"Okay." That didn't seem so strange. Van Worthington was a detective constable with the local police force, and he was dating Polly. After a brief period apart, they were back together, deliriously happy, and talking constantly. A call from him wasn't exactly out of the ordinary.

"He asked if you could come down to the marina. I guess there's a lobster he wants you to take a look at."

"A lobster?" She couldn't have heard that right. Harriet treated all kinds of animals in her practice, from cows and horses to dogs and cats—even the occasional camel, zebra, and iguana. But she'd never been called to care for a lobster. She'd never even heard of a vet being called to care for a lobster.

"That's what he said. Apparently, there's a 'lobster in distress.' He's asking if you can come help them with it."

"What does that mean? How can you tell if a lobster is in distress?" Harriet knew nothing about lobster diseases.

"I have no idea," Polly admitted. "What should I tell him?"

"Tell him I'm on my way."

"I'll take care of the animals and lock up," Polly said. That meant that she would let the clinic pets, Charlie the cat and Maxwell the dog, into Harriet's attached house before she left.

"Thank you." Harriet grabbed her jacket off the coatrack by the door and stepped out into the late afternoon sunlight. The garden was in full bloom, the flowers scenting the air with the sweetest perfume, and her home was beautiful, bathed in the golden light. May was her favorite month in England so far, with its longer days and gleaming sunshine. The lights were on inside the art gallery where her grandfather's paintings were displayed, and several cars sat out front.

Harriet pulled out her phone and called Will. It rang a couple of times, and then he answered.

"Hey," Will said. His voice was rich and deep, and its warmth came through even over the phone. "How are you?"

"I'm doing well," Harriet said. "But I have a change of plans. Van called and asked me to come check out a lobster down at the Whitby Marina."

"A lobster?"

"I have no idea why. But the police are there."

"That sounds serious. What did the lobster do? Do you think it robbed a bank? Are they going to put it in lobster prison?" Will joked.

Harriet laughed. "I'm told it's 'in distress,' whatever that means with a lobster. But I need to head down there now, so I was wondering if you'd want to meet somewhere when I'm done, or if you might want to come with me?"

Will didn't hesitate. "Oh, I must see this distressed criminal lobster. I'll come with you."

That was exactly what she'd hoped he'd say. "Great. How about I come pick you up in a few minutes? Are you at the church or at home?"

"I just got home," Will said. "My commute was terrible today."

Harriet rolled her eyes. Will lived at the parsonage, which was next door to the church. "I'll be there in a few minutes."

"See you soon."

Harriet climbed into the old Land Rover—or "the Beast," as she called it—that she'd inherited from her grandfather along with the clinic. She drove the short distance to White Church, a beautiful old stone building overlooking the sea north of the town. It had quickly become her church home when she'd moved to White Church Bay last summer, and dating the minister had only made her love the place more. She stopped in front of the parsonage, a stone cottage behind the main building.

Before she had a chance to park, Will came out.

"Hi," he said, climbing into the passenger seat. "I wasn't sure if this lobster would be dangerous, so I brought a pocketknife."

"You can never be too prepared."

Instead of setting her GPS for Whitby Marina, she'd rely on Will, since he knew the way. Whitby was about fifteen minutes north of White Church Bay, and Harriet knew roughly where the marina was, but she hadn't yet been in Yorkshire a year, and she wasn't familiar with all the back roads yet.

The country lane was quiet, shaded by mature trees lush with fresh green leaves. She had adapted to driving on the left side of the road, but the narrow country lanes, some too small for two cars to pass each other without one of them going onto the verge, still made her nervous.

She'd wound her way up the hill that led out of town and was driving along a flat section edged by purple heather and bright yellow rapeseed blossoms when her phone pinged with a text.

"Will you read that to me if it's from Polly?" she asked Will.

Will obliged. "'Van says to come to the harbormaster's office when you get there.'"

Harriet had no idea where the harbormaster's office was, but Will did.

He asked her about her day as they drove, and he told her about his day, and it only seemed like a few minutes later that she pulled up in front of a small gray building just beyond the entrance to the marina.

The marina itself was a long, narrow affair, populated with boats of every kind tied up at slips that jutted into the harbor. The parking lot was on one side, and the town of Whitby rose along the cliffs on both sides of the river, neat buildings with terra-cotta roofs set one above the other. Like White Church Bay, Whitby was an old fishing village, and the town had grown up in fits and starts over the centuries, with tourism becoming its main industry.

Harriet parked the car, grabbed her vet bag, and then walked with Will to the harbor office. When she opened the door, she was surprised to see Sergeant Adam Oduba and Detective Inspector Kerry McCormick in addition to Van inside the small building. Both the sergeant and the inspector worked for the county, and they got involved when an issue was beyond the scope of the local police force.

"This must be some lobster," Will said as they walked inside.

"Hello, Dr. Bailey." Sergeant Oduba smiled at her. "Thank you for coming. Good evening, Reverend."

Harriet and Will greeted the officers, the man with gray hair and a mustache at the desk, and Van, who stood by the wall.

"I have to admit I'm quite curious," Harriet said. "I've never been called to treat a lobster before."

"DC Worthington suggested you might be the best one to help, given the odd circumstances," DI McCormick said.

"You're the one I would trust to treat any kind of animal," Van said. "Even a lobster."

"We came right away. We wanted to know what crime this lobster committed," Will said, smiling.

"*Will* wanted to know that," Harriet clarified.

"Theft," Sergeant Oduba said with a straight face. "Grand larceny, to be specific. Breaking and entering, antiquities trafficking, potentially some other charges, but we're not sure yet."

"The lobster did all that?" Harriet asked.

"No. He's just an innocent crustacean bystander," DI McCormick said. "Well, maybe an accessory after the fact. Come on. I'll show you."

More confused than ever, Harriet followed the detective inspector and Sergeant Oduba to a small room at the rear of the office, where a lobster sat in a clear plastic storage bin filled with water. She'd seen enough lobsters in that seafaring part of the country not to be surprised by the fact that it was blue. Most European lobsters were a deep navy blue color, as opposed to the American version, which was more of a muddy brown. Both species turned bright red when cooked.

"See that thing caught in its shell?" Sergeant Oduba asked.

Harriet glanced down and noticed that there was indeed a small rust-colored object caught in a gap between two sections of the exoskeleton that made up the lobster's abdomen.

"What is that?" Harriet asked, leaning forward. Thankfully, someone had slipped rubber bands around the lobster's claws, so she wasn't worried about being pinched.

"It's a coin," DI McCormick said. "A very old and valuable one."

"We were hoping you'd be able to get it out without damaging it," Sergeant Oduba said.

"Or the lobster," DI McCormick added.

"I'll do my best," Harriet said. She rummaged in her vet bag for a pair of rubber tweezers and thick gloves. She grasped the coin with the tweezers and pulled gently. It didn't move. "It's stuck in there pretty tight, isn't it?"

She gently pressed the sections of the lobster's tail on either side of the coin. The tail flexed, and more of the coin was exposed. If she had three hands, she could use the tweezers to get it out now.

"Would you mind trying with the tweezers?" she asked Will.

"This is exciting. I've never done lobster surgery before," Will said, gamely picking up the tweezers. He reached in and pulled gently on the coin. He had to tug for a minute, but then it popped out.

Sergeant Oduba immediately slipped on plastic gloves. He picked up the coin and studied it. "It matches the others," he told DI McCormick.

Others? Harriet studied the lobster for any damage to the soft parts beneath the shell. Though her eye wasn't practiced with lobsters, this one didn't seem to have any wounds. She set the lobster back into the container and straightened up. "What is the coin? What's so important about it?"

DI McCormick spoke. "It's a Norse coin, probably from the ancient Viking settlements near here."

"There were Vikings in England?"

"Yes. A Norse settlement outside of York dates to the early Middle Ages," DI McCormick explained.

"Oh my." Harriet studied the rusty metal. Suddenly, she understood why she'd been called out for a lobster. It wasn't the lobster they cared about—it was the coin. That made much more sense. "If it's that old, it should be in a museum."

"Funny you should mention that," DI McCormick said. "This is part of a collection that was stolen from a local museum last month."

"And it was found this afternoon inside a lobster trap at the bottom of the North Sea," Van said. "Along with other old stuff."

"As in, this is considerably bigger than a single coin stuck in a lobster's shell?" Harriet asked.

Sergeant Oduba sighed. "This is still an active investigation. We can't—"

"She has a right to know at least this much, given that she did surgery on a lobster for us," DI McCormick told him.

Harriet hadn't actually done any surgery, but her curiosity convinced her not to point that out. DI McCormick wasn't usually so forthcoming, so Harriet didn't want to press her luck.

"A man was out on the water this afternoon checking his father's lobster traps, but he got a little turned around," the inspector went on. "He accidentally pulled one up that wasn't his, and he found more than lobsters. He found several sealed rubber containers inside the trap. He thought that was odd, especially since one of the containers popped open and a few old coins spilled out."

"The lobster was inside the trap, along with the containers?" Will asked.

DI McCormick nodded. "He looked inside the container and saw that it held dozens of coins, which he quickly recognized as being very old."

"Good thing he did. I wouldn't have thought they were anything important," Van said.

Harriet didn't want to say it out loud, but she was pretty sure she wouldn't have realized they were important either if she'd come across them. The one she'd seen simply resembled a piece of rusted metal.

"He's a history teacher at the local high school, apparently," Sergeant Oduba said. "He couldn't tell exactly what they were, but he knew enough to figure they didn't belong in a lobster trap at the bottom of the sea."

"You said there were other containers," Will said. "Did he open those to see what was in them?"

"He did. He managed to pry open the other two, and that was when he knew he needed to report it," DI McCormick said. "He radioed the local police."

"We keep a couple police boats in the harbor, so I took one out to meet him and take possession of the trap," Van said.

"What was in the other containers?" Harriet asked.

"An old bust and a bowl," Van said. He pointed to a table nearby, where two more plastic containers sat open. From where she stood Harriet could see one held a small bust and the other a bowl made from some kind of clay. "Really old."

"We're still waiting on analysis, but the man who found them thought the bust might be from Roman times. The bowl he wasn't sure about."

Roman times. Harriet had heard something about that. The Romans occupied England centuries before, and the country still bore remnants of their ancient influence.

"Were those objects stolen from museums too?" Harriet asked.

"We don't know yet," DI McCormick said. "But we're investigating."

Harriet struggled to wrap her mind around what she was hearing. "Viking coins and Roman busts in a lobster trap in the North Sea? How did they get there?"

For a moment, no one spoke. Then DI McCormick let out a breath. "We don't know. But our best guess at this point is that someone was using the trap as a holding station or a dead drop, a place to stash the stolen items where they were very unlikely to be found until someone could pick them up."

"And when they were picked up? What then?" Harriet asked.

"We assume they would have been taken by boat to an international port somewhere," Sergeant Oduba said. "But we don't know for sure."

"You mean someone was trying to smuggle these antiquities out of the country," Harriet said.

The police officers all nodded, and Harriet understood that this thing—whatever it was—went way beyond lobsters.

A NOTE FROM THE EDITORS

We hope you enjoyed another exciting volume in the Mysteries of Cobble Hill Farm series, published by Guideposts. For over seventy-five years, Guideposts, a nonprofit organization, has been driven by a vision of a world filled with hope. We aspire to be the voice of a trusted friend, a friend who makes you feel more hopeful and connected.

By making a purchase from Guideposts, you join our community in touching millions of lives, inspiring them to believe that all things are possible through faith, hope, and prayer. Your continued support allows us to provide uplifting resources to those in need. Whether through our communities, websites, apps, or publications, we inspire our audiences, bring them together, and comfort, uplift, entertain, and guide them. Visit us at guideposts.org to learn more.

We would love to hear from you. Write us at Guideposts, P.O. Box 5815, Harlan, Iowa 51593 or call us at (800) 932-2145. Did you love *A Will and a Way*? Leave a review for this product on guideposts.org/shop. Your feedback helps others in our community find relevant products.

Find inspiration, find faith, find Guideposts.

Shop our best sellers and favorites at
guideposts.org/shop

Or scan the QR code to go directly to our Shop

More Great Mysteries Are Waiting for Readers Like *You!*

Whistle Stop Café

"Memories of a lifetime...I loved reading this story. Could not put the book down...." —ROSE H.

Mystery and WWII historical fiction fans will love these intriguing novels where two close friends piece together clues to solve mysteries past and present. Set in the real town of Dennison, Ohio, at a historic train depot where many soldiers set off for war, these stories are filled with faithful, relatable characters you'll love spending time with.

Extraordinary Women of the Bible

"This entire series is a wonderful read.... Gives you a better understanding of the Bible." —SHARON A.

Now, in these riveting stories, you can get to know the most extraordinary women of the Bible, from Rahab and Esther to Bathsheba, Ruth, and more. Each book perfectly combines biblical facts with imaginative storylines to bring these women to vivid life and lets you witness their roles in God's great plan. These stories reveal how we can find the courage and faith needed today to face life's trials and put our trust in God just as they did.

Secrets of Grandma's Attic

"I'm hooked from beginning to end. I love how faith, hope, and prayer are included...[and] the scripture references... in the book at the appropriate time each character needs help. —JACQUELINE

Take a refreshing step back in time to the real-life town of Canton, Missouri, to the late Pearl Allen's home. Hours of page-turning intrigue unfold as her granddaughters uncover family secrets and treasures in their grandma's attic. You'll love seeing how faith has helped shape Pearl's family for generations.

Learn More & Shop These Exciting Mysteries, Biblical Stories
& Other Uplifting Fiction at **guideposts.org/fiction**

Printed in the United States
by Baker & Taylor Publisher Services